MW00593781

Dishing the Dirt

Rob Johnson

XERIKA PUBLISHING

DISHING THE DIRT COPYRIGHT

For Tilly, Dylan, Peter and Emily

.

ACKNOWLEDGEMENTS

I am indebted to the following people for helping to make this book better than it would have been without their advice, technical knowhow and support:

Yannis Anagnopoulos; Rob Johnson (a different one); Penny Philcox; Colin Ritchie; Petros Stathakos; Dan Varndell; Chris Wallbridge; Nick Whitton; Patrick Woodgate.

And last but not least, my eternal gratitude to my wife, Penny, for her unfailing support, encouragement and belief.

COVER DESIGN BY PENNY PHILCOX AND PATRICK WOODGATE

Special thanks as always to Penny Philcox for the cover artwork and to Patrick Woodgate for the original design.

GREEK LANGUAGE NOTE

There are a few Greek words and phrases used in the text, and these have been transliterated into the Latin alphabet. Where a word has more than one syllable, an accent shows which is the stressed syllable. For instance, the Greek word *póso* (meaning "how much") is pronounced with the stress on the first "o".

When you address someone directly by name in Greek and their name ends in an "s", the "s" is omitted. For instance, a man called Nikos would be addressed as Niko. For the sake of simplicity, however, this rule has not always been observed in the text, and for some of the male Greek characters the "s" has been dropped altogether.

1

'Kill it!'

'What?'

'Kill the bloody thing before it gets one of us.'

'Gets *me*, you mean,' said Sandra. 'I'm the one standing on the floor within a few feet of it while you're perched up on the desk and well out of striking range. Or am I mistaken in believing that scorpions can't actually jump that high?'

There wasn't much that Trevor could say to that, so he switched his attention back to the orangey-brown scorpion on the tiled office floor and stared at it like he was using mind control to make it leave the room or – preferably – spontaneously combust. It was a couple of inches long, not counting the wickedly curved tail that it had used to spear a small black beetle a few minutes earlier.

'It probably came in looking for water,' said Sandra.

'Oh really? Well, to be perfectly honest, I don't give a monkey's whether it was looking for water or the scorpion equivalent of the Holy Grail. I just want it gone. Out of my life forever.'

'And I'm the one to kill it, am I?'

Trevor shrugged. 'Unless you can coax it out with a trail of dead beetles or whatever.'

'But why should *I* have to do it, though? If one of us is going to stomp the thing to death, I think your Doc Marten boots would be far more effective than my flip-flops. Or perhaps we should leave it be and wait for it to die of old age.'

Trevor fleetingly wondered what the life expectancy of the average scorpion might be before he registered the blatant sarcasm in Sandra's tone. 'Why don't we get Grigoris in here? He's Greek after all, and the Greeks must have to deal with this sort of thing all the time. He'll know what to do.'

'Don't be daft. He'll just stomp on it the same as we should and make us look a right pair of—'

Sandra was interrupted by a blur of black and tan that hurtled through the open door of the office, skidded on the tiled floor and crashed heavily into the base of a metal filing cabinet on the opposite side of the room. The scorpion – presumably startled by this sudden intrusion on the enjoyment of its meal – instantly scuttled towards the prone body of the dog, its stinger raised and ready to strike.

'Jesus, Milly!' Trevor yelled, then leapt from the safety of the desk, took two strides and brought the sole of his boot crunching down onto the scorpion less than half a second before it could reach its prey.

Sandra clapped her hands together in mock admiration. 'Ooh, my hero.'

'It was going to sting her,' said Trevor, tentatively raising his foot to make certain that the flattened scorpion had indeed shuffled off its mortal coil.

'So you'd do it for Milly and not for me, eh?'

'She's a defenceless creature... kind of. And you're... not.'

'Why, thank you, Trev. You really do say the nicest things.'

'I didn't mean it like that. All I meant was—'

This time, the interruption was human rather than canine as a short, stocky man with dark, thinning hair swept into the room as if his arse was on fire.

'Some of these people they drive me crazy,' he said,

mopping the sweat from his brow with a slightly off-white tea towel.

'What's up, Grigoris?' said Sandra.

'English guy at Table Four. Face red like a lobster.'

'What about him?'

'He orders stifado, so I bring him stifado. Five minutes later, he call me back and he says it tastes like shit.'

'What?'

'In fact, he says this is worst shit he ever tasted in his whole life.'

'Bit of a connoisseur, is he?'

'Excuse me?'

'Never mind. Did you offer him something else instead?'

'Sure, but he said if the stifado taste like shit, probably everything else here taste like shit.'

'So does it taste like shit?' asked Trevor.

'I dunno,' said Grigoris. 'I not tried it.'

'What did Eleni say?'

Grigoris arched a thick, dark eyebrow and glanced over his shoulder as if making sure he couldn't be overheard. 'You think I gonna tell Eleni some guy say her cooking taste like shit?' he said in a stage whisper and made the sign of the cross.

'Very wise,' said Sandra. 'And what about the guy? He still here?'

'Guy?'

'The customer. The one who—'

'Yeah. He says he gonna finish his beer and he ain't gonna pay for that either.'

'Oh, terrific,' said Trevor. 'As if we're not in enough trouble already.'

Sandra shot him a look that told him in no uncertain terms that the taverna's financial problems weren't for public knowledge and certainly shouldn't be aired in front of the staff.

'Thank you, Grigoris,' she said. 'You'd better get back to work and leave this to us.'

Grigoris nodded and left the office rather more slowly than he'd entered it.

'"Leave this to *us*"?' Trevor repeated as soon as he'd gone. 'You know you're much better at this sort of thing than me. And besides, it's your turn.'

'Eh? How do you figure that out?'

'Er, who was it that killed the scorpion?'

'OK,' said Sandra. 'I'll do a deal with you. I'll go and do what I can to placate Mr Tastes-Like-Shit, and you do tomorrow's surveillance.'

Trevor considered her proposition for several seconds. Sitting in a baking hot van for hours, waiting – usually fruitlessly – for something to happen wasn't exactly his idea of fun, nor probably anyone else who had any kind of life to live. On the other hand, he hated even the most trivial of confrontations, and it was true that Sandra was infinitely more adept at dealing with bolshy customers than he was.

'Deal,' he said.

Sandra smiled and kissed him lightly on the cheek. 'Excellent choice, darling.'

2

After staring at the house across the road for the best part
of two hours, Trevor was fighting an uphill battle to keep
his eyelids from drooping. When he'd first seen it, he'd
been impressed by the sheer size of the long two-storey
villa with its gleaming white walls, terracotta tiled roof
and window shutters in the traditional Greek blue. There
was even a tall circular tower attached at one end which
blended tastefully with the rest of the building. But that
had been a few days ago, and his initial admiration for
the place had rapidly waned to the point where mind-
numbing boredom had resulted in a deep revulsion at its
grandiose opulence. At times, he almost wished someone
would come along and decorate the damned house so
he'd at least have something interesting to look at while
the paint dried.

Trevor took another sip from his almost empty bottle
of tepid water. It was getting on for midday, and even
with all of the camper van's windows open, the heat was
stifling. Early August in Greece wasn't ideal for carrying
out this kind of surveillance operation, but money was
tight, and he and Sandra had been in no position to turn
down any job that was offered to them.

It was nearly a year since Marcus Ingleby had asked
them to take over the running of his taverna – the *Sto
Limáni* – in return for free accommodation and a small
wage, and to make ends meet, they'd re-established the
detective agency they'd previously run in England. Not
that this had done much to help boost their finances.

Cases had been few and far between and had been mainly fairly trivial, such as the recovery of two lost cats and even a missing pet tortoise. Most of their clients had been expats, although the local Greek Orthodox priest did recently hire them to solve the mystery of his stolen bicycle, which turned out to have been relocated after being inadvertently crushed by an inebriated bulldozer driver.

The current case, however, might prove to be their most lucrative so far, given that they had been commissioned by one of the wealthiest people in the area, who suspected his wife was having an affair with a person as yet unknown. Alexandros Barkas owned a string of hotels, all of which were located in the most desirable tourist hotspots on the mainland and islands of Greece, and was married to an ex fashion model called Anastasia, who was twenty years his junior.

'Well, that was a disaster waiting to happen,' Sandra had said after Barkas had filled them in on the details and left them to develop their strategy.

'How'd you mean?' Trevor had said.

'Rich old men and their trophy wives? It's classic.'

'Early sixties hardly counts as "old", does it?'

'Old enough to know better.'

They both knew that to do the job properly, they should be watching Mrs Barkas round the clock, but they didn't have the resources, and they still had a taverna to keep from going under. Mr Barkas suspected that his wife was carrying on her affair during the daytime while he was at work, so Trevor and Sandra had been taking it in turns to watch the Barkas residence for two or three hour shifts every morning or afternoon when the taverna wasn't too busy.

But Mrs Barkas had hardly ventured out of the house since they'd begun their surveillance nearly a week ago. Twice, in fact, and both times while Trevor had been on duty. He'd fired up the engine of the van and waited while she'd backed a white Lexus out of the double garage and then kept behind her at a discreet distance as she headed towards the town. On the first occasion, she'd parked up near the town square and disappeared inside a hairdresser's, which added an extra hour and a half to Trevor's shift by the time she'd re-emerged and he'd followed her back to the house. Her second foray into the outside world had happened yesterday morning and appeared to be for the sole purpose of adding to what was no doubt an already extensive wardrobe of *haute couture*.

Trevor checked his watch.

'Five more minutes and I'm out of here,' he told himself and began counting out three hundred seconds in his head.

He'd got as far as a hundred and eighty-seven when the front door of the house swung open and out stepped Anastasia Barkas. Even from this distance, it was easy to see how she'd once been a top fashion model. Slim and with slightly bobbed, jet black hair, she wore a cream trouser suit over a pale blue blouse that was buttoned to the neck. With the super-sized dark glasses, she could have been a dead ringer for a young Jackie Onassis.

Trevor watched as she made her way along the gravel path that ran beside the front of the house towards the Lexus that was already out on the driveway. But there was something a little different about the way she was walking that he hadn't seen before. Just a touch more jaunty perhaps? Almost as if she was having to restrain herself from actually skipping.

Well, well, thought Trevor. She's in a good mood about something. Maybe today's the day at last.

He turned the key in the van's ignition and, as before, waited until she'd backed out of the driveway. This time, though, she turned left instead of towards the town.

'Dammit,' said Trevor, realising that he'd have to do a three point turn in the van, and he'd have to make it snappy or he'd run the risk of losing her.

He slammed the gear stick into first, took hold of the handbrake and glanced in the rear-view mirror to see a white car with flashing blue lights on its roof approaching at speed. At the same time, the Lexus was rapidly disappearing in the opposite direction.

Trevor revved the engine, mentally urging the cop car to hurry up and get past while he still stood a chance of catching up with Mrs Barkas. But that's when he heard three short blasts of a siren, and the police car screeched to a halt diagonally in front of the van.

'What the—?'

He let go of the handbrake and eased the gear stick back into neutral but kept the engine running.

The driver's door of the police car opened, and a youngish-looking uniformed officer took his time stepping out onto the road. He took nearly as long to put on his cap and adjust it to his liking in the car's wing mirror. Then, as he sauntered towards the van, Trevor recognised the slightly crooked nose, the thin black moustache and the almost permanent hint of a smirk.

'Constable bloody Dimitris,' Trevor said to himself. 'That's all I need.'

He and Sandra had only had a handful of dealings with this particular cop in the past, but none of them had been positive experiences. The guy was overzealous to the point of fanatical in his rigid application of the law – sometimes purely as he himself perceived it. He was also a bully with an utterly misplaced sense of superiority.

'Par for the course,' Sandra had always said of PC Dimitris. 'Put an idiot in uniform and that's what you get. Especially one that's been passed over for promotion as many times as he has.'

Constable Dimitris stooped to peer in through

16

Trevor's open window.

'*Kalıméra*,' he said, the supercilious grin betraying that he couldn't care less whether Trevor had a good day or not.

Trevor gave him the faintest of nods in response. Although he and Sandra had put quite a lot of effort into learning the Greek language, it had become a policy to feign ignorance whenever faced with belligerent officialdom. The hope was that the official they were dealing with wouldn't speak English and, unable to communicate, would wave them away in frustration. From their previous encounters with PC Dimitris, he must have believed that they didn't understand a word of Greek, but this didn't stop him rattling on in his mother tongue for a good thirty seconds.

'I'm sorry,' said Trevor when he'd finished, 'but I didn't understand any of that. Would you mind saying it in English?'

PC Dimitris sighed heavily and closed his eyes. Then he opened them again and pushed the peak of his cap a little further back from his forehead.

'I'm saying that there has been complaint of you sitting here in camping van for two hours and that you been doing the same for days. So you need to explain me why is it you are doing this.'

It was considerably shorter than the Greek version, so maybe Constable Dimitris had edited out the less pertinent remarks or didn't know how to translate them into English.

'Complaint?' said Trevor. 'Who from exactly?'

'Is none of your business. Is confidential police business.'

'I see.'

'So answer my question.'

'Oh, I beg your pardon, officer. I didn't realise you'd asked me one.'

PC Dimitris removed his cap completely, wiped the sweat from his brow with the back of his hand and then replaced the cap firmly on his head.

'I ask you why you keep parking here in same place every day.'

'I like the scenery.'

'The scenery?'

'Vista? Panorama? Basically, it means—'

'Yes, I know what "scenery" means,' Dimitris interrupted, 'but there is nothing but houses all along both sides of road.'

'Ah yes, but they're very *big* houses and very expensive too, I imagine.'

'So why you look at them all this time? You planning robbery?'

'Certainly not. It's the architecture. All the houses are fascinatingly different, and it's a bit of a hobby of mine.'

Constable Dimitris briefly scanned the houses on either side of the street, then pushed his face further in through the open window. 'You bullshit me?'

'Of course not,' said Trevor, recoiling from the stink of garlic on the cop's breath.

Dimitris backed off with his face and wagged a finger at him. 'This is final warning. If I hear any more complaint or I see you here again myself, I arrest you for littering.'

'Actually, I think you mean *loitering*, but I get the message.'

The cop grunted. 'So leave now before I change my mind.'

'OK, but you might need to move out of the way first,' said Trevor and pointed to the rear of the police car, which was little more than three feet from the van's front bumper.

Another grunt, and PC Dimitris stomped off back to his car.

* * *

'And you've no idea who it was that complained?' said Sandra when Trevor had reported back to her at the taverna.

Trevor shook his head. 'He wouldn't say.'

''Cos if it was Mrs Barkas herself, that means she probably knows we're watching her.'

'The thought had occurred to me, which led me on to another thought.'

'Oh yeah?'

'I do have them, you know.'

'I never doubted it.'

'It was the way you said "Oh yeah".'

'What way?'

'With that tone of voice like you're not expecting my ideas to be any good.'

'I didn't mean it like that at all. Maybe it's the heat getting to you. Maybe you're being over-sensitive.'

Trevor had to admit – to himself – that he'd got seriously overheated sitting around in the van for all that time and was urgently in need of a cool shower and something to eat and drink.

'We fix some kind of tracking device to her car,' he said. 'That way, we won't have to keep on watching the house every day, which would be pretty pointless anyway if she really has twigged that we're onto her. Plus we won't have PC Dimitris breathing down our necks, and we'll know whenever she goes out and, more importantly, where she goes *to*.'

'Great idea,' said Sandra, 'but where do you suppose we'd get one round here?'

'Didn't you bring some of your detective kit with you from England?'

'A few bits and pieces, yeah, but not a tracker.'

'What about Vangelis?'

19

'Ah yes. Our local Mr Fixit.'

'He'll know where we can get one if anybody does.'

'I'll ask him tonight. Presumably he'll be in for his usual ouzo or three.'

3

'There's no note or anything?' said Sandra and watched as Trevor peered inside the small Jiffy bag for the third time.

'Just this,' he said, holding up a tiny copper-coloured plastic gun between his forefinger and thumb.

'Bit odd. Maybe it's some kind of death threat.'

'Oh yeah? So who's likely to be sending us a death threat?'

'I can think of two for starters. Donna Vincent and Frank Phelan. They're both doing fairly hefty prison sentences – mostly because of us – and you remember what they said they'd do to us if they ever got the chance?'

Trevor remembered all too clearly, and the image of Donna Vincent screaming at them from behind the bars of a police cell still occasionally woke him in the middle of the night.

'But they won't get out for years,' he said. 'What can they do to us from inside prison?'

'Well, I don't know about Frank,' said Sandra, 'but Donna certainly has the contacts and the money.'

'For what? Put a contract out on us, you mean?'

'It has been known.'

'Oh great,' said Trevor, 'and there was me been thinking we'd be in the clear for at least a few more years.'

As he spoke, he began to examine the tiny plastic gun more closely and discovered that there was a slight ridge at the base of the butt. Wondering if the pistol grip might contain a magazine of miniature bullets, he pulled at it and out slid the business end of a USB memory stick.

'Well, there's a novelty,' he said. 'Maybe it's not a death threat after all.'

'Better see what's on it first before we go jumping to conclusions,' said Sandra and held out her hand. 'Give it here then and we'll have a look.'

They were in the cramped back office of the taverna, and Sandra was sitting on a battered swivel chair at a small, heavily cluttered table that passed for a desk. She took the stick from Trevor and inserted it into the open laptop.

'Make sure you virus check it first,' he said.

'Don't I always?'

'Er, no.'

Sandra muttered something under her breath.

'It's clean,' she said after she'd completed the virus check as instructed.

Trevor stood at her shoulder and watched as she clicked on File Explorer and then the F drive. A single icon appeared on the screen.

'What's that?' said Trevor, leaning forward to get a better view.

'Audio file by the look of it,' said Sandra and double-clicked on the icon.

There was a couple of seconds of silence and then a woman's voice: '*What are we going to do? The whole place is a complete mess, and the kitchen is a total health hazard.*'

Then a man's voice: '*Whatever we do, we just don't seem able to get rid of all the rats and mice.*'

'*Not to mention the cockroaches.*'

'*Only yesterday, I found rat shit on top of the moussaka.*'

'*Oh no. So what did you do?*'

'*Scraped it off and hoped nobody would notice.*'

'*Let's just hope none of the customers get food poisoning.*'

Sandra hit the Pause button and turned to Trevor. 'That's us, for Christ's sake.'

'I know.'

'You and me.'

'I *know*.'

'From the—'

'Recording session.'

About three weeks earlier, Trevor and Sandra had been contacted by a woman called Wendy Gifford, who was a friend of one of their regular customers. She ran an English language school in the town and was planning to put together some audio recordings for her students to practise their listening skills. She was looking for two native English speakers – preferably a man and a woman – to record various passages and pieces of dialogue during a couple of sessions in a nearby studio. The pay hadn't been great, but Trevor and Sandra decided it might be fun, so they agreed, and a date and time were fixed.

When they arrived at the studio – which was actually a small converted back room in someone's house – Wendy handed them each a sheaf of papers and sat them down in a soundproof booth with her and the recording engineer – the owner of the house – issuing instructions from the other side of a glass wall. It had certainly been fun to start with, but both Trevor and Sandra were amazed at how quickly they became tired and their voices began to get hoarse. Most of the passages were fairly banal, including brief descriptions of how to boil an egg and handy hints on how to clean an oven. The short pieces of dialogue were marginally more interesting, but Trevor and Sandra had expressed their serious reservations about recording the one between the co-owners of a taverna who were worried about being closed down by a health inspector. They hadn't been convinced by Wendy's 'It's just a bit of fun' but had eventually agreed when she assured them that it was only her students that would be hearing any of the recordings.

'Bloody Nora,' said Trevor. 'I knew it was weird, getting us to record that bit. What else did we say? I can't remember it all now.'

Sandra clicked the Pause button again:

TREVOR: And what if we get a visit from the health inspector?

SANDRA: Close us down in two seconds flat, I'd imagine.

TREVOR: So what the hell do we do? There's no way we could get this place up to hygiene standards without spending a small fortune.

SANDRA: I don't know, Trevor, I really don't.
(Brief pause)

TREVOR: We'll just have to bribe them, I guess.

SANDRA: Bribe them?

TREVOR: The health inspector or whoever. It's the only way out of this mess, Sandra. Believe me.

There was a faint clicking sound as the recording ended, and Trevor and Sandra simply stared at the laptop in silence for several seconds. Then Sandra picked up the Jiffy bag and checked the inside again. Nothing.

'I think somebody's trying to blackmail us,' she said.

Trevor gulped. 'Blackmail?'

'Seems the most likely to me.'

'So what do they want? Cash?'

'Your guess is as good as mine, but if this recording

ever got out, we'd be screwed, and so would Marcus Ingleby's taverna. Hell, we even used our own names.'

'Not when we recorded it, we didn't. Our names were in the script, but if you remember, we left them out when we did the recording.'

'Yeah, you're right.'

'We must have used our names somewhere else and someone's tweaked the recording to add them in. Probably not that difficult if you know what you're doing.'

'Play that part again,' said Trevor, and Sandra rewound the recording to the relevant section.

Listening intently and replaying it several times, they were certain they could hear a very faint background hum where their names were mentioned. A hum that wasn't present in the rest of the recording.

Trevor took a deep breath and exhaled slowly through his teeth. 'You think Wendy set the whole thing up so she could blackmail us?'

Sandra shook her head. 'Don't think so. She seemed fairly genuine to me. But maybe someone else got her to slip that bit of dialogue in amongst all the other stuff we recorded.'

'Such as?'

'Best guess? I'd say top of the list is Yannis Christopoulos.'

'Mr Angry?'

'The very same.'

Yannis Christopoulos had been a thorn in Trevor and Sandra's sides since almost the first day that they'd taken over the running of Marcus Ingleby's taverna. He was the owner of a much larger taverna a little further along the quayside, but his business had suffered even more than theirs during Greece's economic crisis. The busiest period for both tavernas was the summer, when tourists came flocking to the area, not quite in their

25

droves as they had before the crisis but certainly in good enough numbers to keep the *Sto Limáni* afloat for the rest of the year. The big advantage that Trevor and Sandra had over Christopoulos was that most of these tourists were British, so it wasn't a great surprise that they'd head for a taverna where they could guarantee that English was spoken. Not only that, but Trevor and Sandra had dangled another carrot to attract the less adventurous diners among them. Not literally a carrot, of course, but more traditional British fare such as eggs, beans and chips, shepherd's pie and toad in the hole.

Christopoulos had tried all kinds of tricks and gimmicks in an attempt to lure their customers away – free wine with every meal, happy hours and even karaoke nights – but with minimal success. And this was when he'd begun to adopt a completely different approach, which was along the lines of "If you can't beat them, sabotage them". It had started relatively innocuously when Trevor and Sandra became aware of a sudden increase in the number of damning comments about their taverna on TripAdvisor and some of the other major review sites. They were all posted under different – and presumably fictitious – names, but although they had no proof, Christopoulos appeared to be the obvious suspect. They didn't notice any significant drop-off in trade, however, and they assumed that Christopoulos hadn't seen much improvement in *his* because the gloves finally came off and matters took a potentially far more damaging turn for the worse.

First, there were the unexplained power cuts, which only affected Ingleby's taverna. Then there was the highly unusual plague of wasps smack in the middle of one of their busiest lunchtimes, forcing most of the customers to flee the scene. The snake in the kitchen that made Eleni the cook down tools for nearly two hours before someone could be fetched to remove it. The list of near disasters went on and on, but as with the spate of negative reviews, there was never any hard evidence against Christopoulos himself.

Sandra played the audio file again while she and Trevor listened in concentrated silence.

'So now what do we do?' said Trevor when the recording had finished.

'Not much we *can* do,' said Sandra, 'except wait till whoever sent this gets in touch and tells us what they want.'

'It might be worth having a word with Wendy Gifford in the meantime, though. If somebody *did* give her that script, maybe we can find out who it was.'

'Well, aren't *you* full of good ideas today.'

'Is that supposed to be sarcasm?'

'Not at all. We'll pay her a visit soon as we can tomorrow.'

4

It was the middle of the morning when Trevor and Sandra pulled up outside The Wendy Gifford School of English, which was located on the ground floor of a three-storey house halfway along a row of almost identical buildings in one of the town's many side streets. What set it apart, however, was the brightly coloured mural that covered almost every inch of its front wall that wasn't taken up by the spotlessly clean picture window. It had been painted with considerable skill and consisted almost entirely of characters from children's books, including Winnie the Pooh, Pinocchio, Peter Pan and, somewhat bizarrely, the Incredible Hulk.

The wooden door to the right of the mural was painted a bright yellow and was slightly ajar. There was no bell, so Trevor knocked on the door, which caused it to open by another couple of inches.

'Door's open, so we might as well go in,' said Sandra when there was no response, but when she took hold of the handle and pushed, nothing happened.

'That's odd,' she said and tried again – harder this time – but with the same result.

'Must be something stopping it from inside,' said Trevor.

'You think?'

She put her shoulder to the door, but still it didn't budge, so she called out through the narrow opening, 'Hello? Anybody there?'

Again there was no answer, so Trevor added his not

very substantial weight to Sandra's efforts but with negligible effect.

'What the *fuck*?'

It was a woman's voice from low down on the other side of the door. Muffled and heavily slurred.

'Is that her?' said Trevor. 'Wendy, I mean.'

'Not sure,' said Sandra. 'Doesn't sound posh enough somehow.'

'Maybe whoever it is has had a stroke or something.'

Sandra squatted on her haunches and spoke through the gap again. 'Is that you, Wendy? Are you OK?'

'I was doing fine until you started shoving at me with the damn door.'

Trevor couldn't be certain it was Wendy's voice. In all their dealings with her, she'd never spoken with any discernible accent at all. Not quite "posh", as Sandra had said, but this woman sounded heavily East London. Bordering on cockney even.

The grunting and groaning from inside the door grew steadily louder, as did the sound of shuffling feet, and the door clicked shut. Presumably, the woman was using the handle to haul herself upright.

Seconds later, the door opened slowly inwards, and there stood a taller than average woman in her mid fifties with shoulder-length salt-and-pepper hair that looked as if it hadn't seen a comb in weeks. She was wearing a pastel-coloured floral print summer dress with half sleeves and a dark stain that spread from the centre of the neckline almost down to the waist. It was Wendy Gifford all right, but barely recognisable from the invariably immaculate Wendy Gifford they'd come to know.

'Who the hell are you, anyway?' she said, squinting at each of them in turn through bloodshot eyes and smudged mascara.

'Sandra Gray and Trevor Hawkins,' said Sandra. 'We

29

did the recording for you.'

'The what?'

'You wanted somebody to—' Trevor began but broke off when the stink of ouzo and something unidentified but deeply unpleasant on Wendy's breath hit him full in the face.

'Wait a minute,' she said. 'Where's me sodding glasses?'

She scoured the floor around her while Trevor and Sandra took in their surroundings. They were in an almost square entrance hall, the walls of which were festooned with children's paintings, group photographs – probably of Wendy's students through the years – typewritten notices on a corkboard, and a variety of uplifting quotations. These included "You're braver than you believe, and stronger than you seem, and smarter than you think" and "It always seems impossible until it is done". Three closed doors lined the hallway. One on each side and another straight ahead. Most likely the classrooms.

'Bollocks,' said Wendy. 'Bloody broken.'

She stooped unsteadily to pick up a pair of blue-framed spectacles from the floor next to an empty bottle of ouzo that lay on its side, a tiny puddle of liquid beneath the open neck. One arm of the glasses had snapped off, so she did her best to balance them on her nose and forced herself upright again, using the wall for support.

'Oh yeah, I remember now,' she said, peering at Trevor and Sandra through the lopsided lenses.

'Are you all right?' said Sandra. 'Did you have a fall or something?'

'You could say that, yeah,' said Wendy, and the beginnings of a laugh turned into a hacking cough.

'I need to sit down,' she said after she'd recovered enough to speak.

30

She opened the door on the left of the hallway, and Trevor and Sandra followed her into a large room with pale blue walls and yellow ceiling. There were six rows of four tables, each with an orange plastic chair neatly parked beneath it. A whiteboard dominated the wall at the far end of the room, and below that was a substantial wooden desk and an office chair that looked decidedly more comfortable than the orange plastic ones. Wendy slumped down onto it and immediately began to rummage through one of the desk drawers.

'Where the hell are they?' she muttered. 'They're in here somewhere. I know they are.'

She slammed the drawer shut and wrenched open another one.

'Gotcha,' she said after a brief search and took out a disposable lighter and a packet of cigarettes.

She lit one and inhaled deeply, which produced another prolonged coughing fit.

'Bloody things'll kill me one o' these days,' she spluttered eventually and studied the glowing tip of the cigarette.

'Are there no classes today?' said Sandra.

Wendy looked up at her as if she'd forgotten she wasn't alone. 'Summer holiday, thank fuck. Not that you'd notice a fat lot of difference if it was termtime.'

'Not many students then?'

'How many parents have got the cash to send their kids for private English lessons these days?'

'Very few, I guess,' said Trevor, even though he realised this was probably a rhetorical question.

'Spot on,' said Wendy and took another cough-inducing drag on her cigarette.

'Mind if we sit down?' said Sandra. 'There's something we need to ask you about.'

Wendy waved a dismissive hand around the classroom. 'Help yourself. Plenty of room.'

Trevor and Sandra pulled out two of the orange plastic chairs and sat.

'It's about that recording session we did for you,' said Sandra.

Wendy raised an eyebrow and adjusted her one-armed spectacles, which had become even more lopsided. 'I paid you for that, didn't I?'

'Yes, you did, thanks. It was one of the pieces we read that we wanted to talk to you about.'

'Oh?'

'The one about the taverna,' said Trevor. 'Where Sandra and I are supposed to be worried about how unhygienic it was and that it might be closed down by a health inspector.'

Wendy blew half a dozen smoke rings and watched them disintegrate as they headed towards the ceiling. 'There were quite a few pieces we recorded that day. I can't say I remember that one particularly.'

Trevor filled her in on a few more of the details.

More smoke rings and more staring at the ceiling.

'Did you write that one yourself or did someone give it to you?' said Trevor, struggling to suppress his impatience.

'Could be.'

'Could be *what*?'

Wendy lowered her gaze and eyeballed him. 'Could be somebody gave it me. I dunno. Can't remember now.'

'Oh for—'

'The thing is, Wendy,' Sandra cut in, evidently deciding that Trevor was fast turning into "bad cop" and it was time for "good cop" to take over. 'This is really important. If that recording gets into the wrong hands, we could be seriously in the shit.'

'Join the club, love.'

'Excuse me?'

Wendy wafted a hand around the classroom again.

32

'Short of a bleedin' miracle, this place'll be flat bust by the end of the year – at the latest – and I'm not a great one for believing in miracles.'

'I'm really sorry to hear that, Wendy. I really am. But unless you can help us, we—'

'Fuck it,' said Wendy, exhaling twin streams of smoke through her nostrils. 'So what if they carry out their threats? I'm past bloody caring, to be honest.'

'Threats? Do you mean someone *did* give you the script?'

Wendy dropped her cigarette onto the floor and crushed it beneath her foot. Then she went through the drawer-rummaging routine again until she found what she was looking for.

'Here,' she said, brandishing a single sheet of paper that looked like it had been crumpled and then roughly smoothed out afterwards.

Trevor scraped back his chair and hurried to snatch the paper out of Wendy's hand.

'Yeah, this is it,' he said, 'but there's a handwritten bit at the bottom: "*To be recorded. Tell no-one you did not write this yourself or you will suffer consequences. Type out script again and destroy this note*".'

Sandra turned to Wendy as she lit another cigarette. 'Who gave you this?'

'One of the kids,' said Wendy after she'd overcome a brief fit of coughing. 'Student of mine. She said some bloke stopped her in the street when she was on her way here for a lesson.'

'Did she say who it was?'

Wendy shook her head. 'Couldn't describe him either – or so she claimed.'

'Oh?'

'I dunno, but I somehow got the impression he must have slipped her a few euros to keep her trap shut. Either that or he threatened her like he did me.'

'So that's why you got us to record it?' said Trevor. 'Because he threatened you?'

'Can't you read? He only threatened me if I told anyone.'

'So why then?'

''Cos along with that bit of paper, there were a couple of fifty euro notes, and like I say, I'm pretty strapped for cash right now, and I thought it was just some kind of prank.'

'A prank?' said Sandra. 'You didn't think the part about suffering the consequences was a little suspicious?'

'I need a lie down,' said Wendy, getting to her feet. 'You can find your own way out.'

'Hang on a minute,' said Trevor and took hold of her arm as she attempted to pass him. 'What about this kid? The student? Who is she and where can we find her?'

'Sofia something-or-other. Lives on a farm in some village a couple of miles out of town, I think. There's a filing cabinet in the classroom opposite with all the kids' details, so help yourself. Now let go of me arm and let me get some kip.'

Trevor released her from his grip, partly because he realised they were unlikely to get any more information out of her, but mainly as an instinctive reaction to avoid another blast of tobacco smoke and ouzo breath that were delivered from a distance of less than twelve inches. Then he and Sandra watched Wendy make her unsteady way to the back of the classroom and out of the door.

Sandra opened her mouth to speak but was interrupted by the opening bars of Survivor's *Eye of the Tiger* alerting her to an incoming call on her mobile phone. She fished it out of her pocket and checked the display.

'Unknown,' she said and hit Answer. 'Hello?'

5

'Hang on a second,' said Sandra and switched the phone to speaker. 'Sorry, what was that again?'

'*I said I assume you have listened to the little recording I sent you?*'

The voice on the phone was heavily disguised and sounded like Mickey Mouse doing an impersonation of R2-D2 after a massive dose of helium. Male rather than female, but even that was open to doubt.

'We did indeed, Mr Christopoulos.'

'*Who?*'

'Look, just because you're using some kind of fancy app on your phone, it's not exactly difficult to work out who would want to get us closed down.'

'*I've no intention of getting you closed down as long as you pay me not to make the recording public.*'

'Oh, so it's purely blackmail, is it? And not because you're the owner of a taverna that's likely to go tits up as long as ours is still up and running.'

'*I don't know what you're talking about. I don't own a fucking taverna, so I don't give a shit if it goes "tits up" or not. All I'm interested in is the money.*'

'OK, I'll play along for now. So how much do you want?'

'*Fifty thousand.*'

'What's that? Drachmas?'

'*Don't get funny with me, lady. Fifty thousand euros.*'

Sandra snorted with laughter. 'Me being funny? I think you're the comedian here, Christopoulos. Fifty thousand euros? Where the hell do you think we're gonna get that kind of money even if we wanted to?'

'*Marcus Ingleby. He's the owner of the taverna, right? He's got the money. I'm damn sure of it. – And stop fucking calling me Christopoulos.*'

'How about I call you Yannis then?'

'*Are you listening to me? Maybe you should be taking this a lot more seriously because if you don't pay up, your little recording goes public and you can kiss goodbye to your poxy taverna. Not only that, but I wouldn't be at all surprised if the police didn't decide to press charges for conspiracy to bribe an officer of the state.*'

Trevor felt the blood drain from his face. He and Sandra had come within a whisker of spending time in a Greek prison before, and the prospect terrified him as much now as it did then.

'I'm not sure it's such a good idea to keep winding him up,' he whispered in Sandra's ear. 'I mean, perhaps it really isn't Christopoulos after all.'

'Well, who else is it going to be?' she whispered back.

'I dunno, but I think we should—'

'*You still there?*' Mickey/R2-D2 interrupted.

'Course we are, Yannis. So what was it you were saying?'

There was a weird noise over the speakerphone which was presumably intended as an extended grunt of irritation, but the helium voice app made it sound more like the squeal of a wounded chicken.

'*I'll call you again same time tomorrow, so you'd better have got hold of the cash by then or you and your taverna are screwed.*'

'Sorry, Yannis, but I thought we'd already established that it's Marcus Ingleby that actually owns the—'

'*And don't even think of going to the police.*'

The line went dead.

'So what do you reckon?' said Trevor. 'Was it Christopoulos or somebody else?'

'Couldn't tell from the voice, of course, but like I said, who else would it be?'

'Anybody who might want to blackmail us, I guess.'

'True, but given recent history, Christopoulos has got to be the prime suspect. I mean, if we don't pay up, who else is gonna care if the taverna gets shut down? Seems to me that he's the only one that'll benefit whichever way it goes.'

Trevor scratched his head. 'There was one thing that struck me as odd, though. His English was a bit... *too* good?'

'I've probably had more conversations with him than you have – and that's not very often – but he speaks English pretty much like a native. Grigoris told me once that he was educated somewhere in the UK. Bit of an accent, sure, but you couldn't tell that from the voice-mangling he was using on the phone.'

'So whether it's him or not, what do we do now?'

'First off, I reckon we track down this Sofia girl and see if we can get some information out of her about who it was that gave her the script. At least then we'll know for sure if it really is Christopoulos. And if it isn't, we just have to take it from there, I suppose.'

6

Lunchtime had been unexpectedly busy at the taverna, so Trevor and Sandra had had to lend Grigoris a hand waiting on tables. After that, it had been all hands on deck to help Eleni with the washing up. So, by the time they'd set off in the van to track down Sofia Tsoukala, it was already late in the afternoon.

As it turned out, the village where the girl lived was much further than the couple of miles from town that Wendy had told them. About eight miles, in fact, and way up into the hills, some of the steeper inclines putting a considerable strain on the camper van's elderly engine.

'Here we are then,' said Trevor, parking up at the side of the road in what appeared to be roughly the centre of the village. '*Kremmídia*. That means "onions", doesn't it?'

'Uh-huh,' said Sandra as she massaged her feet, which had become badly swollen in the heat. The absence of air-conditioning in the van hadn't helped, and even with all the windows fully open, the sluggish pace had created little more than the occasional influx of a warm blast of air.

'Onions,' said Trevor. 'Why on Earth would you call a village "Onions"?'

'Perhaps they just really like onions. Or maybe that's mainly what they grow round here.'

'There was another village I came across a while ago called "Fish" – *Psári*. It was miles inland and nowhere near a lake or even a river, so how does that work?'

'I have absolutely no idea, Trev, and quite frankly, at this precise moment, I really couldn't care less. What I *do* care about is finding some kind of café where we can get a nice cold beer and preferably a very large bowl of equally cold water that I can soak my massively swollen feet in.'

'You'll be lucky,' Trevor snorted, and instantly regretted having been quite so blunt when he clocked the narrowing of Sandra's eyes.

The truth was, though, that Sandra had been too busy massaging her feet to be aware of their surroundings even before they'd entered the village. There were no more than thirty or forty small houses, all built from stone and several in a state of mild disrepair, with the newest-looking house probably having been constructed nearly a century ago.

'We'll just have to hope we get offered a drink when we get to Sofia's place,' said Trevor in an attempt to placate Sandra and to fend off a repeat of her previously expressed irritation that he'd forgotten to bring any drinking water with them. 'It's a farm too, so they're bound to have a big bowl you can soak your feet in.'

'Oh yes?' Sandra sneered. 'That would be a good start, wouldn't it: "Hello, we'd like to speak to you about a serious blackmail attempt and, by the way, would you mind if I soak my feet in that trough your cows are drinking out of?".'

'They don't usually have cows round here,' said Trevor. 'It's mostly sheep and goats from what I've seen.'

It was the second remark in less than a minute that he'd regretted as soon as the words were out of his mouth, and he deliberately avoided eye contact with Sandra. His ears provided quite enough information as to her response. The only person he'd ever known who could sigh and grunt simultaneously.

39

'Milly must be gasping too,' he said in an epic fail to change the subject.

He glanced in the rear-view mirror to see that the dog – who had been sleeping peacefully on the back seat of the van until a few minutes ago – was now sitting up and returning his gaze, panting heavily and her lolling tongue producing an impressive torrent of drool.

'Well, we'd better find this farm fast then before we all die from dehydration,' said Sandra.

'I didn't spot anything on the way in,' he said. 'Maybe we should carry on past the end of the village.'

'Or we could just ask somebody.'

'Like who? We haven't seen a single person yet. Not even a dog or a cat.'

Sandra checked her watch. 'Probably still having siestas.'

Trevor decided against querying whether dogs and cats actually had siestas and opted instead for: 'Perhaps it's one of those deserted villages. You know, like when the older generation dies out and the young ones all bugger off to try and find a better life in the cities – or other countries.'

'Hmm, it's an interesting theory,' said Sandra, 'but do you think they'd also have abandoned all their cars as well?'

Trevor looked back and forth along the road at the twenty or so cars, vans and pickups.

'Good point,' he said.

'Only one thing for it,' said Sandra, returning to her foot massaging. 'You'll have to knock on one of the doors and ask for directions.'

'Me? Why me?'

'Have you not seen the state of my feet? I doubt I could hardly cross the road.'

'Yeah, but there's probably nobody here that speaks English, and you know your Greek is a lot better than mine.'

'You're only after directions. Tell 'em the name and then watch which way they point.'

An image flashed into Trevor's mind of the time a few months ago when he'd had to go into a pharmacy and mime that he wanted haemorrhoid ointment.

'That's easy for you to say, but what if—'

He broke off abruptly, startled by the sudden appearance of a face at his open window. It was a boy of about eleven or twelve years old with lank dark hair and a beaming grin.

'*Yeia sas*,' he said.

'*Yeia sas*,' Trevor and Sandra responded in unison.

'You German?'

'Er, no,' said Trevor. 'English.'

'Bravo,' said the boy. 'It's good I practise.'

'You speak English?'

The kid gave him a "Why would you doubt it?" kind of shrug. 'Of course.'

'That's great,' said Sandra, partly leaning across Trevor to get closer to the boy. 'I wonder if you could help us.'

Another shrug. 'Sure. Why not?'

'We're looking for a girl called Sofia Tsoukala.'

'Sofia?'

'Yes. Do you know her?'

'We are in the same class.'

'At the English language school?'

'And also at ordinary school. Why you look for her? She done something bad?'

Sandra shook her head and smiled. 'No, no. Nothing like that. We just need to ask her a few questions.'

'What about?' said the kid with the beginnings of a frown.

'Oh, er, nothing important. But if you could tell us where—'

The boy's frown developed rapidly. 'You with the police?'

Before Sandra could reply, a woman's voice shouted something in Greek from across the road.

The boy turned towards her. '*Naι, Mamá*?'

The woman was in her mid to late thirties with long straight hair that was so red it could only have come out of a bottle.

There then followed a brief shouting match across the road between the boy and his mother, little of which Trevor or Sandra could understand. The kid gestured towards the van a couple of times, and the woman went back into her house, leaving the door open behind her.

'Pah!' said the boy. 'I try to practise my English like a good student, and she shouts at me like I just shit on the carpet.' Judging by the broad grin, he was clearly pleased with this remark but added, 'Is correct, yes? "Shit on the carpet"?'

'Kind of, yes,' said Trevor. 'But you were going to tell us how to find where Sofia lives.'

'Sure thing. Is easy as peas.'

* * *

The boy's directions were rather more complicated than they needed to be – probably because he wanted to milk the opportunity to practise his English as much as possible – but he was right that the farm was easy to find. Getting to it was, however, another matter altogether. A little over a mile past the end of the village, Trevor spotted the elaborate shrine on the right, and a few yards beyond that, a track that wound its way up a steep incline and disappeared over a ridge.

He eyed the track with a growing sense of alarm as he took in the hard packed earth that was liberally strewn with stones and sharp-edged rocks. Here and there were foot-deep gouges in the earth that had no doubt been caused by torrential rain or the passage of heavy farm vehicles when the track had been wet.

'There's no way the van'll get up there,' he said. 'Not without shredding its tyres or completely knackering the suspension.'

'It'll be fine,' said Sandra, exuding a confidence that Trevor had little difficulty in dismissing.

'Yeah, you won't be saying that when the sump gets ripped out and we're stuck up here and miles from anywhere for God knows how long.'

'OK then. So what do you suggest?'

'We'll have to walk it.'

Even as Trevor said the words, his heart sank at the prospect of trudging up the hill in this heat. And how far was it anyway? The kid had told them the farm was a kilometre or so from the road. Or so? What the hell did that mean? It could even be double that at least.

'Walk it?' said Sandra. 'In case it slipped your mind, my feet happen to be nearly twice their normal size, and not only that but all I have with me is a pair of flimsy sandals that I probably won't be able to get on anyway.'

Given his own serious misgivings about conquering the track on foot, Trevor quickly conceded the point and decided to risk it in the van. 'Sorry, Sand, I wasn't thinking. You're quite right, of course. As long as I take it slow, I'm sure we'll be fine.'

So slow, in fact, that it took nearly ten minutes to cover the first hundred metres of the track with Trevor managing to dodge the largest of the rocks and the deepest gouges whilst narrowly avoiding putting the van into the drainage ditches that ran along each side. Even so, he winced every time he heard the faintest of scraping sounds from underneath the van and the frequent rasping of overhanging olive branches against its sides.

But after these first hundred metres, the surface of the track improved dramatically, and although by no means perfectly smooth, Trevor was able to make considerably faster progress. He still kept his foot hovering above the brake pedal in case a sudden chasm appeared in front of them – which is what eventually happened. A rough trench of about half a metre deep and a little less than a metre wide ran the entire width of the track, and even Sandra agreed that this would prove a step too far for the van's undercarriage. By now, however, the farm was in sight and only a short walk away. Mercifully, it had turned out to be a lot less than the "kilometre or so" from the road that the boy had told them.

'You think you can make it?' asked Trevor with a nod at Sandra's feet.

'I guess I'll have to,' she said, 'unless you're gonna carry me.'

Although she could hardly be described as "willowy", Sandra was constantly concerned about putting on weight, which Trevor considered to be totally unnecessary, and he was about to tell her that he'd be perfectly happy to carry her when she laughed and said, 'Don't worry. I'm only kidding. We don't want you putting your back out, do we?'

'Sandra, I don't know how many times I've told you this, but you really don't have a—'

'Besides,' she interrupted, 'it might look a bit odd if we arrived at a farm where we don't even know the people, looking like we're just married and you're carrying me over the threshold.'

'Well, if you're sure.'

'It's not far, and as long as I can get these sandals on...' She tailed off as she opened the straps on one of the sandals as far as they'd go and began to force her swollen foot into it.

'We'll have to take Milly with us, though,' said

Trevor. 'She'll fry if we leave her in the van.'

At the sound of her name, and despite her obvious heat exhaustion, Milly leapt from the back seat and launched herself onto Trevor's lap, dousing him with unwelcome gobbets of drool.

'OK, OK,' said Trevor, 'but you'll have to have a lead on.'

Love the dog dearly as he did, Trevor was well aware that she was what might be called "a free spirit" or, more accurately, a dog that was utterly unresponsive to any form of training, however hard he'd tried. Letting her loose to run amok on a farm – especially one that would almost certainly have livestock – would be asking for a whole lot of trouble that he could really do without right now.

'Right, let's get this done, shall we?' said Sandra, scowling as she loosely fastened the last of the sandal straps, and they headed off up the track with Trevor supporting her as best he could with one arm while Milly attempted to pull the other out of its socket by relentlessly lurching forward on her lead.

The farmhouse itself was a single-storey cement rendered block of a building with a flat roof and, like several of the houses in the village, was in need of some serious care and attention. The once white paintwork was stained and peeling, and the open wooden shutters on all of the windows were already well beyond the capabilities of a renovation expert. In front of the house, a substantial dirt yard was scattered here and there with a dozen foraging chickens, a couple of goats and a ginger and white cat with three kittens who were dozing in the shade of a rusting tractor that was missing a driver's seat. There was also a dog. Large, yellowy white and of indeterminate breed, it was chained to the trunk of an olive tree in the far corner of the yard, barking manically and repeatedly lunging towards them, seemingly unaware of the restrictions of the heavy chain, which was made even shorter by being wound several times round the tree trunk. Inevitably, Milly joined in the barking and lunging contest with gusto.

At a short distance beyond the house were two wooden outbuildings, one the size of a garden shed and the other a small barn, but apart from the various animals, there was no living creature in sight. Knocking on the door of the house produced no response, so Trevor and Sandra made their way towards the outbuildings, giving the farm dog as wide a berth as possible. The doors of both outbuildings were open but there was not a soul inside either.

'This place is giving me the creeps even more than the village did,' said Trevor. 'Did you ever see *Deliverance*?'

'Is that the one where a bunch of rednecks do unpleasant things to some blokes from the city?' said Sandra. 'Duelling banjos and squeal like a pig?'

'*Ποιοι είστε*?'

At the sound of the voice from behind them, Trevor and Sandra both spun on their heels to see an old man in a flat cap, check shirt and denim dungarees who couldn't have been more than five-foot-six even without the stoop. Frail though he appeared, he seemed perfectly capable of using the double-barrelled shotgun that he was pointing directly at them.

7

'We might be experiencing a slight amount of turbulence shortly, so please remain in your seats with your safety belts securely fastened.'

Jimmy MacFarland tightened his belt by another millimetre. Any tighter and it had the potential to cause lasting damage to some of his internal organs. He'd been busting for a piss for the last half hour or so, but once he'd boarded the flight at Gatwick, he'd been determined not to budge from his seat or undo his seat belt until the plane had safely touched down on solid ground again.

This was the first time in his life that he'd ever been on an aeroplane and only the second time he'd even been abroad, if you could count the Isle of Man as "abroad". That was about ten years ago now, and the only reason he'd been was to catch some of the TT motorcycle racing. Getting there had been fine. The sea had been calm as a millpond, and he'd whiled away the best part of three hours in the ship's bar, chatting to a couple of bikers who happened to come from roughly the same area of Glasgow as he did. As for the return journey, he'd divided his time between the bogs and hanging over the guard rail of the boat and puking his ring during a force eight gale.

The experience had left him in little doubt that foreign travel – by any mode of transport – was definitely to be avoided in the future. What was the point anyway? Yeah, there were some amazing places around the world, but he could see them all on the telly without so much as lifting his arse from the comfort of his own armchair. The beer would probably be shite, and he'd heard all about frogs' legs and fried bloody scorpions in some of these supposedly civilised countries. Fuck that for a lark.

The only reason he was thirty-five thousand feet up in the air right now was that the money had been far too good to turn down. Not that he'd jumped at the chance straight away. Hell, no. There'd been many a sleepless night before he'd called back and said he'd take the job. Maybe he'd have turned it down if he'd realised at the time quite how long he'd be banged up in a hermetically sealed metal tube. Four palms-sweating hours, not to mention all the pratting about before he'd even got on the damn thing.

He'd arrived at the airport about three hours before the flight was due to leave, not through wanting to spend any longer there than was strictly necessary, but mainly because he'd heard about checking in and security checks sometimes taking forever. As it happened, he hadn't been misinformed. Getting through security in particular had been a complete nightmare, and it seemed to MacFarland that he'd been singled out for unnecessarily close attention. Maybe it was the trembling hands and the sweating brought on by the impending flight that made him look suspicious, or perhaps it was the long black hair swept back into a ponytail or the heavy scar on his cheek. Either way, they'd done a proper job on him.

First it was the tan-coloured cowboy boots.

'You'll have to take those off, sir,' said the security officer with a stern expression and close-cropped fair hair.

'Oh aye, and why's that then? Every other bugger's gone through wi'oot tekkin' theirs off.'

'Shoes, sir. Yours are boots.'

48

'And there's a difference, is there? I mean, I know what the difference is between a shoe and a boot, for Christ's sake, but the thing I dinnae get is—'

The security officer had puffed out his barrel of a chest. 'It's entirely up to you, of course, sir, but if you want to keep them on, this is as far as you go.' Then he'd leaned forward and whispered, 'And we wouldn't want you to miss out on a leading role in the remake of *The Magnificent Seven*, now would we... *sir*.'

MacFarland had come within an inch of telling the guy to go fuck himself but had managed to suppress the urge and carefully laid the boots in one of the plastic trays along with his small canvas holdall and leather jacket.

The next challenge came when he set the alarm off on the walk-through metal detector and had one of the female officers run a paddle thing up and down his body until that too started to bleep loudly.

'Do you have anything metallic in your pocket, sir?' she asked, pointing to the right-hand pocket of his jeans.

'Aye, just a wee bit o' shrapnel is all.'

The woman had frowned and taken half a step back. 'Shrapnel? What, like a war wound, you mean?'

MacFarland had found himself smiling for the first time that day. 'Naw, hen. No a war wound. Just some loose change.'

So it was back to the crop-head to find that his jacket, holdall and boots had already disappeared through the X-ray machine.

'What do I do with this then?' he said, holding out the dozen or so coins for inspection.

The officer had told him he'd have to put the money in a plastic tray on its own, even though MacFarland was well aware from the look on his face that he had another suggestion he would have preferred.

As he set off back towards the walk-through scanner,

MacFarland had wagged a finger at him. 'And just so you know, I've counted every penny, so don't you be gettin' any ideas.'

This time, he sailed through the metal detector only to find that one of the other female officers was having a good old rummage through his holdall after it had come through the X-ray.

'Is there some problem?' he asked, stopping short of adding "officer", which he decided would be giving these people an even greater sense of authority than he felt they deserved.

'Well, there's this for starters,' she said, holding up a half-used tube of Colgate toothpaste.

'Aye, yer quite right,' said MacFarland. 'Me ma used to play merry hell wi' me 'cos I always squeezed it in the middle 'stead of at the end.'

The officer looked at him as if she wasn't sure whether he was being serious. 'I'm not talking about whether you've squeezed this particular tube of toothpaste in the middle or anywhere else. What does concern me, however, is that it's actually a liquid.'

'A wha'?'

'A liquid.' She spoke the words as if she was speaking to a five-year-old who was hard of hearing.

'Nae, hen. If it wuz a liquid, it'd all leak out if you took the cap off and turned it upside doon. Giz it here and I'll show ye.'

MacFarland held out his hand but got a frosty stare in return. 'I do hope you're not trying to be amusing, sir, because this is a very serious matter indeed.'

'Aye, of course.'

'The regulations are quite clear as to what does and doesn't constitute a liquid, and all liquids must be placed in one of the...'

MacFarland let her carry on quoting the rule book at him, only half listening until she reached the end of her speech. She then held the tube of toothpaste at arm's length between her finger and thumb and let it drop into a nearby wastebin like it was a used condom or something equally disgusting.

'So perhaps you could remember that next time you fly,' she said and closed the zip of his holdall, handing it to him with a cheesily false smile and adding, 'I hope you enjoy your flight.'

If it hadn't been for the sheer terror of having to part company with solid ground for the next four hours, MacFarland would almost have been relieved to have got through all that shit and finally got himself strapped into his seat. As it was, he'd spent the next half hour before takeoff flicking through the in-flight magazine and making certain he could quickly lay hands on the paper sick bag if needed. He'd also studied and memorised the laminated sheet of safety instructions but still listened attentively to the flight attendants as they explained what to do "in the unlikely event of an emergency". He did, however, have to tell the middle-aged couple sitting next to him to "Shut yer yakkin', will ye? I'm tryin' to fuckin' listen here". Not surprisingly, this had been the one and only communication between MacFarland and his neighbours for the rest of the flight.

'Ladies and gentlemen, this is your captain speaking. We shall shortly be beginning our descent to Kalamata Airport, so please remain seated and make sure your safety belt is securely fastened.'

MacFarland took a deep breath to enable him to tighten his belt by another couple of millimetres and squeezed his eyes tight shut.

8

Trevor and Sandra were no further forward in their quest to get positive proof that it was Yannis Christopoulos who was trying to blackmail them. The old man with the shotgun had turned out to be Sofia Tsoukala's grandfather, and it also turned out that the gun had not been loaded. But this they only discovered when Sofia's dad had come running to find out why the dog was barking its head off. He couldn't speak a word of English, so he'd demonstrated by snatching the shotgun from his father-in-law and opening it up to show them the empty barrels.

After that, his profuse apologies in Greek were easily understood, even with Trevor and Sandra's rudimentary knowledge of the language, and they'd also managed to convey that they were hoping to be able to speak to his daughter. Not unnaturally, he was clearly perturbed by this, but they'd quickly assured him that Sofia wasn't in any trouble and they just needed to ask her a few questions. The cloud had lifted from the man's face as instantly as it had appeared, and he'd beckoned them enthusiastically towards the house.

'*Apó ethó. Eláte,*' he'd called out over his shoulder as he strode on ahead and added something about Sofia being in the kitchen helping her mother.

Milly had had to be left outside, tied up out of range from the other dog and both engaging in a constant barking match while Trevor and Sandra were plied with homemade wine and cakes as they sat around the kitchen table with Sofia and her mother and father. There was plenty of laughter, made possible only by Sofia's impressive skills as a translator, but when they'd come to the real reason for their visit, she'd been unable to be of much help. She admitted that she'd been given an envelope to pass on to Wendy Gifford, but when Sandra asked her who it was that had given it to her, she said it was nobody she knew.

'All I can tell you,' she'd said, 'is that it was a boy on a *papáki* – a small motorbike.'

'A boy?'

'Teenager. Sixteen or seventeen maybe?'

Trevor had asked if she might be able to recognise him if she saw him again, but Sofia had said that it had all happened very quickly and that he was wearing a crash helmet, so his hair and part of his face were hidden beneath it.

'Blimey,' Trevor had said as they'd collected Milly and made their way back to the van. 'Christopoulos or whoever it is has gone to a lot of trouble if they're using *two* go-betweens.'

'Doesn't seem likely it's just some teenage kid on a motorbike, that's for sure,' said Sandra, noticeably slurring her words.

Trevor, on the other hand, had had the presence of mind to stick to half a glass of wine and was certainly sober enough to realise that Sandra had apparently forgotten all about her swollen feet and that her somewhat hesitant progress as they walked was for an entirely different reason.

During the slow drive back to town, they had plenty of time to discuss what their next step should be. Not that they needed much of that time to come to the conclusion that there were only three options open to them – pay the blackmailer their fifty grand, go to the police or confront Christopoulos directly.

They dismissed the first option almost immediately. There was no way they could raise that kind of money themselves, and they both agreed not to get Marcus Ingleby involved unless it became absolutely unavoidable. The guy was in his mid seventies with some potentially serious health issues. The news that they were being blackmailed and that his taverna might get closed down could very possibly tip him over the edge.

Option Two had to be kept on the back burner for now. If the blackmailer caught wind of them even chatting to a cop in the street, they might very well carry out their threat and go ahead with making the recording public. Besides, what evidence did they have other than the recording itself and the script that an unknown person had given to a lad on a motorbike who in turn had given it to a twelve-year-old girl to pass on to Wendy Gifford? There was the handwritten note on the script, of course, but it was unlikely that the police in a town of this size had a resident graphologist to analyse it.

'Maybe we should do that ourselves,' said Trevor. 'Rather than simply confront Christopoulos and demand to know if he's the one who's blackmailing us – which he'd obviously deny anyway – we somehow get hold of a sample of his handwriting and compare it to what's on the script. I mean, we're no experts, but at least it might give us a rough idea before we go in all guns blazing.'

Sandra considered the possibilities for several seconds. 'Yeah, it's worth a go, I guess. And even if there was only a slight similarity, it would give us something a bit more solid to take to the police if it came to it.'

While she was speaking, her smartphone bleeped, and she pulled it out of her pocket. 'Looks like Mrs Barkas is on the move.'

'Can't be up to much. Not in the evening.'

'Oh, I forgot to tell you,' said Sandra. 'Her hubby phoned earlier to say he'd be away on business for a few days, so it might be worth our while keeping a closer eye on her.'

'You tell him about the tracker we'd put on her car?'

'Uh-huh. He didn't even ask how much when I told him we'd have to add it to our expenses.'

'Which way's she going?'

Sandra looked back at the screen of her phone and the little red dot on the map. 'Not towards the town. Heading south at the moment.'

'So what do we do? Follow her?'

'Seems like it might be an opportunity we can't afford to miss, but we'll probably be needed back at the taverna. It'll be getting busy soon and there's only Eleni and Grigoris there to feed the masses.'

'Might not be too many on a Tuesday. Why don't you call them and find out if they can manage on their own? And if not, maybe we can get Maria to go and help out.'

Five minutes later, the decision was made. Grigoris had told them that things were fairly quiet so far, and yes, they'd get Maria in if they needed her.

'Great way to spend our evening off,' said Trevor.

'Why, did you have something else in mind?'

'It only ever happens once in a blue moon, so I hadn't given it a lot of thought, to be honest.'

'If Christopoulos gets the taverna closed down, we'll be having plenty more evenings off in the future.'

Trevor didn't answer, and they carried on in silence until they came to a major fork in the road.

'Which way?'

'Right,' said Sandra. 'Keep following the coast road.'

For the next twenty minutes, they passed through the inevitable armies of olive trees on either side of the road, occasionally catching glimpses of the sun beginning to set and casting a path of flaming orange across the flat calm of the sea. It was just clipping the horizon when the little red dot on Sandra's phone came to an abrupt halt.

9

The car park of the Thalassa Resort Hotel was almost full, but it didn't take Trevor and Sandra long to spot Anastasia Barkas's white Lexus, which was even more conspicuous by being skewed diagonally across two spaces.

'Must have been in quite a hurry,' said Trevor, parking up in one of the few remaining spaces.

'Horny is as horny does,' said Sandra.

Trevor wasn't exactly sure that made any sense, but he got the gist. 'Might be our lucky night at last.'

'Although possibly not Mrs Barkas's.'

'Given that she seems to have been in such a hurry, I think we can assume that lover-boy is already in the hotel.'

'Or girl.'

'What?'

'I'm just saying that, as yet, we have no evidence that she really is having an affair, and if she is, who's to say it's not with a woman?'

'Fair point,' said Trevor. 'So how are we gonna find out?'

Until they'd known where the little red dot on Sandra's phone ended up, they'd been unable to give any thought to how they'd proceed once they'd caught up with Mrs Barkas, so neither of them spoke for several seconds while they stared at the front of the hotel and tried to work out what their next step should be. The Thalassa Resort wasn't much to look at from the outside.

Modern with a sloping tiled roof and painted a kind of sandy magnolia. Three storeys, the top two having individual balconies for each room. Fifteen on each floor and presumably the same at the back of the hotel where they'd be overlooking the sea.

'I suppose it's always possible she wanted to get here first to doll herself up before lover-boy – or girl – turned up,' said Trevor.

'Could be,' said Sandra, 'although I don't see how that'll help us. Sit here and twiddle our thumbs till the next car arrives and presume that's who she's waiting for?'

'Unless it's somebody we recognise.'

'Bit of a long shot, isn't it? No, I reckon we have to go in and see what we can find out. If we can at least find out what room she's in, we can keep an eye on any comings and goings.'

'Or maybe they'll be going for dinner in the restaurant. I'm guessing there must be one, and it's getting on for that sort of time.'

Sandra smirked. 'Yeah, I'm doubtful that their first priority will be stuffing their faces with calamari.'

'Hmm,' Trevor nodded. 'I see what you mean.'

'It's still too hot to leave Milly on her own in the van, so you stay here while I go and check things out.'

'OK,' said Trevor as Sandra opened the passenger door and stepped out onto the tarmac, 'but make sure you come back and let me know if anything's happening.'

Sandra blew him an exaggerated kiss and set off towards the hotel entrance, which was Milly's cue to hurtle from the back of the van and leap onto the recently vacated passenger seat, gazing after her and beginning to whine.

Trevor attached a lead to her collar.

'Come on, you,' he said. 'Let's go for a bit of a stroll.'

* * *

'Well, that didn't do us much good,' Sandra had said when she came back out of the hotel and caught up with Trevor and Milly wandering around the car park. 'Miserable git on reception gave me some crap about how he couldn't possibly give out any information about their guests, even when I told him that Mrs Barkas was my sister-in-law and that I'd brought the medication she'd forgotten and she could die without it.

'"In that case, madam," he said, "if you'd care to leave it with me, I will contact Mrs Barkas and she can come and collect it herself." Course, I didn't have so much as a packet of aspirin on me, so that was a non-starter, and I don't even know if she's *got* a sister-in-law, never mind a life-threatening disease. And you should've seen how snotty he got when I offered him a bribe.'

'So now what?' Trevor had said.

'You'll have to create a diversion to get him away from the reception desk, so I can at least try and find out what room she's in.'

'A diversion? What kind of diversion?'

'The kind of diversion that gets him away from the reception desk.'

'Such as?'

They'd then spent the next few minutes suggesting various possibilities, most of which were almost immediately dismissed for being totally impractical or

59

just plain crazy or both. The only one that seemed to have any chance of succeeding meant that Trevor was now walking Milly around the side of the hotel to the back while Sandra hovered near the hotel entrance where she had a clear view of the reception desk.

A wide crazy-paving path sloped downwards past well-maintained lawns and flowerbeds towards the sea, and between the back of the building and the beach an impressively large swimming pool was surrounded by a vast area of ceramic tiles of a similar sandy magnolia colour as the hotel. The strategically placed pseudo streetlamps were subtle but effective, and the lighting beneath the surface of the pool gave the water an unnaturally turquoise tinge. Of the multitude of white sun loungers, only half a dozen were occupied, and these were all close to the open-fronted bar, from which came the muted strains of Greek bouzouki music.

There was no-one in the pool itself, and Trevor made his way to the far side with Milly excitedly lunging on her lead as she vainly attempted to reach the water. She'd never been overly fond of getting wet, but within a few days of arriving at Marcus Ingleby's villa a year ago, she'd begun to recognise that a plunge in his pool was an excellent antidote to the heat of the day. Just to be sure, however, Trevor had brought her favourite rubber ball with him, and when he unclipped her lead and tossed the ball into the middle of the pool, Milly was after it in a flash of black and tan fur.

The noise of the splash was more than loud enough to rouse the attention of the drinkers on the sun loungers.

'Oh, good grief,' shouted one of them, a middle-aged woman in a gaudy swimsuit and equally gaudy sarong. 'There's a damn dog in the pool.'

Her additional pointing at Milly was entirely redundant as all of the others were already looking in that direction. One of the men, who was a little older and sported a bright pink T-shirt and knee-length shorts, jumped to his feet and yelled at Trevor to, 'Get that bloody dog out of there.'

'It is disgusting, the water it is polluting,' shouted another man with a Germanic accent.

Milly was having far too much fun splashing around in the pool to take any notice. Not that she would have done even if Trevor had told her to get out, and he wasn't about to do that anyway. Annoying the residents was the whole purpose of the exercise, and it seemed to be working perfectly, especially when he saw that the first man had turned his back and was scurrying into the hotel.

Excellent, thought Trevor. He's off to complain to the— Hang on a minute, though. He's going into the bar.

From where he was standing, he could clearly see the man speaking to the woman behind the bar and gesticulating wildly. Seconds later, the woman strode out onto the terrace and joined in with the rest of the pointers and shouters before making her way around the pool towards Trevor.

Oh, bloody Nora. This wasn't supposed to happen at all.

He edged away from her, speeding up as she increased her pace, while Milly apparently decided that she'd had enough watery fun for one evening and began to clamber out of the pool. After three attempts, she made it up onto the tiles and shook herself vigorously, right in front of the approaching barmaid and scoring a direct hit with a heavy shower of water.

Meanwhile, Trevor's peripheral vision had caught sight of the Germanic-sounding man hurrying around the pool in the opposite direction with the likely intention of creating a pincer movement. Trevor quickly weighed up his chances. The man was in his mid to late thirties, tall and evidently worked out on a regular basis. The woman from behind the bar was early twenties, below average height and with the physique of an undernourished stick insect.

No contest, he thought, and turned towards her at the precise moment that the sodden Milly arrived at speed and with a grossly inefficient braking ability. The sudden and unexpected impact caught him in the crook of his right knee, spinning him round while he clutched frantically at the air to try and remain upright. The laws of physics were, however, not on his side, and the inevitable splash was far greater than Milly had achieved.

Trevor was not the strongest of swimmers by any means, and he employed much the same arm flailing technique that he'd used a moment earlier to return to the surface. Spluttering and coughing out a mouthful of heavily chlorinated water, he became aware that all of the shouting and yelling from before had now transformed into rapturous applause and gales of hysterical laughter. On this occasion, though, the sound was coming not only from the small group of previously irate poolsiders but also from higher up.

Through streaming eyes, his gaze drifted upwards to the first and second floor balconies, several of which were now occupied, presumably by those hotel guests who had been alerted to the shouting and yelling commotion. He was about to flounder his way to the side of the pool when a particular couple on one of the second floor balconies caught his attention. A woman with jet black hair in a white towelling robe and a slightly older man in a matching robe.

'Bloody Nora,' Trevor said aloud and inadvertently swallowed another mouthful of pool water.

10

'Are you sure it was him?' said Sandra as Trevor squirmed around in the back of the van to get out of his soaking wet clothes.

'Not a hundred per cent, no,' said Trevor, his voice partially muffled by the T-shirt that was refusing to detach itself from his head and shoulders. 'I had a bit of trouble focusing, which isn't that surprising when you're drowning.'

'But you're sure as you can be?'

'Pretty much. And judging by the way he scuttled back into his room when he spotted me, I'd say it had to be Christopoulos, and I'm absolutely certain it was Mrs Barkas.'

'So he obviously recognised you then?'

'Seems like it.'

'Pity we didn't get a photo as evidence.'

'Yeah, well, taking photos is also a bit tricky while you're drowning. Not to mention that my phone might not have been up to the job by then.'

So saying, he pulled his dripping wet smartphone out of his back pocket and held it out for Sandra's inspection.

'No more *Angry Birds* for you for a while then.'

'Sandra, you know perfectly well that I have never in my life played *Angry Birds* or any other—'

'I know, I know,' Sandra chuckled and fired up the van's engine. 'We'll probably have to get you a new phone, though. Maybe even get Barkas to stump up for one on our expenses.'

Trevor finished dressing in the dry clothes from the cupboard next to the back seat where Milly was lying and apparently enjoying licking the chlorinated water from her fur.

'Where are we going then?' he said as he flopped down onto the passenger seat.

'Back to base unless we can think of any better option on the way.'

'You don't think we ought to tell Barkas about his missus first?'

Sandra waggled her head from side to side while she gave it some thought. 'I dunno. We're fairly sure we know who it is now, but without any real proof, it'll just be our word against Christopoulos's.'

'But who knows how long it'll be before we can *get* proof? I reckon we owe it to him to at least let him know we've made some progress. We haven't hardly had anything to report since he gave us the job, and he's paying us a fair bit of money. Maybe he's already thinking of giving up on us.'

'Tell you what,' said Sandra. 'Perhaps we should sleep on it and make a decision in the morning.'

As they retraced their route north along the coast, it occurred to Trevor that Christopoulos might have given them a way out of his little blackmail scheme. What if they turned blackmailers themselves and threatened to tell Barkas it was him that was having an affair with Mrs B unless he handed over the recording and any copies he might have? Barkas was well known in the area as a rich and powerful man who didn't suffer fools – and very probably adulterers – lightly, and there were more than a few rumours that he had some rather unpleasant contacts in the world of organised crime. Surely that would be more than enough to make Christopoulos drop the whole blackmail thing if he believed he might be about to lose his kneecaps – or worse.

On the other hand, if Barkas ever found out that they'd held out on him by not revealing the identity of his wife's lover, the same fate might end up being theirs rather than Christopoulos's. Besides, not telling him the truth about what he'd paid them to find out would be massively unethical, and his conscience wouldn't allow that to happen and nor would Sandra's.

Trevor was forced to admit to himself that any idea of trying to cancel out one blackmail with another was absurd, and apart from being unethical, Barkas would probably want more than simply their word that it was Yannis Christopoulos who was making the two-backed beast with his wife. By the same token, they could hardly go to the police with some half-baked story that Christopoulos was trying to blackmail them unless they had at least some kind of evidence to back it up.

'Whichever way you look at it, that's what we need to get,' he said.

'What?'

'Evidence. In both cases. Evidence that it's Christopoulos that's having an affair with Barkas's wife and evidence that it's also Christopoulos who's trying to blackmail us.'

'Any suggestions?'

'What about the handwriting on the script he gave to Wendy Gifford? We were going to try and match that with his.'

'Sounds good in theory, but he's hardly likely to give us a sample voluntarily, so how else are we gonna...?'

Her voice tailed off before she finished the sentence, which was a sign that Trevor knew all too well.

'You've had a brilliant idea, haven't you?' he said.

'Not for me to say whether it's brilliant or not, but it's the best I can do for now.'

65

* * *

Even though it was a clear, moonlit night, there were still plenty of pitfalls for the unwary in the shadows of the rough ground behind Christopoulos's taverna, and Trevor found one easily.

'Ow, bugger,' he said as he turned his ankle in a hidden dip in the earth and ended up on his backside.

'You OK?' said Sandra, turning back to see what was wrong.

'Yeah, fine. Just thought I'd have a sit down for a minute.'

'And you go on at *me* about sarcasm.'

Trevor rubbed his injured ankle. 'I'm not convinced this is such a brilliant idea after all.'

'Well, if you've got a better one, you'll be sure to let me know, won't you?'

'And thanks for the sympathy, by the way.'

'Not broken anything, have you?'

Trevor detected a softening in her tone, which appeared to indicate her genuine concern.

'Don't think so,' he said. 'Slight sprain maybe.'

Sandra held out her hand to help him up. 'Come on then. We need to get this done in case Christopoulos decides to come back early from his love nest.'

'Not very likely, I'd've thought,' said Trevor and gingerly tested his injured ankle until it supported his full weight.

'No point taking any more risks than we are already. You all right to keep going?'

'Take it slow, though, eh?'

The back door of Christopoulos's taverna was wide open. Inside, a brightly lit corridor turned at right-angles to the left after about seven or eight metres. Judging by the sound of clattering pots and pans and the heavy aroma of cooking meat, the kitchen was immediately round the corner. The first two doors in the hallway were the men's and women's toilets, although it was hard to tell which was which from the rather cryptic symbols mounted on them since one bore the image of an elephant and the other a giraffe. The third door was closed and, as Sandra quickly discovered, locked.

'This must be his office,' she whispered and took a small leather wallet from her pocket.

Selecting two of the half dozen thin-bladed instruments it contained, she stooped and inserted them into the lock. Seconds later, there was a sharp click, and she slowly opened the door.

'Blimey, that was impressive,' said Trevor as they both stepped inside the room.

Sandra replaced the picks in their wallet and winked. 'Don't forget I was in the private detective business quite a while before I even met you.'

Trevor closed the door and flicked on the light switch.

'Jesus, Trev. What are you doing?' Sandra hissed at him. 'Turn it *off*. Somebody might notice the light under the door.'

Trevor did as instructed, and Sandra switched on her pen torch, scanning it around the room.

It wasn't unlike the back office at their own taverna. Small, needing a good clean and cluttered with all kinds of stuff that had no business being in an office at all – crates of bottles, a couple of broken chairs stacked in the corner and an entire set of scuba gear, including a harpoon gun. The walls had the usual quota of religious icons to be found in almost every office, bar, shop and home in Greece. Sometimes painted on wood, they were mostly pictures of Christ, the Virgin Mary or some saint or other. A basic six-drawer desk stood against the far wall beneath a barred window, its surface littered with an untidy assortment of papers, files and unopened mail.

'You check that lot out,' said Sandra, 'and I'll do the drawers.'

Trevor switched on his own pen torch. He dismissed the sealed envelopes on the basis that Christopoulos was hardly likely to be writing to himself and began sifting through the loose sheets of paper. Most were in typescript, and the few that were handwritten were letters addressed *to* him and nothing that could be attributed to Christopoulos himself. He flipped open one of the cardboard pocket folders and rifled through the contents.

'Hello. What have we got here then?' said Sandra.

She was on her knees and pointing into the open bottom drawer on the left side of the desk with one of her lock picks. Trevor leaned over to see that the only item in the drawer was a semi-automatic handgun.

'Interesting office equipment,' he said.

'Worth knowing he's got a weapon, I suppose,' said Sandra.

'You think he might shoot us?'

'Unlikely, but forewarned is forearmed.'

'What does that mean? We get a gun ourselves?'

Sandra ignored the question. 'Found anything useful yet?'

'Nothing handwritten so far.'

'We'd best crack on then before somebody comes.'

She closed the drawer with the gun in it and opened the top one on the right while Trevor continued searching through the folders on the desktop. Again, there was nothing of any use except for half a page of handwriting that could have been written by anyone. It was also hardly a big surprise that it was all in Greek, which would have made matching the handwriting to the note on the script even more difficult.

He was becoming increasingly despondent that this whole exercise was a complete waste of time and, more importantly, not worth the risk of being caught breaking and entering, when there was a knock at the door.

'*Kýrie* Christopoulos?'

At the sound of the woman's voice, Trevor and Sandra froze and exchanged anxious glances before simultaneously flicking off their pen torches.

The woman called out Christopoulos's name again and then slowly opened the door. She switched on the overhead light to reveal the tableau of Trevor standing next to the desk with a sheaf of papers in his hand and Sandra on her knees beside him.

'*Ti kánete ethó*?' said the woman, her eyes popping as she wiped her hands on her somewhat grubby apron.

'Er...' Sandra began and got to her feet. 'Sorry, we were looking for the *toualétes*.'

'Toilets not in here,' said the woman with a disbelieving frown and pointed at the wall that separated the office from the toilets. '*Oi toualétes eínai thípla*.'

'Yes, of course,' said Sandra. 'How silly of us.'

She set off towards the open door with Trevor following closely in her wake, but the woman hesitated before stepping aside to let them pass.

'*Sas xéro*,' she said. 'You are the English at *Sto Limáni* taverna.'

Neither Trevor nor Sandra bothered to answer as they scurried to make their escape.

11

Christopoulos's visit wasn't at all unexpected, but it didn't happen until about eleven the next morning. Presumably it had taken him this long for him to tear himself from the arms of Anastasia Barkas, return to his taverna and be informed of the previous night's break-in.

'How dare you?' he roared as he burst into the back office at the *Sto Limáni* taverna with a face like he hadn't had much sleep but could still summon up the energy to tear somebody limb from limb if the fancy took him. And judging by the solid, slightly squat physique, he'd have had no problem following it through.

'Mr Christopoulos. What a pleasant surprise,' said Sandra, all teeth and flashing blue eyes as she spun round on the swivel chair to face him.

'How very odd,' said Trevor, who was perched on the edge of the desk with his legs stretched out in front of him. 'We were only just talking about you.'

'Cut the bullshit,' said Christopoulos. 'I wanna know what you were doing in my office.'

Trevor and Sandra gave him their innocent no-idea-what-you're-talking-about looks that they'd been practising earlier.

'Sorry, but I've no idea what you're talking about,' said Sandra.

'Me neither,' said Trevor.

Christopoulos took a step closer to them, his fists clenched and the weight of his heavy dark eyebrows

70

seeming to force his eyelids into narrow slits. 'You were recognised, dammit.'

'Oh really?' said Sandra. 'Who by?'

'A member of my staff. She said it seemed like you were searching for something.'

Trevor pursed his lips and slowly shook his head. 'Not us, I'm afraid. Must have been somebody that *looked* like us.'

Christopoulos's knuckles visibly whitened. If he clenches his fists any harder, thought Trevor, he'll be drawing blood from his palms.

'You do realise I could report you to the police for this.'

'For what exactly?' said Sandra.

'For breaking into my fucking office, that's what.' Christopoulos's voice had almost trebled in volume, but it instantly dropped back down again when he added, 'And for robbery.'

'Robbery?' said Trevor. 'So what was it we're supposed to have stolen?'

'Especially as we weren't even there in the first place,' Sandra put in.

The slits of Christopoulos's eyes opened wide, and his menacing expression morphed into a leer of a grin. 'Oh, I'm sure I can think of something. Nothing *too* valuable perhaps. I mean, I'm not a cruel man, and I wouldn't want you to spend quite so many years in prison. But unless you tell me what it was you were searching for in my office...'

He let the sentence hang, unclenched his fists and held his hands at his sides, palms towards them.

'Well now, Yannis... You don't mind if I call you Yannis, do you?' said Sandra but didn't wait for a response. 'If you want to get into trading threats, how about this one? How about we go to the cops ourselves and tell them all about your little blackmail scheme?'

Trevor and Sandra had been expecting Christopoulos and had already agreed they would confront him about the blackmail, so Trevor watched closely to see how he would react. Surprise, certainly, but it was impossible to tell whether it was genuine or not.

'Blackmail?' said Christopoulos. 'What the hell are you talking about?'

Sandra picked up the recording script from the desk behind her and held it out for his inspection. 'How about this?'

Christopoulos reached out to take the paper from her, but she snatched it back out of his range.

'I can't read it from there,' said Christopoulos. 'What is it?'

'It's a script that you gave to Wendy Gifford for us to record so that you could get our taverna closed down.'

Christopoulos laughed unconvincingly. 'Are you insane? I don't even know anybody called Wendy Gifford. And in any case, why would I want your taverna to be closed down?'

It was Trevor and Sandra's turn to laugh, but rather more convincingly.

'Oh, come off it,' said Trevor. 'You've been trying to sabotage us for months. The negative reviews, the wasps, the unexplained power cuts. None of that worked, so you resorted to outright blackmail.'

'That's absolutely ridiculous. And don't think that accusing me of blackmail is going to stop me going to the police about—'

He was interrupted by Sandra playing the incriminating recording, which she'd already cued up on the laptop before Christopoulos's arrival.

'Well, that was very stupid of you,' said Christopoulos when the recording ended. 'Especially the part about bribing a health inspector. That could land you in a lot of trouble, that could.'

'Which is precisely what you intended,' said Sandra.

Christopoulos snorted his derision but did not respond.

'And by the way,' said Trevor. 'Speaking of landing in a lot of trouble, you must be terrified that Alexandros Barkas might find out about your little... dalliance with his beloved wife. I suppose you're aware of his connections with organised crime?'

The faint grin that Christopoulos had been wearing vanished in a flash. 'That's none of your damned business.'

'But that's where you're wrong, you see, Yannis,' said Sandra. 'It's very much our business because Mr Barkas is paying us – quite handsomely, I might add – to find out who it is that's been having their wicked way with Mrs Barkas.'

Christopoulos took a plain white handkerchief from his pocket and dabbed at the beads of sweat that had begun to appear on his forehead. 'You have no proof. Why should Barkas believe it's me?'

'I saw you at the hotel. You know I did because you saw me too,' said Trevor.

'Your word against mine.'

'That's true, of course, but I consider it our duty to at least inform our client of our suspicions at this stage.'

'And what did you see exactly?' said Christopoulos, his hands clenching into fists once again.

'You and Mrs Barkas on a hotel balcony.'

'So?'

'In matching bathrobes? I think Mr Barkas might have a few doubts about that, don't you?'

'I see. First you accuse me of blackmailing *you*, and now you're trying to blackmail *me*. So what's your price, eh? You keep your mouths shut about me and Anastasia, and I forget all about going to the police about you breaking into my office?'

'Not at all,' said Sandra. 'As Trevor just told you, we have a duty to our client to keep him informed of any developments in our investigation.'

'Pah! What developments? You think that fat old fart will set his gangster dogs on me purely because you *say* you saw me on a balcony with his wife. And in any case, Barkas should be grateful to me for keeping her happy because from what she tells me, he's not what you might call much of a stud in the bedroom.'

'Is that right?' said Sandra.

Christopoulos fell silent for a few seconds, his eyes cast downwards as if trying to decide whether his anger had caused him to say more than he should have done.

Then he pointed to each of them in turn. 'I've had quite enough of all this nonsense, and if you want my advice, you ought to prepare yourselves for a visit from the cops.'

The moment he left the office and was safely out of earshot, Trevor nodded to the smartphone on the desk behind Sandra. 'Not much help with the blackmail side of things, but I reckon there should be plenty on here to convince Barkas.'

Sandra picked up the phone and tapped on the white square icon to stop recording.

12

Trevor and Sandra wasted no time in paying Alexandros Barkas a visit at his office in the town to inform him of the recent progress in their investigation. He listened intently to the part of the recording where Christopoulos had let his guard slip and admitted to having an affair with Mrs Barkas. His fury was hardly surprising and involved a great deal of shouting in Greek and much pounding of his fists on his desktop, and he seemed to be just as incensed about being called a "fat old fart" and the reference to his lack of prowess under the duvet as he was about the affair itself.

'Wait till I get my hands on that little bastard!' he yelled, momentarily lapsing into English. 'By the time I finish with him, he will be praying for death to come.'

'Wow,' said Trevor as he and Sandra stepped out of the air-conditioned office block into a wall of midday heat. 'I hope that was an exaggeration about what he was going to do to Christopoulos.'

'Quite,' said Sandra, sliding her sunglasses from the top of her head to the bridge of her nose. 'Pretty inevitable he'd react like that, but maybe he'll calm down before he gets the opportunity to do something stupid.'

'But what if he *does* carry it through and kills Christopoulos – or, more likely, has one of his gangster mates do it for him? I can't help thinking it'll be our fault.'

'I know what you're saying, Trev, but he paid us to

find out if his wife was having an affair, and that's what we did.'

'Just doing our job, eh?'

'Jesus, Trevor, don't go making me out to be some kind of "only following orders" guard at a Nazi death camp.'

'You know that's not what I meant,' said Trevor and gently took hold of her arm, but she shrugged herself free and strode on ahead.

'Oh bollocks,' he muttered to himself, realising that he could have expressed himself rather more delicately but also suspecting that Sandra's anger probably had more to do with her own feelings of guilt than her annoyance with him.

He caught up with her as she was opening the van door and was about to apologise when *Eye of the Tiger* announced an incoming call on her phone.

'Unknown,' she said, checking the screen before answering and switching on the speakerphone.

'*I think you know who this is*,' said the Mickey Mouse/R2-D2 voice with the helium addiction.

'Of course,' said Sandra chirpily, 'but we hadn't expected to hear from you quite so soon after our little meeting. So what's up, Yannis?'

'*Yannis?*'

'Christopoulos. Or have you forgotten your own name already?'

'*Jesus Christ. We had all this bullshit the last time, and I told you then that my name is* not *fucking Christopoulos.*'

Even through the heavy distortion of the voice, it was abundantly clear that the caller was getting decidedly pissy. As before, Trevor wondered whether Sandra's winding him up was the most sensible of strategies.

'*So what's it to be?*'

'Pardon?'

The sound from the phone was probably a sigh, but it was hard to be sure through the distortion. '*I gave you twenty-four hours to come up with the money, so do you have it or not?*'

'I'm sorry, I didn't quite – *kerrreeeshooweeh* – signal here is – *sheeshaaashooo* – have to call me back – *kerroooshwoosh*—'

'I'm not really sure how that's going to help us,' said Trevor as Sandra disconnected the call.

'Just to buy us a bit more time, that's all.'

'To do what? Even if we had the fifty grand, we're not gonna pay it, and we still don't have any real evidence to take to the police that it's Christopoulos who's blackmailing us.'

Eye of the Tiger blasted out again, and Sandra checked the display before switching off her phone altogether.

'I dunno,' she said. 'If it *is* Christopoulos, then maybe he'll be otherwise occupied when Barkas catches up with him and won't be able to carry out his threat of making the recording public.'

'Or reporting us to the cops about the break-in.'

Sandra shrugged and climbed into the passenger seat of the van. 'Christ, it's like a bloody oven in here.'

'And what if it *isn't* Christopoulos that's blackmailing us?' said Trevor when he'd fired up the engine.

'Then I'd say we're a wee bit screwed,' said Sandra and randomly selected a cassette, which she shoved into the ancient player on the dashboard.

Trevor recognised the opening notes of Steppenwolf's *Born to be Wild*, which instantly reminded him of when he and Milly had first set off in the van "lookin' for adventure". It was a little over two years ago, and since that time, he'd experienced far more adventures than he'd bargained for and mostly not the kind he'd been looking forward to. He'd been falsely accused of murdering his wife, hounded by the British Secret Service, come within inches of being rubbed out by a bunch of vicious gangsters, kidnapped and shot in the arm, to name but a few of his unexpected and most certainly undesirable ordeals. And now here he was, quite possibly on the verge of being thrown into jail for breaking and entering, robbery, and conspiring to bribe an officer of the Greek state.

Bloody hell, he thought. How much worse could it get?

13

On their way back in the van, Trevor and Sandra had decided that they should go to the police with the Wendy Gifford recording and the handwriting on the script as soon as possible. Even though they had no hard evidence against Christopoulos – and the blackmailer might not be him at all – they could see no other way forward without some outside assistance. The Mickey Mouse voice on the phone had warned them against going to the cops, of course, but what had they got to lose at this stage? Either way, unless they paid up the fifty grand, the taverna was doomed.

However, as soon as they arrived back at the taverna, they saw that it was busier than usual for a weekday lunchtime, and Grigoris and Eleni were run off their feet. Maria had been unavailable to come and help out, so Trevor and Sandra had no choice but to roll up their sleeves and get stuck in themselves.

They both knew next to nothing about the culinary arts, but there was still plenty to do under Eleni's instruction in the kitchen, which mainly consisted of chopping veg and washing dishes. Eleni was not the most patient of chefs, and as far as Trevor was concerned, was like the Greek equivalent of Gordon Ramsay – except a lot more shouty and much more sweary.

'*Pio grígora*! *Pio grígora*!' was her oft repeated mantra when they were taking too long to peel spuds or wash a particular saucepan that she needed urgently.

Trevor had a natural inability to do anything in a hurry and didn't work well under pressure, which probably explained why he cut his finger quite badly while chopping an onion. This meant that valuable time was lost while Sandra administered first aid and a plaster, which put Eleni into even more of a strop than before.

Meanwhile, Grigoris could barely keep up with racing into the kitchen with trays of dirty plates and glasses and immediately rushing back out again with the same trays seriously overladen with the latest orders. The poor guy was getting dangerously close to a complete meltdown, made even more imminent when he made his next appearance in the kitchen and said, 'There is a man out there, I don't understand a word he says.'

'A customer?' said Sandra while she carried on scrubbing at a particularly stubborn stain at the bottom of an enormous saucepan.

'Customer, yes. I ask him for his order, and he talks nonsense at me.'

'What nationality?'

Grigoris shrugged. 'I got no idea. Is no language I ever heard.'

'*Katsaróla*! *Tóra*!' Eleni yelled without turning her attention away from the equally enormous frying pan she was wrestling with on the hob.

'Don't worry, Grigoris,' said Trevor. 'Show me who it is, and I'll go and see if I can figure out what the guy wants.'

Part of the reason for Trevor's volunteering was that he knew full well that Sandra was far more useful in the kitchen than he was, even before the injury to his finger. Just as importantly, however, it was the perfect opportunity to escape Eleni's constant yelling and the hellish inferno of the kitchen, if only for a minute or two.

He followed Grigoris through the indoor area of the

taverna, which, as usual in the summer, was totally devoid of customers, and across a narrow road onto the large wooden terrace, where every table and chair was occupied by noisily chattering diners. Trevor took a deep breath of the blissfully cooler, sea-scented air as Grigoris pointed to a table at the far end of the terrace. A man in his early forties with long black hair scraped back into a tight ponytail was sitting alone, his forearms resting on the wooden balustrade and staring down into the gently lapping water beneath.

Trevor weaved his way between the tables, sidestepping the occasional child's pushchair and the more frequent obstacles of brightly coloured beach bags, but as he came closer to his goal, there was something about the man he thought he recognised. Something about the ponytail? The chunky gold earring in the left ear? Neither were particularly uncommon, so maybe he was imagining it.

'Hello there,' he said, addressing the side of the man's face and speaking distinctly and unnecessarily loudly to compensate for the guy's apparent lack of English. 'I'm sorry, but I'm afraid our waiter couldn't—'

He broke off as the man turned his head and looked up at him, removing his wraparound sunglasses as he did so. Until that moment, the heavy scar on his right cheek had been hidden from Trevor's view, and so too had the dark brown eyes, which bore less of the piercing malice that he remembered all too well, even after all this time.

'Aye,' said the man. 'I dinnae ken wass up wi' yer wee man, but he didnae seem tae understand a word I were sayin'.'

Trevor swallowed hard, his heart pounding to the rhythm of an over-enthusiastic band of Japanese taiko drummers in his chest. It was a sensation he hadn't experienced in quite some while, but now it had returned with a vengeance.

'Oh, er, yes,' he stammered. 'Grigoris is... He's the waiter in fact and er... Well, he's kind of Greek, you see, and er—'

'Kinda Greek? So he's nae proper Greek then?'

'No, he *is* Greek, but er—'

The man grinned, which accentuated the deep scar on his cheek even more. 'Hey, dinnae fret, pal. I'm just messin' wi' ye. So just tell us what's good tae eat here?'

'Er, right, OK. Well, the calamari is fresh today and the—'

'Cala what?'

'Um, it's basically squid that's cut into rings and deep fried in—'

The man's grin evaporated instantly. 'You tekkin' the pish?'

'Sorry?'

'Just 'cos I'm from Glesgae, ye assume I'll eat any old shite as long as it's been deep fried, eh?'

'Well, no, I—'

The grin returned. 'Ach, dinnae wet yer pants, pal. Ye need tae get yersel a sense o' humour.'

Trevor did his best to return the grin, aware that his quivering upper lip made it less than convincing.

The man picked up the laminated menu card from the table and jabbed a finger at it. 'I see ye dae a full English breakfast. Nae a Scottish one then?'

'Is there a difference?'

'Course there's a difference, but I kinda think ye'll nae have white puddin' or tattie scones, so I guess I'll have tae make do wi' the English version.'

Trevor was about to lean over and point to the phrase on the menu which made it perfectly clear – in bold type – that the full English breakfast was only served until twelve noon, but decided against it. Eleni would just have to make an exception for once.

'Aye, and a mug o' strong tea tae wash it doon,' the

man called out as Trevor scuttled back to the relative safety of the kitchen.

'You OK, Trev?' Sandra asked him once he'd put in the order for the full English and Eleni's expected tongue lashing had run its course. 'You look like shit.'

'Like I've seen a ghost?' said Trevor and slumped down onto a wooden chair in the corner.

'Sort of, yeah.'

'It's him. I'm bloody sure it is.'

'Him? Him who?'

'The Scottish bloke. You know. The one who... Oh, what was his name?'

'You don't mean the one who was here last week and kicked up a fuss because his eggs were overcooked?'

'No, no, not him. The one back in England. Harry Vincent's bloke. The one who tried to kill us.'

Sandra's eyes popped. 'The one whose foot we ran over when we were getting away from Vincent?'

'Uh-huh,' said Trevor, aware that the taiko drummers in his chest were still beating away up-tempo.

'Mac-something-or-other, wasn't it?'

'Farland. That's it. MacFarland.'

'And he's here?'

'Large as life and demanding a full English breakfast.'

'You're absolutely sure it's him, though?'

Trevor waved a hand in the general direction of the terrace. 'Go and take a look for yourself if you don't believe me.'

Less than a minute later, Sandra came back into the kitchen, her face flushed and breathing heavily. 'It's him all right, but what the hell's he doing here?'

'Coincidence? On holiday perhaps?'

'You think?'

Trevor remained sitting and put his face in his hands. 'Nope.'

14

Trevor and Sandra were sitting on the now empty terrace, sipping cold beers and still trying to come up with a plausible theory to explain MacFarland's appearance at their taverna.

'He didn't let on that he recognised me,' said Trevor, 'but I'm bloody sure he did.'

'Well, that's hardly surprising,' said Sandra. 'Since it's highly unlikely to be a coincidence that he just turned up here out of the blue, then he must have been looking for us specifically.'

'Maybe he's after revenge for what you did to him.'

'Me?'

'As I recall, it was you that half blinded him with pepper spray, smashed his hand with the butt of your gun and very probably mashed his foot when you drove over it.'

'So, it's all my fault if he really is after revenge, is it?'

Trevor didn't answer straight away. Although it was true that it was Sandra who'd done the physical damage to MacFarland, none of it would have happened if Trevor hadn't inadvertently messed up the job she'd been working on at the time.

'No, of course it's not all your fault,' he said at last, 'but whether it's you or me or both of us, why has he waited so long?'

'Could be that it's taken him till now to track us down.'

'Seems like he's gone to a lot of trouble over a smashed hand and a crushed foot.'

'Perhaps that wasn't the whole story. You know what an evil bastard that Harry Vincent was. What d'you think he'd have done to MacFarland for letting us escape with a load of his dosh?'

Trevor rolled the cold glass of beer slowly back and forth across his forehead. Even though they were sitting at a table in the shaded area of the terrace, the mid afternoon heat was still intense, and despite their proximity to the sea, there was barely the hint of a breeze. As always in such conditions, Trevor felt his brain turning to mush and therefore incapable of anything involving rational thought. Fatigue was also getting the better of him, so he decided that an hour's siesta in their air-conditioned apartment above the taverna was the only solution.

'Sorry, Sand, but I'm gonna have a bit of a doze,' he said and drained his glass. 'All this MacFarland, Christopoulos, Barkas stuff is doing my head in.'

'Good idea,' said Sandra. 'I think I might join you.'

They both got to their feet and were about to cross the narrow road that separated the terrace from the taverna building when a marked police car appeared around the corner and cruised to a halt in front of them.

'The best laid plans, eh?' said Sandra and took a step back to allow the passenger to open his door.

'Sergeant Pericles,' said Trevor as the officer stepped out of the car. 'Haven't seen you for a while.'

'It's lieutenant now,' he said, pointing to the two stars on one of the epaulettes on his shirt. 'And Pericles is my first name. You should address me by my family name, Tomaras.'

Trevor and Sandra had had almost no contact with Sergeant Pericles – now Lieutenant Tomaras – in the twelve months since he'd interviewed them about Harry

Vincent's wife Donna's attempt to frame them for murder.

'Congratulations on your promotion,' said Sandra. 'I see the constable hasn't done quite so well, though.'

She nodded at PC Dimitris as he climbed out of the driver's seat and carefully adjusted his cap.

Pericles responded with a strange combination of a scowl and a grin, just visible as he lowered his head and ran a hand over his neatly groomed thick black hair.

'I am here on business of the greatest importance,' he said, eyeballing Trevor and Sandra in turn.

'Not for a quick ouzo then?' said Sandra.

Pericles bristled. 'I am on duty, *kyría*.'

'Oh, OK, it's only that we've had officers here before who—'

'The sun is very hot,' Pericles interrupted, clearly unwilling to discuss the unprofessional drinking habits of his colleagues. 'You wish to speak here or somewhere more comfortable?'

Trevor led the way back to the table that he and Sandra had just vacated and pulled up a couple more chairs.

'So, what do we owe the pleasure?' said Sandra.

'Pleasure?' said Pericles. 'This is not about pleasure, *kyría*. This is a very serious matter indeed.'

'Sorry, it's just an expression. I mean, what can we do for you?'

'You can answer my questions is what you can *do* for me.'

Sandra slapped her palms on the edge of the tabletop. 'Fire away then.'

The two officers briefly exchanged puzzled frowns before Pericles asked if Trevor and Sandra knew a man called Yannis Christopoulos.

'Of course we do,' said Trevor, 'and we were going to come and talk to you about—'

'He has made a complaint against you that you illegally broke into the office at his taverna.'

'Is there a legal way to break into someone's office then?' said Sandra, and Trevor gave her a gentle kick under the table.

'This is not a time for comedy, *kyría*. Did you or did you not do this crime?'

'Well, if it's a crime to be desperate to use the toilet and we happened to choose the wrong door, then yes, I suppose we did.'

'But the office door was locked.'

Sandra slowly shook her head. 'I don't think so, no.'

'And there is a witness who says she saw you searching for something.'

'The toilets, as I said.'

'Searching *kyríos* Christopoulos's desk.'

'Why would we be doing that?'

'This is what I am asking *you*,' snapped Pericles.

'Look,' said Trevor, deciding that winding the cop up wasn't the best approach in the circumstances. 'I don't know who your witness is, but she must be mistaken.'

'Ah,' said Constable Dimitris, who had been quietly taking notes and hadn't spoken until that moment. 'So how you know it was a "she"?'

'Because the serg— lieutenant said it was "a she" about five seconds ago.'

Pericles gave PC Dimitris a withering glance and muttered something to him in Greek. Dimitris returned to his note taking.

'You do realise I have the right to demand your finger patterns?'

'Fingerprints?'

'Fingerprints, yes,' said Pericles, clearly irritated with himself for using the wrong term.

'And what would that prove?' said Sandra. 'We've already admitted that we were in Christopoulos's office,

87

so our fingerprints would be all over the place.'

'Including on his personal and private papers?' Seemingly recovering from his gaffe of a moment ago, Pericles sat upright in his chair and there was a definite sense of triumph in his tone.

Trevor's brain scrambled for an appropriate response but failed, and judging by her silence, the same went for Sandra too.

'Christopoulos is blackmailing us, you know,' said Trevor, blurting out the words in the belief that attack might be the best form of defence.

PC Dimitris stopped taking notes, and Pericles's tone was more of shock than triumph. 'Blackmail?'

'It's when someone threatens to do something you don't want them to do unless you pay them money.'

'Yes, yes,' said Pericles with a dismissive wave of his hand. 'I know what blackmail is.'

'Blackmile?' said Dimitris.

'Black-*mail*,' Pericles corrected. '*Ekviasmós*.'

Dimitris nodded and wrote in his notebook.

Pericles frowned. 'This is a very serious allegation. In what way is he blackmailing you?'

Between them, Trevor and Sandra explained about the recording they'd done for Wendy Gifford, the threatening phone calls and the heavily disguised voice. Finally, Trevor produced the script with the note that they believed had been written by Christopoulos.

'You *believe* this was written by *kýrios* Christopoulos?' said Pericles when he had finished reading. 'You have no *proof* that it is he who is blackmailing you?'

'Not exactly, no,' said Sandra, 'but we were rather hoping you could help us with that.'

Pericles handed the script back to Trevor, but he rejected it with an outstretched palm. 'We thought you might be able to analyse the handwriting. You know, like get a sample of Christopoulos's and compare it with the note on the script.'

'This is most irregular,' said Pericles, having given the matter several seconds' consideration. 'I come to interview you about a complaint that *kýrios* Christopoulos has made against *you*, and now you make a complaint against *him*.'

'Confusing, isn't it?' said Sandra.

Pericles wagged a finger at her. 'This better not be a case of... What is your expression? Tat for tit? He accuses you, so you accuse him. One does not cancel the other. This is not how the law works.'

'Absolutely,' said Sandra.

'Quite right,' said Trevor.

Pericles pushed back his chair and stood up. 'So, it is my decision that – in the interests of justice – you will both come to the police station tomorrow morning to have your finger... prints taken, and I shall also invite *kýrios* Christopoulos so that he can give a sample of his writing.'

'Fair enough,' said Sandra. 'And then you'll find out who's the real villain in this case.'

'We shall see,' said Pericles and headed for the police car with Constable Dimitris hurrying to keep up.

15

The police station was mercifully cool when Trevor and Sandra stepped inside the following morning. A small group of cops and ancillary staff were in earnest conversation in front of the reception desk, and one of them was PC Dimitris. He scowled at them as they approached and then raised an eyebrow as if he'd no idea why they were there.

'Yes?' he said.

'Lieutenant Pericles asked us to come in today, if you remember,' said Sandra.

'I know. And it's Lieutenant *Tomaras*.'

'So is he here?'

PC Dimitris seemed to have some trouble arriving at what he considered to be a satisfactory answer, which turned out to be a sideways nod of the head and, 'Follow me.'

At the far end of the reception area, he knocked on a plain wooden door and opened it without waiting for a response. He said something in Greek and stepped aside to let Trevor and Sandra enter a small, brightly lit room that smelt of fresh paint and stale cigarette smoke even though Pericles didn't smoke. Directly in front of them, Pericles was sitting behind a large desk that was cluttered with cardboard folders, the usual office paraphernalia and an impressive array of rubber stamps, which appeared to be obligatory in almost every Greek office. Pericles was busily writing on an official looking form and didn't acknowledge their presence for several seconds.

'So,' he said at last, replacing the cap on his pen. 'Correct me if I'm wrong, but I think the last time that we were together in this room was about a year ago when I questioned you about the Donna Vincent woman and how she murdered my cousin Manolis.'

'Seems like only yesterday,' said Sandra.

'It was lucky for you that the case was solved satisfactorily or both of you might have taken her place in prison for a very long time.'

'Which is why she tried to frame us,' said Trevor.

Pericles sat back in his chair and folded his arms across his chest. 'And will you tell me it is the same this time?'

'I'm sorry,' said Sandra, 'but I don't understand what you mean.'

'This business with Yannis Christopoulos,' said Pericles. 'He claims you broke into his office. You claim he is trying to blackmail you. It is obvious to even a simple policeman like myself that you do not much like each other.'

'You could say that, yes, but I thought that was the purpose of this meeting today. To try and clear up some of these things. And Christopoulos isn't even here.'

Leaning forward, Pericles unfolded his arms and placed his palms flat on the desktop. 'It is unfortunate that *kýrios* Christopoulos will not be joining us today.'

'What?' said Trevor, unable to conceal his annoyance. 'But that was the whole point of—'

'In fact,' Pericles interrupted, *'kýrios* Christopoulos will not be joining us today, tomorrow or any other day. *Kýrios* Christopoulos is dead.'

'Dead? What do you mean, he's dead?'

'It is, of course, a very early stage in our investigation, but it is most probable that he was murdered.'

Trevor was aware that his mouth was opening and closing involuntarily, and there was a deeply unpleasant sensation in his guts. The only sound was the faint buzzing of the overhead strip-light until Sandra managed to find her voice.

'When did—' She put her fist to her mouth and cleared her throat before beginning again. 'When did this happen?'

'We cannot yet be certain of the time, but it was at some point during last night at the office of his brother Tassos Christopoulos.'

'I didn't even know he had a brother.'

Pericles clicked his tongue. 'He is not often here. As a big lawyer, his work is mainly in Athens and sometimes Thessaloniki.'

'Big?'

'*Epitychís*. Successful.'

Trevor was still struggling to digest the news of Christopoulos's death – murder – when a sudden chill ran up his spine.

'Just now, when you were talking about how Donna Vincent had tried to frame us,' he said. 'What did you mean about it being the same this time?'

'There was a... How do you call it? A feud. A vendetta between you,' said Pericles. 'You yourselves tell me he was trying to blackmail you.'

'So you're saying we're *suspects*?'

'It seems to me that you have a strong motive for wanting *kýrios* Christopoulos out of your lives. Or perhaps, as before, someone is wanting to frame you.'

'That's absolutely ridiculous,' said Sandra. 'Why on Earth would we tell you he's trying to blackmail us and almost immediately go and murder him?'

'That is not for me to say, but as I said before, it is very early in our investigation, and it is very possible that there are other suspects. For the moment, however, I must ask for your passports, and there is now even more need for your fingerprints. The constable will show you the way.'

Trevor glanced over his shoulder, his heart pounding louder than ever, to see that PC Dimitris was leaning against the frame of the open door and smirking with such glee it was as if they'd already been convicted and sentenced.

16

The lunchtime trade was nowhere near as hectic as on the previous day, so Trevor and Sandra had escaped to the office, but ready to leap into action if the need arose.

'Here it is,' said Sandra, leaning forward in her chair to get a better view of the laptop screen.

She'd only had to search for a couple of minutes before finding what she was looking for. The online newspaper *Greek News in English* carried the story of Yannis Christopoulos's death, but details were scant since the news had only broken in the last hour.

'"More to follow", it says.'

'So, what have they got so far?' said Trevor, who was sitting on the tiled floor with his back against the wall and absentmindedly stroking Milly's upturned belly.

'The usual blurb about where, how old he was, divorced, no kids, etcetera and then: "The body of Mr Christopoulos was found early this morning in the office of his brother Mr Tassos Christopoulos, a prominent lawyer. According to Mrs Monica Raducanu, the Romanian cleaner who discovered the body, Mr Christopoulos was lying face down on the floor of the office with his head in a large pool of blood. There was some kind of thin metal rod protruding from his neck, which Mrs Raducanu believes may have been a souvlaki skewer. She also added that the office was in a state of disarray with papers and folders strewn around as if someone had been searching for something. When Lieutenant Pericles Tomaras, who is leading the investigation, was asked to confirm that Mr Christopoulos had indeed been murdered, he replied that it was much too soon to jump to any conclusions. More to follow".'

Trevor launched himself up off the floor and peered over Sandra's shoulder to read the article for himself. 'A souvlaki skewer?'

'That's what it says.'

'Funny way to murder somebody.'

'Not so funny for our Mr Christopoulos, I guess.'

'No,' said Trevor and scratched the back of his head. 'Still, at least we'll be in the clear once they've checked the place for our fingerprints.'

'You think?'

'We didn't even know he *had* a brother, never mind been to his office.'

'Gloves?'

'What?'

'You don't think the police will expect the killer to have been wearing gloves?'

'Shit, I see what you mean.'

Trevor's brain whirled as he tried to come up with something – anything – that would categorically prove their innocence. As Pericles had said, the feud with Christopoulos and the blackmail business could possibly be construed as sufficient motive, and their alibi probably wouldn't stand up either. Depending on when the police decided what time the murder had happened, it was more than likely that he and Sandra would have been asleep in bed with Milly as the only witness.

'You fancy a walk?' he said. 'I need some fresh air to clear my head, and Milly could do with some exercise as well.'

* * *

95

Having first checked that Grigoris and Eleni could cope on their own for a while, but telling them to call if they needed help, Trevor and Sandra strolled along the quayside with Milly racing ahead. Ordinarily, they would have taken at least a passing interest in the variety of fishing boats, speedboats and yachts that rocked lazily on their moorings, but not today. Today they only had eyes for the few feet of concrete before them as they alternated between deep in thought and deep in conversation.

When they reached the point on the quayside where the promenade turned sharply to the right towards the mouth of the harbour, they carried straight on, down onto a sandy beach that stretched in a gradual arc as far as a low outcrop of rocks in the distance. Milly had already made a fairly detailed inspection of the first thirty yards or so of the beach – thankfully ignoring the picnics that many of the sun-worshippers were tucking into – and came hurtling back towards them with an impressively large piece of driftwood clamped between her jaws. In an instinctively automatic response, Trevor wrestled it from her and hurled it as far as he was able into the gently rolling waves. Milly plunged into the sea and set off in frenzied and ungainly pursuit.

'So, do we tell the police or not?' said Trevor, breaking the silence of the previous couple of minutes and referring to their earlier conversation about Alexandros Barkas being a likely suspect for Christopoulos's murder.

'Tricky,' said Sandra. 'Client confidentiality and all that.'

'Yes, but we both heard what he said he'd do to Christopoulos when we told him about his wife's affair. Even if it wasn't Barkas himself, maybe he hired one of his gangster pals to do it, like we thought he might.'

'Perhaps the cops will figure that out for themselves.'

'I don't see how. At the moment, we're the only ones that know Barkas had a motive.' Trevor stooped to pick up the piece of driftwood that the soaking wet Milly had dropped at his feet and sent it spiralling back into the sea. 'We could always give them a bit of a nudge in the right direction, I suppose.'

'What do you mean?'

'Anonymous tipoff?'

'And that wouldn't be breaking client confidentiality?'

Trevor was well aware that the question was entirely rhetorical, and he resisted the temptation to mention the various occasions in the past when Sandra hadn't been quite so scrupulous in her investigative methods. Instead, his already overheated brain resumed its quest for a plausible solution to their problem, and they continued along the beach in silence.

Silence, that is, until Milly came crashing out of the sea, minus the driftwood, and raced across the sand towards a small group of people she'd spotted about fifty or sixty yards ahead.

'Milly!' Trevor yelled after her, justifiably afraid that she was about to cause her own particular brand of havoc.

Since the early summer, hundreds of loggerhead sea turtles – *Karétta karétta* – had been coming ashore to lay their eggs on this stretch of beach, as they did every year, and because they were a protected species, teams of volunteers were almost constantly on patrol to protect the nesting sites. Inquisitive dogs with a fondness for digging were particularly unwelcome, and their irresponsible owners were often treated to a well deserved talking-to.

Of course, the small crowd might simply have been a bunch of holidaymakers playing some kind of beach game, but Trevor wasn't prepared to take the risk, and he broke into a run, with Sandra following close behind. By the time they were halfway there, Milly had already arrived and was running round and round the group of people and barking in a frenzy of excitement. Several members of the group were shouting at her and gesticulating wildly to shoo her away.

'Oh, bloody Nora,' Trevor said aloud with the sickening awareness that his worst fear was very probably about to be realised.

He carried on shouting her name as he ran, but Milly was clearly having far too much fun to take any notice.

'I'm so sorry,' he gasped as he fought to recover his breath.

'This your dog, is it?' said one of the group, but Trevor was too busy chasing Milly around the circle to respond.

After the third lap, Sandra circled in the opposite direction, and they caught Milly in a pincer movement. Trevor took the lead that hung loosely round his neck and clipped it to the dog's collar.

He repeated his apology and pointed at the metre square of wire mesh in the sand. 'I know how important these nests are, and I really do appreciate everything you do to protect them.'

He was instantly aware of how much this sounded like a lame platitude, and apparently so did one of the members of the group.

'Well, if you're so concerned, why don't you keep your dog on a lead?'

She was a woman in her early twenties and spoke with a middle-class English accent. Like three of the others in the group, she was dressed in shorts and a blue T-shirt bearing a loggerhead turtle logo. Trevor assumed that these were the official volunteers, whereas the other half dozen in the group were merely interested spectators, who were all in swimming costumes apart from one guy with a black ponytail and a heavy scar on his right cheek.

Trevor's jaw dropped as MacFarland met his eye and gave him a wry smile.

It took Trevor several seconds before he remembered to breathe. Then he took a firm grip on Milly's lead and dragged her away, still barking frantically, while he called out more apologies over his shoulder.

17

Trevor and Sandra were already ten minutes late for their regular Thursday afternoon meeting with Marcus Ingleby as Trevor skidded the van to a halt on the gravel driveway in front of his villa.

'He's gonna go ballistic,' said Trevor.

Sandra shrugged and stepped out of the van. 'Like we haven't got plenty of other stuff to deal with right now.'

As the owner of the *Sto Limáni* taverna, Ingleby had adopted a fairly hands off position since he'd passed the running of the place to Trevor and Sandra. He had, however, insisted that they kept him up to date on how things were doing by coming to see him once a week with a full report, although they suspected that this was less of a reason than his need for some intelligent company. He also adored Milly, and the feeling was entirely mutual, judging by the way she was now hurtling round to the back of the villa in hot pursuit of whatever treats Ingleby had in store for her this time.

Trevor and Sandra followed at a more leisurely pace – but not by much. 'Three-thirty *sharp*' is what Ingleby had told them when he'd first arranged for these weekly meetings to take place, 'so don't piss me about, OK?'

It wasn't as if he had a busy schedule to keep up. After retiring from a lengthy and generally successful criminal career, he was rapidly approaching his mid seventies and had little else to do but drink, smoke and watch TV, all of which he indulged in to extraordinary excess. The old boy had been a total pain in the arse when they'd first met him a year ago, but they'd got used to his miserable-old-git act eventually – mainly when they came to realise that most of the time it *was* just an act – and had even grown very fond of him.

The sliding glass patio door at the back of the house was already open, and Trevor and Sandra sidled into the enormous open-plan living room as if hoping that Ingleby wouldn't notice their late arrival. It was not to be.

'Where the fuck 'ave you been?' he said without so much as a glance in their direction, apparently too intent on tossing peanuts up in the air for Milly to catch. Most of them, she missed, and had to resort to chasing after them on the slippery pale grey marble tiles.

Ingleby was sitting in his usual armchair at the far left of the room and furthest away from the kitchen area. In between the living and kitchen areas was a large oval dining table surrounded by a dozen chairs, all of the furniture chrome-framed and upholstered in pale grey to match the rest of the decor.

Ingleby's white short-sleeved shirt was open to the waist, revealing a deeply tanned narrow chest and a sparse sprouting of white hairs. Almost entirely visible below the hem of his khaki knee-length shorts was a half-full catheter bag attached to his left leg with Velcro straps.

'Sorry we're late, Marcus,' said Sandra. 'We've got quite a lot on at the moment.'

'Running my taverna, I hope.'

'And some... other stuff.'

For the first time, Ingleby slowly swivelled his heavily lined face in their direction. 'Other stuff?'

'Nothing to worry about really.'

'Well,' said Ingleby, taking a cigarette from the pack on the occasional table next to his armchair, 'there's a particular word in that sentence that I'm not at all keen on and that, Sandra my love, is the word "really". Care to explain?'

On their way to the villa, Trevor and Sandra had discussed how much they should tell the old man and what they should keep quiet about. In the end, though, they'd agreed that it would probably be best to come clean about all of it. News travelled fast in a small place like this, and despite the fact that Ingleby rarely ventured far from home, he kept himself remarkably well informed of all the local goings on. If he later found out about something they'd kept back from him, the shit wouldn't only hit the fan but would be plastered all over the pair of them as well.

'We're being blackmailed,' said Trevor, uncharacteristically deciding to get straight to the point – or one of them at least – in the certain knowledge that Ingleby hated waffle as much as he despised being lied to.

'Blackmailed?' said Ingleby, abruptly sitting forward in his chair. 'What about?'

'The state of the taverna.'

'The taverna? What's the matter with it?'

'Nothing.'

Trevor and Sandra perched themselves on the edge of the long L-shaped settee facing Ingleby and took turns to explain about the incriminating recording, the previous attempts to sabotage the taverna, and how they suspected it was Yannis Christopoulos who was blackmailing them.

'Christopoulos? That wanker?' said Ingleby before they'd quite reached the end of their explanation.

'Except he's dead,' said Trevor.

'Murdered,' Sandra added. 'And the police think we're prime suspects.'

Ingleby stubbed his cigarette out in the onyx ashtray on the arm of his chair with such force that the ashtray overbalanced and crashed to the floor. Milly briefly examined the scattered contents before deciding that there was nothing edible among the dozen or so cigarette butts and resumed her search for any peanuts she may have missed.

'Christ on a bike,' said Ingleby. 'I suppose I don't 'ave to ask if it *was* you that done 'im in?'

'No. You don't,' said Sandra, clearly indignant that he should even consider such a thing.

'I can't say I'd blame you if you did, but if it wasn't you, d'you 'ave any idea who else might be a likely contender?'

Trevor filled him in on how they'd found out that Anastasia Barkas was having an affair with Christopoulos and what Barkas had threatened to do to him. As far as he and Sandra were aware, Barkas was the only other possibility, but the police wouldn't have any reason to suspect him unless they got a tipoff.

Ingleby took a deep breath and exhaled slowly through his lips. 'From what I know of Alexandros Barkas, he's not the sort of bloke you'd wanna mess with.'

'There's also the issue of client confidentiality,' said Sandra.

'Client confidentiality? Bollocks to that. If I were you, I'd be a fuck sight more worried about what he might do to you if he found out you'd grassed 'im up to the cops.'

Trevor felt his stomach churn. Oddly enough, he and Sandra had only been considering the ethical aspect of informing the police about Barkas's possible involvement in the Christopoulos murder, and until that moment the prospect of violent retribution hadn't even crossed their minds.

'Still, every cloud has a silver lining, eh?' said Ingleby, lighting up another cigarette. 'If it's

Christopoulos that was blackmailing you, the fact that he's now croaked clears up that little problem, doesn't it?'

Unlike the possibility that Barkas might do them serious harm if he found out that they'd dropped him in it with the cops, this *had* already occurred to them, but it was scarcely compensation for becoming prime suspects in a murder case.

'I reckon the blackmail business is the least of our problems right now,' said Sandra, putting Trevor's thoughts into words. 'I mean, the taverna might well be safe from getting closed down, but what if Trev and I end up doing life in prison for a murder we didn't commit?'

Ingleby went to flick ash from his cigarette into the ashtray, but realising it was no longer on the arm of his chair, flicked it onto the floor between his feet. 'I guess I'll have to hire somebody else to run it.'

He was a cantankerous old bugger at the best of times, thought Trevor, but this kind of utter callousness was something new even for him, and he was unable to conceal his shock when he said, 'Oh great. Thanks very much.'

Ingleby held Trevor's gaze for several seconds until his expression suddenly transformed from deadly serious to a beaming grin. 'For God's sake, I'm jokin' with yer. You've done a great job running the taverna for me, so why the fuck would I wanna lose you now?'

'Well, thanks, Marcus, I—' Sandra began, but Ingleby waved her to silence.

'All right, don't go all soppy on me,' he said. 'And one of you make yourself useful and fetch me a drink.'

'Water?' said Sandra.

'Piss off. Single malt whisky, and make it a large one.' He must have caught Trevor glancing at his watch when he added, 'Listen, sonny, at my time of life, the sun's always over the yardarm, so I can 'ave a snifter whenever I bloody well please, OK? And in any case, I've got some hard thinking to do.'

Trevor held up his hands in mock surrender. 'Of course. I was just... making sure my watch was still working.'

Ingleby grunted, and Sandra made her way over to the semi-circular glass and chrome bar in the corner of the room. As she reached up for one of the bottles that lined the shelves behind the bar, the familiar strains of *Eye of the Tiger* blasted out from somewhere within the shoulder bag that she'd dropped by her feet when she'd first entered the room.

'Get that for me, will you, Trev?' she called out over her shoulder.

Trevor rummaged through the myriad objects inside the bag, eventually located her phone and answered it without checking who was calling.

'S*o you still think I'm Yannis Christopoulos, do you?*' said the helium-fuelled Mickey Mouse voice.

18

The concept of "holidays" was rapidly growing on Jimmy MacFarland. In his current line of work, he was usually employed in fairly short bursts, so during the sometimes lengthy periods when he wasn't employed, he just hung around waiting for the next job to come along. Until he'd embarked on a freelance career, he'd spent several years working full time for Harry Vincent but had never considered asking for even a day off because he knew all too well what the malicious bastard's answer would have been. "What you want time off for, Haggis Bollocks? You don't do fuck all as it is." Something like that, anyway.

MacFarland couldn't remember even having had what might be called a proper holiday throughout the whole of his childhood. Not that this was a big surprise. Nearly all of the foster parents he'd had – and there'd been plenty of them – were mostly in it for the money they'd get, so they were hardly likely to go lashing out on so much as a day trip to the seaside, never mind a week's holiday in Largs or Helensburgh or wherever. And as for the smattering of young offenders' institutions he'd passed through? Yeah, right.

Largs? Helensburgh? He'd never visited either of them, but sure as hell they couldn't hold a stick of rock to where he was right here and right now. This place had everything. All the S's, in fact. Sun, sea, sand and shite beer. Well, OK, maybe not "everything", and the S for sex was still missing, but the prospects for that were improving by the day. And on top of all this, he had plenty of cash to splash around since Donna Vincent had already paid him half his fee up front with the second half due when the job was done. He could of course have been sensible and stashed some of his fee and expenses away for the next inevitable rainy day, but when would he ever get another chance to stay in a top hotel with all the trimmings and a well stocked mini-bar in the room, which he could raid at will without freaking out at the cost of a miniature bottle of Glenfiddich.

He also hadn't stinted when it came to hiring a car from the airport and ignored all the Corsas, Twingos and other cheaper options and went straight for a silver Jeep Renegade. He was sitting in it now with the engine idling and the aircon cranked up to almost full blast as he scanned the vast expanse of sandy beach below. Even though it was early August and the height of the holiday season, there was masses of empty space between the hundreds of sunseekers dotted along the sand in both directions. Empty, that is, apart from the dozens of turtle nests, made visible by the bamboo canes at the corner of each and the red and white tape surrounding them.

MacFarland had never even heard of loggerhead sea turtles until earlier that day when he'd been taking a leisurely stroll along the beach and come across a small group of people clustered around something in the sand and had stopped to see what the fuss was about. Once he'd spotted that the object of their fascination was simply a square metre of wire mesh, he was on the point of moving on when something held him back. Or rather, some-*one*. Mixed in among the group were two men and two women, their ages ranging from late teens to early thirties and all dressed in identical blue T-shirts with some kind of turtle logo on the front. They seemed to be explaining to the rest of the group about how this entire beach was one of the most important nesting areas for something called a loggerhead sea turtle, which was apparently an endangered species.

Not that MacFarland was at all interested in any of that stuff. After all, he was a firm believer in the survival of the fittest, and if some creature or other was on the brink of dying out, well, that was their own fault, wasn't it? No, it wasn't *what* was being said, but *how* it was being said that kept him rooted to the spot. More specifically, it was the voice of one of the blue T-shirt brigade. MacFarland wasn't much cop at recognising foreign accents, but he guessed it was either Italian or French. Whichever it was, he found himself strangely mesmerised by the slightly husky way her words flowed into each other and how her "th" sounds were more like a "z". He couldn't begin to describe the effect properly, and all he really knew was that it was bloody sexy. And it wasn't only the voice either. The young woman it belonged to had long dark hair, blue-grey eyes, a mouth that appeared to be set in a permanent smile, and her smooth flawless skin was tanned to a golden honey colour.

MacFarland knew he was staring at her but couldn't bring himself to shift his focus in any other direction. He was also aware of his irritation when one of the other blue T-shirts took over the spiel about the turtles and their nesting habits. He didn't want to listen to anyone else, and he found the woman with the English accent was particularly annoying. Not only because she was English, but also because she was clearly desperate to show off her knowledge and repeatedly deprived him of his listening pleasure by interrupting the Italian/French woman when she was in mid glorious flow. And it was this same English woman who'd almost completely broken the spell when she'd yelled at some dog that was racing around the nest and barking its head off. But not just any old dog. A dog he thought he recognised, and a dog that belonged to two people that turned up a few seconds later. Trevor Hawkins and Sandra Gray, he *definitely* recognised. Their arrival had been the only thing that had been able to distract him fully from staring at the Italian/French woman, and it was almost worth it when he clocked the look of horror on their faces and how they'd scurried away like frightened rabbits.

Unlike his visit to their taverna, this had been a chance encounter, but it all heightened MacFarland's enjoyment of scaring the crap out of them, and all the while he was being handsomely paid he had no intention of putting them out of their misery any time soon. Besides, since a few hours ago, they were no longer top of his list of priorities. That position was now occupied by a certain Italian/French turtle volunteer, and as if right on cue, two figures in blue T-shirts came into view on the beach a couple of hundred yards to his right. At this distance, it was impossible to tell if one of them was the Italian/French woman or even if either of them was a woman at all, but he switched off the engine anyway and stepped out of the car.

19

'I'm sorry,' said Lieutenant Pericles, sitting back in his chair, 'but I do not see how that is relevant to Yannis Christopoulos's murder.'

As soon as Trevor and Sandra had left Marcus Ingleby's villa, they'd gone straight to the police station to tell Pericles the latest news.

'But like we told you,' said Sandra, 'we had another call from the blackmailer, and since Christopoulos is dead, it can't have been him.'

'So our supposed motive for murdering Christopoulos doesn't stand up any more,' Trevor added.

'But at the time when the murder happened, you *thought* he was the blackmailer, and that is all that matters,' said Pericles.

It was a fair point, of course, and Trevor was surprised that neither he nor Sandra had figured that out for themselves. In their defence, though, they'd still been in shock from getting the latest call from the blackmailer and had spent most of the journey from Ingleby's to the police station with one single thought in their minds: "So if it's not Christopoulos that's blackmailing us, then who the hell is it?"

Sandra had been much less antagonistic with Mickey Mouse/R2-D2 than she had been on previous occasions when they'd been convinced that the voice belonged to Yannis Christopoulos, which probably helped in getting the blackmailer to give them a little more time. Sandra had insisted that they were prepared to pay the fifty thousand euros, but they'd need at least a week to put that amount of cash together. R2-D2 had told her she was talking nonsense and that another twenty-four hours should me more than enough before abruptly ending the call.

'So,' Pericles continued, 'since your motive for murdering *kýrios* Christopoulos has not been eliminated, I have no reason to remove you from my list of suspects.'

'Oh,' said Sandra, 'so you have a list, do you?'

Pericles hesitated before answering. 'That is... confidential information.'

'But you don't have any actual *evidence* against us. All you've got is a possible motive.'

'That looks like a nasty cut you have there,' said Pericles, leaning forward and pointing to the small bandage on Trevor's finger.

Despite having a very low pain threshold, Trevor had almost forgotten about his wound, and he looked at it with an expression of mild surprise.

'Oh, this?' he said. 'Bit of an accident cutting up vegetables.'

'*Nai?*'

'What's that supposed to mean?'

'Then, of course, there is the matter of the *soúvla*. The metal souvlaki skewer in the neck of *kýrios* Christopoulos.'

'What?'

'You manage a taverna, do you not?'

Trevor and Sandra shared a fleeting look of realisation.

'Seriously?' said Sandra. 'That's your evidence, is it? Trevor has a cut on his finger and the murder weapon was a souvlaki stick?'

'I did not say that a *soúvla* was the murder weapon.'

'So if a metal skewer in the guy's neck didn't kill

him, what did?'

'That, again, is confidential information as it is part of our ongoing investigation.'

'OK,' said Trevor, 'so is it also confidential what time the murder happened?'

Pericles picked up a pen and tapped it on the desktop while he considered his response. 'The pathologist report is not yet complete, so all I can tell you at the moment is that it was late last night or in the early hours of this morning.'

'Aha! So we're in the clear then.'

'Excuse me?'

'Sandra and I were both at Marcus Ingleby's villa yesterday evening and stayed the night as well.'

A blatant lie, of course, but it was Ingleby himself who'd suggested the alibi.

'*Kýrıos* Ingleby?'

Pericles spoke the name as if Trevor had told him it was Beelzebub himself. Not a big surprise as Pericles had had various "difficult" dealings with the old man in the past.

'That's right,' said Trevor. 'Marcus Ingleby. I think you know him.'

'I know him, yes.' Pericles put his fist to his mouth and cleared his throat. 'We will have to... interview him to confirm this, of course.'

'And what about our blackmail case?' said Sandra. 'Will you be investigating that too?'

'Sadly, *kyría*, my captain is off sick and I do not have the resources to investigate a murder *and* an alleged blackmail.'

'It's not bloody "alleged". It's actually happening.'

'I'm sorry, but solving *kýrıos* Christopoulos's murder must be my priority. When that is done, perhaps I will be able to look into—'

'But we've got less than twenty-four hours until we

have to pay up or we're screwed,' Trevor interrupted.

'Screwed?'

'Er... up shit creek without a paddle.'

Pericles frowned and shook his head to indicate that he had no idea what Trevor was talking about.

'If we don't pay up, the taverna will be closed down once the recording's made public,' Sandra explained.

'Ah, yes,' said Pericles with a half smile of understanding. 'That would be most unfortunate.'

'*Unfortunate*?' Trevor echoed. 'It wouldn't be "unfortunate". It would be a complete bloody—'

He broke off when the door of Pericles's office burst open, and he looked over his shoulder at a woman that he recognised all too well. Anastasia Barkas. Still elegant in a brightly coloured silk dress, the faint streaks of mascara on her cheeks spoke for themselves, but she was also very, very angry.

Completely ignoring Trevor and Sandra, she marched up to Pericles's desk and launched into a high volume tirade with plenty of finger pointing and hardly a pause for breath. Since this was delivered at such speed and entirely in Greek, Trevor was only able to pick up the odd word of what she was saying. These included "Alexandros", "husband", "Yannis Christopoulos", "death", and "wanker", which were repeated several times, but it was impossible to fathom precisely what she was so furious about, although Trevor guessed that at least part of the reason was that her lover had been murdered.

Pericles attempted to interject on a couple of occasions but clearly decided that he would have to wait for her to finish her rant before he'd have any chance of commenting. However, when his opportunity finally arrived and he opened his mouth to speak, Mrs Barkas took a deep breath, turned on her heel and walked briskly out of the office, pausing momentarily when she acknowledged Trevor and Sandra's presence for the first time and yelled at them that 'You are to blame for all of this, you...' Trevor didn't catch the last few words as they were spoken in quickfire Greek, but there was little doubt that they weren't terms of endearment.

Pericles puffed out his cheeks and exhaled loudly. Then he picked up his pen again and stared fixedly at it while he repeatedly tapped it on the desktop.

'So what was all that about?' said Sandra after a few seconds when the only sound in the room was the tap-tap-tapping of Pericles's pen.

There was a lengthy pause before he carefully set the pen back down on the desk and said, 'I probably should not tell you this, but as she said this in your presence...' He paused again as if trying to make the right decision. '*Kyría* Barkas tells me that her husband Alexandros discovered that she was having an affair with Yannis Christopoulos and had threatened to kill him. She was demanding that we arrest him immediately and charge him with the murder.'

20

'It's not the greatest of plans, I agree,' said Trevor as they drove back to the taverna, 'but if we're gonna do it, we need to act fast before the cops get to Barkas and he thinks it's us that's grassed him up. 'Cos if he does, we'll be the last people on Earth he's going to want to help.'

'You don't think Mrs B will have told him already? That it was her, I mean?'

Trevor shrugged. 'I wouldn't have thought so. She knows better than anybody the temper he's got on him and what his gangster pals are capable of.'

'Well, *we're* not gonna tell him, that's for sure,' said Sandra, 'but if something goes wrong, we'll be totally in the shit.'

'As if we aren't already? We've got less than twenty-four hours to find out who the blackmailer is, and now that Christopoulos is dead, I don't have the slightest idea where to start.'

Sandra was silent for a few seconds before she took her phone out of her pocket. 'OK, I'll give him a call. Hopefully we can meet up somewhere fairly neutral. I don't want to drop by the house and run the risk of bumping into she who is not our greatest fan right now.'

* * *

The "fairly neutral" venue – as chosen by Alexandros Barkas himself – was aboard his own motor yacht, which was moored in the harbour within sight of Trevor and Sandra's taverna. It wasn't one of those massive ocean-going gin palaces that are often seen in the most exotic marinas such as Monaco or Saint Tropez, but large enough to have a couple of berths and a galley down below and a pair of enormous outboard engines.

It was a lot less neutral and rather more public than Trevor and Sandra would have preferred, but since the purpose of the meeting was to ask Barkas for a huge favour, they hadn't felt in much of a position to quibble over his choice of location. This was particularly so because he'd been more than a little reluctant to meet them at all when Sandra had suggested it.

'You've completed the job I asked you to do,' he'd said, 'and I have already transferred the money I owe you into your bank account. I don't understand what else there is for us to discuss.'

Sandra had told him that it wasn't something they could talk about over the phone and it was a matter of the utmost urgency. Whether it was Sandra's persuasiveness or his curiosity that had got the better of him, he'd eventually capitulated and agreed to see them at eight o'clock the following morning.

'Let's just hope the police don't get to him before then,' Sandra had said when she'd ended the call.

'And also that he's not planning to take us out on the bloody thing,' Trevor had said. Even being on a boat that was securely moored in the harbour was enough to make him seriously queasy.

'So what is it you wish to see me about that is so urgent?' Barkas asked as Trevor and Sandra stepped down from the quayside onto the afterdeck.

He was sitting on one of the padded white bench seats that lined three sides of the deck and smoking a fat cigar. He was dressed in an open-necked white shirt and immaculately pressed cream chinos with tan-coloured leather slip-ons and, unusually for a Greek man, was completely bald, which gave him an uncanny resemblance to Telly Savalas, but with a cigar instead of a lollipop.

Uninvited, Trevor and Sandra sat on the bench seat opposite him. The expression on Barkas's face made it perfectly clear that this was to be no occasion for small talk, so Sandra got straight to the point and explained as concisely as possible about the blackmail threat and the plan they'd come up with, 'Which is why we need to borrow fifty thousand euros.'

Barkas took a deep draw on his cigar and slowly exhaled a plume of blue smoke but failed to respond.

'It would only be for a few hours,' said Sandra.

'As you know,' said Barkas after another lengthy pause, 'I am a businessman and therefore not in the habit of investing my money in anything unless there is the definite prospect of a financially beneficial outcome.'

'We totally understand that,' said Sandra, 'and we do realise that it's a really big favour we're asking you for, and we wouldn't be asking you at all if we weren't so desperate and there were any other options.'

Barkas flicked cigar ash over the side of the boat. 'As an alternative, I do have certain... contacts who I'm sure would be able to discover the identity of your blackmailer and deal with them accordingly.'

Trevor swallowed hard at the thought of what "deal with them accordingly" would involve. 'That's very kind of you, Mr Barkas, but I'm not sure if there'd be enough time for that. We have to pay up by four this afternoon or we lose the taverna.'

'That would indeed be a terrible tragedy for you,' said Barkas, 'but if I agree to lend you the money, what guarantee do I have that you will be able to repay it?'

Trevor and Sandra looked at each other. They couldn't *absolutely* guarantee it, of course, but they were as certain as they could be that their plan was sufficiently well worked out that nothing could possibly go wrong, and Sandra told him so but without revealing any of the details.

'I see,' he said, and for the first time, the hint of a smile broke across his face, accompanied by the *non sequitur* of all *non sequiturs*. 'So what do you think of my boat?'

'Er... lovely,' said Sandra.

'Very nice,' said Trevor. 'And very expensive, I expect.'

'Precisely,' said Barkas, prodding his cigar in Trevor's direction. 'And how do you think I can afford such expensive luxuries?'

'By having a lot of money?' said Trevor, realising too late that Barkas's question was almost certainly rhetorical and that his response was not only unnecessary but also incredibly inane.

'Because,' Barkas continued, understandably ignoring Trevor's remark, 'I have been in business long enough to know when it is wise to take a risk and when to simply walk away. I have also developed an acute sense of whether I can trust someone or not.' He took another long pull on his cigar. 'I must admit that I was impressed with your work in discovering my wife's infidelity, and I therefore believe you are worthy of my trust in this matter.'

Trevor was aware that this last comment was directed specifically at Sandra, but his eagerness to hear Barkas's verdict spelled out overcame any thought of wounded pride. 'So you'll lend us the money?'

'I shall make the arrangements immediately.'

Trevor and Sandra began to gush their undying gratitude, but Barkas held up his hand to silence them.

'You will have until midnight tomorrow to return my money,' he said, 'but I should emphasise how displeased

I shall be if I find that my trust in you has been misplaced. I would also remind you of the contacts I mentioned earlier.'

21

The little kiosk on the seafront wasn't exactly doing a roaring trade. From what Jimmy MacFarland had discovered on the previous evening when he'd spent a couple of hours with some of the volunteers on the beach, it was set up every year during the summer months by Archelon, the organisation responsible for protecting the nesting sites and resulting hatchlings of the loggerhead sea turtle. The idea was that the kiosk would act as an information point but, just as importantly, raise much needed funds by selling T-shirts, soft toy turtles, turtle keyrings and a range of other turtle related knick-knacks. It was staffed by two volunteers at a time, working in shifts, and this lunchtime – as MacFarland had also found out the previous evening – was to be the turn of the Italian/French woman with the amazingly sexy voice.

MacFarland was halfway between his car and the kiosk when his phone rang, and having checked the display, he diverted his course further along the quayside. He'd deliberately avoided Donna Vincent's last half dozen calls and not even bothered to listen to the voicemails she'd left each time. He couldn't put it off any longer, so he clicked on the answer icon.

'Where the fuck have you been?'

As expected, she was seriously pissed off.

'Aye, well, it's no a great signal where I am.'

'Oh really?'

'Back o' beyond place like this, it's amazing I get a

signal at all.'

'What you seem to be forgetting, MacFarland, is that I know exactly where you are because I used to bloody live there.'

MacFarland held the phone a couple of inches further from his ear as her voice had risen to yelling level by the time she reached the end of the sentence. There wasn't much he could say in response, and he didn't have to wait long for her to carry on.

'So, is it done yet?' she said with a slight decrease in volume.

'Not as such.'

'What the hell do you mean, "not as such"? Either it is or it isn't.'

'These things take time.'

'Yeah, and according to my accountant, you've been using most of that time to run up some pretty hefty bills.'

'Aye, well, all legitimate expenses.'

Donna mumbled something inaudible and then: 'I'm not gonna keep shelling out indefinitely, so when do you reckon you'll get the job done?'

'Couple o' days? Maybe more?'

'Jesus Christ, I'm not asking you to assassinate the president of the United States.'

'Aye, that'd certainly take longer.'

'Don't get smart with me, MacFarland. If I hadn't been stuck in this shithole of a prison, I'd have done it myself.'

'Uh-huh.'

'Harry always said you were a useless waste of space, but I didn't exactly have a lot of options.'

True enough, thought MacFarland. Useless waste of space was just one of the many insults Harry Vincent had hurled at him over the years he'd worked for him, even though he'd saved the bastard's cockney arse more times than he could remember.

'You listen to me,' Donna went on. 'I'll call you again in two days from now, and you'd better have it sorted by then, OK?'

The line went dead, and MacFarland briefly wondered what the "or else" might be that she presumably had in mind as he set off back up the quayside towards the turtle kiosk.

There were no other customers, and the Italian/French woman was inside, chatting to some guy in his early twenties with the physique of a beanpole and a lame excuse for a beard.

'Hi there. Youse have any o' they in ma size?' said MacFarland, pointing at the half dozen T-shirts in different colours that were laid out on the small counter at the front of the kiosk.

He'd addressed the question to the Italian/French woman, who returned his smile but left it to Crapbeard to answer.

'Hi,' he said, giving MacFarland the once-over. 'I'd say you're either a large or extra large.'

'Aye, probably. Ye have any other colours or is it just these ye have here?'

Again, he directed the question at the Italian/French woman, but again it was the lad who answered, his accent clearly English middle class. 'We did have some in yellow, but we've sold out, I'm afraid.'

'Nae bother,' said MacFarland. 'It's no exactly ma favourite colour anyway.'

'Ah.'

'I don't suppose you have any in green and white stripes? That's ma favourite colour.'

'No, I'm sorry. We only have—'

MacFarland laughed and turned to Crapbeard for the first time. 'I'm joking, son. Dae ye no follow the footie?'

'Well, I—'

'Glasgow Celtic FC. Green and white stripes.'

'Yes, of course.'

The lad smiled nervously, and MacFarland narrowed his eyes at him. 'Just dinnae be tellin' me yer a Rangers fan or there'll be big trouble.'

'No, I—'

MacFarland laughed again. 'Hey, dinnae fret, son. I'm only havin' a wee laugh wi' ye, like I say.'

Crapbeard forced an anxious grin, and MacFarland instantly switched his attention back to the Italian/French woman.

'So then, I'll tek wan o' the green and wan o' the white. How's that for a compromise, eh?'

'Large or extra large?' said the lad.

'Better make 'em extra large. It's no that I'm a fat bastard, but I dare say they'll shrink in the wash, yeah?'

The Italian/French woman crouched down and spent a few seconds rummaging under the counter before re-emerging with the two T-shirts, each individually wrapped in plastic.

'Well, and there's me thinking you conservationist types were dead against using all this plastic.'

'It *is* biodegradable,' said Crapbeard.

'Glad to hear it,' said MacFarland and reached for his wallet in his back pocket. 'So what dae I owe ye?'

'They're fourteen euros each, so that's—'

'Twenty-eight euros,' MacFarland interrupted. 'Aye, I can dae the *math* as them Yanks are so fond o' sayin'.'

He wouldn't normally pay the best part of twenty-five quid for a couple of T-shirts, and especially not with pictures of turtles on them, but this was all in a good cause – and not just for the benefit of the turtles.

'Keep the change,' he said as he placed a ten and a twenty euro note into the Italian/French woman's outstretched hand.

'*Merci beaucoup*,' she said, her almost permanent smile spreading even wider.

'Ah, so you're French then.'

'*Mais oui, monsieur*. Yes, I am French.'

'I thought so,' said MacFarland. 'An' I'll bet ye have wan o' them lovely French names like most o' youse French lassies have.'

He knew it was cheesy as an opening line, but he had to start somewhere.

'It is Coralie,' she said with the faintest of blushes. 'Coralie Cormier.'

MacFarland clicked his fingers and beamed at her. 'There y'are. Like poetry, that is.'

Coralie's blush deepened. He couldn't tell whether this was a good sign or not, but he decided to press on regardless. 'So what time d'ye knock off?'

'Excuse me?'

MacFarland pointed at his watch as if to give a visual clue to what he was asking. 'What time dae ye finish work here?'

22

An intense fear of heights was just one of several phobias that Trevor had acquired over the years, so he wasn't at all keen on the arrangements for the handover of the cash. The blackmailer had called at exactly two o'clock that afternoon, and despite the heavily disguised Mickey Mouse/R2-D2voice, it was abundantly clear how astonished he was to discover that Trevor and Sandra had the fifty thousand euros and were willing to pay up.

Naturally, Sandra had asked what guarantee they had that the incriminating recording would be destroyed.

'*I'll leave it where I pick up the cash*,' R2-D2 had said.

'But how do we know you don't still have copies other than the one you sent to us?' Sandra had asked.

'*You don't. You'll just have to trust me.*'

Trusting the word of a blackmailer was up there with getting a fox to look after your chickens, but Trevor and Sandra's options were limited to none whatsoever, so they'd listened carefully to R2-D2's instructions concerning when and where the handover was to take place. The "when" was in two hours' time at four o'clock. The "where" was an abandoned water park about a couple of miles up the coast from Trevor and Sandra's taverna. The detailed instructions concluded with the inevitable warning as to what would happen if the blackmailer spotted anyone besides the two of them, especially if they so much as *looked* like they might be cops.

Trevor checked his watch for the umpteenth time, holding it up close to his face to avoid his peripheral vision catching sight of the ground forty feet below. They were standing on a small metal platform at the mouth of a tubular plastic water slide that twisted and turned its way down to what had once been a large swimming pool but had now been completely filled in with rubble and earth. This was allegedly by order of the local council for health and safety reasons, although Trevor wondered why they hadn't also removed the decaying and rather rickety water slide itself or the rusting metal steps that led up to the top.

'What's the time?' said Sandra.

'Five to,' said Trevor. 'About a minute since you last asked me.'

'You ready?'

'I guess.'

Trevor let go of the metal guard rail, but only for as long as it took to wipe his sweating palms on his trousers, and quickly grabbed hold of it again. Not too tightly, though, as he had little faith that it wouldn't give way under even minimal pressure. The Japanese taiko drummers in his chest had been warming up for so long now that he'd almost forgotten their presence. Almost, but not quite, and they began to get seriously stuck in to an up-tempo pounding rhythm when Sandra suddenly announced that: 'Somebody's coming.'

Trevor realised that his eyes were tight shut, and he opened them to see she was pointing to a small figure that was hurrying along the seafront towards the water park.

'Looks like a dwarf,' he said.

'Or a kid,' said Sandra. 'It wouldn't be the first time R2 has used a kid as a go-between, remember.'

As the figure came closer, Trevor could make out that the kid (or dwarf) was wearing a black hoodie and also

126

some kind of mask. Possibly one of those plastic Guy Fawkes ones that had become quite popular since the *V For Vendetta* movie got itself a cult following and the Anonymous movement started up.

Sandra opened the lid of the attaché case at her feet and glanced at the bundles of banknotes, on top of which was a thick layer of loose notes and three large flat stones they'd collected from the beach for added weight. Closing the lid again, she made sure that the two latches remained unfastened and held the case horizontally at the mouth of the water slide.

When the figure in the Guy Fawkes mask reached the opening at the bottom end of the slide, they looked up at Trevor and Sandra and gave the prearranged signal, which basically meant waving both arms in the air. Sandra then launched the attaché case into the chute, and Guy Fawkes took a couple of steps back.

It was several seconds before the case appeared out of the water slide and dropped close to Guy Fawkes's feet. As it did so, the lid of the case burst open, and about thirty of the loose notes flew out and scattered across the ground in every direction.

'*Yamóto!*' Guy Fawkes shouted, and scurried around, frantically gathering up the banknotes that were escaping on the breeze.

'That worked well,' said Trevor. 'Should give us a few extra seconds to catch the bugger.'

'Best not waste them then,' said Sandra, and he climbed into the mouth of the slide, using his hands and elbows to launch himself towards the bottom.

He gritted his teeth and wished they'd had the foresight to have put a mattress or some other soft object in place to cushion his fall when he came hurtling out at the end of the tube. However, he quickly realised that this would have been an entirely unnecessary precaution when he came to a dead stop after little more than two feet.

'Damn it,' he said. 'This isn't gonna work, Sand.'

Their plan to get to ground level as fast as possible in order to apprehend – or at least follow – the blackmailer or their intermediary clearly had a major flaw. The absence of even the merest trickle of water inside the abandoned slide meant that the friction between Trevor's clothing and the dry plastic was never going to allow a rapid descent.

'Shit,' said Sandra. 'I'll have to use the steps. Get yourself out of there and you might be able to see where they go from up here.'

The inside of the tube echoed to the sound of Sandra's feet hurrying down the metal steps, and Trevor sighed heavily. It was partly a sigh of frustration that their plan had failed so miserably, but also, if he was honest, a sigh of relief that he hadn't gone shooting out at the bottom of the slide and ended up as a mangled heap of blood and shattered bones.

* * *

Sandra was sitting on the low wall of one of the seafront hotels and looking distinctly gloomy when Trevor caught up with her.

'No joy then?' he said.

'What do *you* think?'

Trevor was aware that her snarky tone was directed at herself just as much as at him for the catastrophic failure of their plan.

This was confirmed when she said, 'Why did it never occur to me that those water slide things don't work properly unless they've got water in them? I mean, there's a pretty heavy clue in the phrase *water* slide.'

'What happened to your knee?' said Trevor, noticing the nasty looking cut where she'd hoisted up the hem of her cotton dress.

'Little bugger chucked a flowerpot at me.'

'A flowerpot?'

Sandra pointed a dozen yards back down the road to where a large terracotta pot was lying on its side. 'Believe it or not, I was actually gaining on them, so they must have panicked and they grabbed it off that wall there. It didn't hit me directly, but it landed close to my feet, and I tripped. Not much chance of running after that, so I gave up.'

'Looks painful.'

'It is. And here's some more bad news.'

She handed him her phone, and it took him a moment to register the significance of the big red warning symbol on the screen. 'The tracker battery died?'

'Uh-huh.'

Trevor decided that this wasn't the most appropriate time for recriminations, although he definitely remembered Sandra saying that she would put the tracking device on charge once they'd retrieved it from Anastasia Barkas's car. But her fault or not, the tracker's failure had totally scuppered their backup plan.

'Oh well,' he said, vainly attempting to inject even a modicum of nonchalance into his voice. 'It was only in one of the case's compartments, so they'd probably have discovered it sooner rather than later and trashed it anyway.'

Sandra's only response was to grunt and dab at the wound on her knee with her handkerchief.

Trevor sat down beside her on the wall and contemplated the full horror of their situation. There was no denying that their plan had turned out to be a massive cockup, and they were now in an even bigger mess than ever. They may have saved the taverna, but in so doing, they'd lost fifty thousand euros of Barkas's money, and he'd left them in no doubt what the consequences would be if he didn't get it back.

'So now what?' he said after neither of them had spoken a word for a good two minutes.

Sandra exhaled through her teeth. 'Make a run for it?'

'Seriously?'

'Course not. Tempting though it might be, we're still on the list of suspects for Christopoulos's murder, so what are the cops gonna think if we disappear all of a sudden? Plus also, we'd be dumping Marcus in it with nobody to run his taverna, and I've got a sneaking feeling that Barkas's "contacts" are likely to be able to track us down wherever we went.'

'But we've still got no more idea who the blackmailer is than we had before, and unless we know that, we haven't got a hope in hell of getting Barkas's money back. Even if we could identify who it was that picked up the case from the water park, I'd lay bets that it was only one of R2-D2's go-betweens again.'

There was another lengthy silence while they both considered their extremely limited options.

'It's a long shot, I know,' said Sandra eventually, 'but there's always the flowerpot.'

'The what?'

'The flowerpot. The one the bastard threw at me.'

Trevor shook his head. 'Sorry, Sandra, I'm not quite—'

'Fingerprints. I can't be certain, but I'm fairly sure they weren't wearing gloves.'

'OK, even if there *are* fingerprints on it, I don't see how that's gonna help us. If it was a kid – as seems to be the most probable – their prints are hardly likely to be on the police database, are they? And even if by some miracle they were, how's that gonna help us find out who the real blackmailer is? We'll just end up having the same problem as before when we talked to that Sofia girl and she had no idea who gave her the script. And being able to identify the blackmailer is only part of it. We've then got to somehow get the money back off them and return it to Barkas – and all that by midnight tomorrow.'

'Well, if you've got any better ideas, Sherlock, then please do enlighten me.'

Trevor hadn't, so he picked up the empty flowerpot, and they made their way back to the water park to retrieve the recording that Guy Fawkes had hopefully left at the bottom of the slide.

23

'Do not think you can bribe me by bringing me such a gift,' said Lieutenant Pericles, eyeing the large terracotta flowerpot that Trevor had placed on his desk.

'No, no,' said Sandra. 'This isn't a gift. It's evidence.'

'Of what?'

Sandra briefly explained what had just happened at the water park but left out the part about borrowing the money from Barkas. She and Trevor had decided beforehand that, as far as the police were concerned, the fewer links there were between them and Barkas the better.

'So,' she concluded, 'we were hoping that you might be able to check the flowerpot for fingerprints.'

'There's also the three stones inside it that they left behind,' Trevor added. 'They probably touched at least one of those too.'

Pericles raised his eyes to the ceiling. 'I have already told you that I am too busy trying to solve the murder of *kýrios* Christopoulos. I don't have the resources for something like this.'

'Look, this isn't just a few quid we're talking about,' said Trevor. 'It's fifty thousand euros, for God's sake.'

'Yes, I appreciate that this is a very large sum of money but— '

'Surely you have people who do this kind of thing. Fingerprinting, I mean.'

'We have *a* person,' said Pericles, 'but she too is

working on the Christopoulos murder.'

'Haven't you done all the fingerprinting you need to do for that already. It's one office, isn't it? What else is there?'

'I'm afraid you do not understand the complexity involved in investigating a murder, *kýrie* Howkins.'

'Hawkins.'

'Hawkins,' Pericles repeated. 'In any case, if you are correct that the person who collected the money was a child, it is most unlikely that we will have a record of their fingerprints in our files.'

'It could have been a dwarf,' said Trevor, more in desperation than any real conviction.

'A what?'

'A dwarf. An adult who has very short arms and legs. Like that actor who plays Tyrion Lannister in *Game Of Thrones*.'

'I have never seen this programme, but I—'

'Seriously? You've never seen *Game Of Thrones*? Blimey, you must be about the only person on the planet who—'

Sandra cut him off with what Trevor considered to be an unnecessarily forceful elbow in the ribs.

'I believe that you mean a *nános*, as we say in Greek,' said Pericles, 'but I do not remember ever seeing such a person in this area.'

'Maybe they came from outside the area,' said Trevor, realising that there weren't many straws left to clutch at.

'You think that your blackmailer would have gone to the trouble of hiring someone – a *nános* – from outside the area simply to act as their... what is the word?... go-between?'

Trevor looked down at the floor as if he'd just had a telling off from the head teacher and mumbled, 'Perhaps not.'

'No, I'm sorry,' said Pericles, picking up his pen and tapping it on the rim of the flowerpot. 'Doing what you ask would be very much a waste of police time, which, as I said, we have very little of at the moment.'

'OK then, if that's your final answer,' said Sandra after several seconds of silence had passed between the three of them. 'But you should also be aware that if we don't find out who this blackmailer is by midnight tomorrow at the latest, you might very possibly have two more murders on your hands.'

'Excuse me?'

'Ours,' said Sandra, pointing to herself and Trevor in turn.

Pericles leaned forward in his chair, his normally neutral expression morphing into a heavy frown. 'What are you talking about?'

'I can't tell you who we borrowed the fifty thousand euros from, but he made it perfectly clear what he'd do to us if he didn't get it back to him by tomorrow night.'

'You are sure of this?'

'Uh-huh. No doubts at all.'

Pericles sat back in his chair again and tapped at his teeth with the tip of his pen. 'This is, of course, a far more serious matter than I'd realised.'

'Finally we're getting somewhere,' said Trevor, more to himself than anyone else in the room.

'However,' Pericles continued, 'my position is still the same as I explained to you before.'

'Oh, so you'd rather spend your time attempting to solve a murder that's already happened than preventing two more from happening at all.'

Another jab in the ribs from Sandra and a look that said, "Pissing him off isn't going to get us anywhere".

It was perhaps fortunate that Pericles chose to turn a deaf ear to Trevor's barb and changed the subject altogether – or so he believed. 'I should also take this opportunity to remind you that you remain the chief suspects in our ongoing investigation into the murder of Yannis Christopoulos, so you must not leave this district until our enquiries have been completed. Now, if you'll excuse me—'

'What about Mr Barkas?' Trevor interrupted. 'The last time we were here, his wife told you he'd threatened to kill Christopoulos, so how come *he's* not your main suspect?'

'This is confidential information, although I can tell you that we have interviewed *kýrios* Barkas and confirmed that he has an alibi for the night of the murder that is entirely beyond question.'

'But so have we,' said Sandra. 'Have you spoken to Marcus Ingleby yet?'

Pericles cleared his throat and seemed to find something fascinating about the stapler on his desk. 'We have, yes.'

'And?'

'*Kýrios* Ingleby is a very rude man, but he did eventually tell us that you were both with him at his villa at the time when we believe the murder was committed.'

'So we're in the clear then.'

'Not quite, I'm afraid. There are no other witnesses who can confirm *your* alibi, and I am aware from past experience that *kýrios* Ingleby is not always the most truthful of people.'

'You're accusing him of lying?'

Pericles shrugged. 'All I am saying is that I cannot yet eliminate you from our list of suspects.'

'Ah, the famous list again,' said Trevor. 'How many on it now, or is it just me and Sandra?'

'This also is confidential information.'

'I'll take that as a "yes" then.'

'You must take it as you wish,' said Pericles with undisguised irritation, 'but perhaps if you could leave me to get on with my work, it is possible that I might discover other suspects.'

'So, that's it, is it?' said Trevor, scraping back his chair and getting to his feet. 'Well, don't blame us if we both end up dead in a ditch tomorrow night and you have two more murders to solve.'

Pericles ignored the remark, and taking a buff-coloured cardboard folder from a drawer in his desk, he opened it and began to read with studious concentration.

'Come on, Sandra,' said Trevor. 'We're obviously wasting our time here.'

He headed for the door and Sandra followed, but before they reached it, Pericles called out, 'And you can take this thing with you.'

Trevor turned to see that he was once again tapping the flowerpot with his pen.

'Consider it a gift after all,' he said. 'And you might want to drop the stones back at the beach the next time you're passing. It's against the law to remove them, isn't it?'

Immediately outside the door, they spotted PC Dimitris crossing the reception area towards them. His almost permanent smirk spread into a leering grin.

'*Yeia sas*,' he said. 'Has *kýrios* Barkas spoken to you yet?'

'What?' Trevor and Sandra chorused, and Trevor felt his knees begin to buckle with the shock of the question.

'I believe he is not very happy with you.'

Trevor and Sandra were too stunned to respond, so the constable carried on, clearly warming to his theme. 'Yes indeed, because although he is innocent of the murder of *kýrios* Christopoulos, he is very much angry that he was made a suspect and demanded to know who it was that had made him so. The lieutenant refused to tell him, of course, as this is private police information, but he seemed to have the idea that it was you. I cannot imagine how much *more* angry he will be when he finds out about the money.'

He ended the sentence with a malevolent chuckle and a 'Have a nice day', then continued on his way.

24

It was still only early evening, but this being a Friday, it was likely that the taverna would be busy, so Trevor and Sandra took the opportunity to take a short breather before the hordes descended and it would be all hands on deck. They were relaxing in their apartment on the floor above and promising Milly that they'd take her out for a walk soon as long as she gave them half an hour's peace and stopped jumping on top of them and whimpering. She didn't.

Trevor glanced up at the clock on the wall from his prone position on the settee. 'Twenty-nine and a half hours until we have to get Barkas's money back to him.'

'Can you please stop counting down the time every few minutes?' said Sandra as she wrestled with Milly to prevent her trying to climb onto her lap. 'It really doesn't help.'

'God, we must have been insane to borrow the money from someone like Barkas. I dread to think what he'll do to us if we don't pay it back.'

'We went through all this before, Trev, and if you recall, he was the only person we knew of that would have that kind of cash. And keeping on repeating the shit that we're in isn't getting us anywhere nearer to a solution.'

'And you getting pissy isn't much help either.'

The silence that followed was interrupted only by Milly and her increasingly insistent demands to be taken for a walk.

Trevor closed his eyes, aware that he could very easily have nodded off to sleep if it hadn't been for the racket Milly was making. It was difficult to concentrate, but he did his best, and his mind ran through the events of the last few days as he tried to put his finger on even the tiniest of clues that might help to identify the blackmailer. He'd got as far as the last couple of hours and was mentally replaying their conversations with Pericles and PC Dimitris when something struck him as distinctly odd.

He pushed Milly's paws off his chest and sat upright on the settee. 'You remember what that prick Dimitris said?'

'Most of it, unfortunately,' said Sandra, halfheartedly suppressing a yawn. 'Why?'

'The last bit. Something about Barkas being even more angry when he finds out about the money.'

'Yes, well, I think we're perfectly well aware of that already.'

'But how did *he* know that we'd lost Barkas's money?'

Trevor waited for Sandra to digest what he'd said, surprised that this hadn't occurred to her first. Normally she was far quicker on the uptake than he was.

'I see what you're getting at,' she said at last. 'Apart from the blackmailer, the only person who would have known was Pericles, and he hadn't yet had a chance to tell Dimitris. And we didn't even tell Pericles it was Barkas that lent us the money.'

'So where does that leave us? Dimitris is the blackmailer?'

Sandra tilted her head from side to side. 'Not necessarily, but it certainly looks like he must be involved somehow.'

'But what if he *is* the blackmailer? Why him?'

'A fifty thousand euro boost to what is probably a

fairly mediocre income wouldn't go amiss, I'm sure.'

'Yeah, although if we hadn't paid up, how would he benefit from getting the taverna closed down?'

'He wouldn't have to if all he was interested in was the fifty grand. It's the threat behind it that's the important thing. And whether he's the blackmailer himself or it's someone else, at least we've finally got a lead to follow.'

Trevor checked the clock on the wall once again but refrained from pointing out how much time they had left to pay Barkas back his money.

* * *

As expected, every seat on the terrace of the taverna was occupied by the time Trevor and Sandra came downstairs to help out – Sandra in the kitchen with Eleni and Trevor waiting on tables with Grigoris. It was a purely expedient division of labour, based on the fact that he was marginally more useful as a waiter than as a chef's assistant. On this particular evening, however, his mind was so occupied with other matters that his ability to accurately pass on customer orders to the kitchen was even wider of the mark than usual.

'What's this supposed to be?' said one of the English diners when Trevor deposited a plate of moussaka in front of him.

'Er, moussaka?' said Trevor, stooping slightly to confirm what was actually on the plate.

'But that's not what I ordered.'

'Isn't it?'

'No, I ordered shepherd's pie.'

'Oh, right. They're really quite similar, you know.'

As on the several previous occasions when Trevor

had taken an uneaten plate of food back into the kitchen and admitted his mistake, Eleni shook a metal ladle in his face and yelled at him in Greek. Translation was unnecessary. The gist was perfectly clear.

Half an hour later when he was delivering the bill – calculated by Sandra – to a middle-aged German couple at a table near the middle of the terrace, he spotted two new arrivals sitting down at the only other table that had become available. Without waiting for the German couple to pay, he raced back into the kitchen and grabbed Sandra by the arm, causing her to drop the empty saucepan she'd just finished washing.

'Jesus, Trev,' she said as she bent to pick it up. 'Mind what you're doing, will you?'

'It's him,' said Trevor, gasping for breath.

'Him who?'

'The Scottish bloke. MacFarland. He's here again.'

'Oh.'

'And he's got a woman with him. I think she's one of the turtle people.'

'The what?'

'The turtle people. You know. One of the volunteers.'

'Got himself a girlfriend, has he?'

'*I* don't know, but that's hardly the point, is it?'

Eleni shouted something and, applying the five second rule, Sandra handed her the saucepan.

'Maybe he really is just here on holiday,' she said.

Trevor shook his head. 'Too much of a coincidence for my liking. Shit, Sandra, the guy's a maniac and he's out for revenge – on *us*. I'm bloody sure of it.'

Before Sandra could respond, Grigoris bustled into the kitchen supporting a huge tray of empty plates and glasses on the palm of his hand at shoulder height.

'He is here again,' he said. 'That man I don't understand a word he says.'

He caught Trevor's eye with a look of mild desperation.

The heavy hint was unmistakable, and Trevor slouched out onto the terrace, cursing under his breath.

25

Trevor and Sandra had sent Eleni and Grigoris home as soon as there was no more cooking to be done and there was only a handful of customers left. Fortunately, MacFarland and his girlfriend – or whoever she was – weren't among them as they'd finished their meal, paid their bill and left more than an hour ago. MacFarland had behaved in much the same way as when he'd come to the taverna a couple of days earlier, still not openly acknowledging that he recognised Trevor or Sandra, but they were certain he must have done. If anything, he'd been politeness itself, probably because he was out to impress the young woman he was with. From the brief times Trevor had spent at their table, however, it was clear that she was having a major struggle to understand a word MacFarland said.

It had been a lucratively busy evening, and Trevor had regretted letting Eleni and Grigoris go early as soon as he'd gone into the kitchen and seen the mountain of washing up there was to be done. But exhausted as they both were from everything else they'd been having to deal with, he'd rolled up his sleeves and set about it while Sandra cleared up the debris from the tables out on the terrace.

It was well after midnight when Trevor hung the last of the saucepans on its hook above the stove and unsuccessfully dried his hands on an already wet tea towel.

Sandra's taking her time, he thought, so he went out

to see if she needed some help and if she was ready to shut up shop and head upstairs to their apartment for their customary nightcap or two.

The moment he stepped out onto the terrace, it was blindingly obvious what had been taking her so long. Her face was ashen white, and two men were standing either side of her, one of them gripping her firmly by the arm. But these were no ordinary men. They were well over six feet tall and so massively built, they made Dwayne Johnson look almost skeletal. Both wore black T-shirts stretched across their enormous chests and black combat trousers. With their dark complexions and shaven heads, they could possibly have been twins.

'What's going on?' said Trevor.

'You come with us,' said the man holding Sandra's arm.

'What for?' said Trevor.

'I'm not sure we have a lot of choice,' said Sandra.

This fact became even more apparent when the man who didn't have hold of her arm pulled a pistol from the back of his waistband and pointed the muzzle at the side of her head.

'Come now or we kill,' he said with the same heavy accent as his twin.

'OK, OK,' said Trevor, raising his hands in surrender. 'Just put the gun away, yes?'

Perhaps the guy didn't understand, although it was much more likely he wanted to maintain the threat because he kept the gun exactly where it was.

* * *

The combination of physical discomfort and sheer terror was causing a very unpleasant feeling deep within Trevor's guts, and he was struggling to stop himself from throwing up. The weird smell from the inside of the hessian sack wasn't helping either. The thug twins had tied one over his head and another over Sandra's soon after they'd bundled them into the back of a van that was parked close to the taverna. Their hands had been tied behind their backs, which made it next to impossible to prevent themselves being thrown violently around on the metal floor as the van sped off and hurtled round bend after bend.

Despite having no idea what horrors awaited them, it was almost a relief when the van had finally come to a halt about twenty minutes later. They were then marched a dozen or so yards across what felt like an area of concrete beneath their feet. There was the sound of a large metal door grating on its hinges, and Trevor had stumbled forward, encouraged by the unmistakable muzzle of a gun being prodded into the small of his back. In the two and a half years since being made redundant as a low grade sales assistant at a DIY superstore, he'd had far more experience of precisely how this felt than he could ever have anticipated.

The metal door had been slammed shut behind them, the noise echoing around what must have been a very large empty space. Some kind of warehouse or factory floor perhaps? The air was surprisingly cool considering the relative heat of the night, and Trevor had fought hard against the notion that this might even be an abattoir. He'd seen enough gangster movies to know that being blindfolded and brought to an abattoir at gunpoint in the middle of the night was unlikely to end well.

Another twenty yards of concrete and then down a flight of steep stone steps, the temperature gradually dropping even further as they went. Two enormous hands had gripped Trevor by the shoulders and manoeuvred him into position before forcing him down onto a straight-backed wooden chair. Seconds later, the thug twins exchanged a few words that were in some language that definitely wasn't Greek, immediately followed by the sound of heavy footsteps retreating back up to ground level.

Trevor and Sandra had remained silent for several minutes until they'd been sure that they couldn't be heard. Even then, they spoke in whispers. Trevor's head was still throbbing from the rap he'd received from the butt of a gun when he'd started talking to Sandra in the back of the van and told to 'Keep shut your mouth.'

'You OK?' he said.

'Oh yeah. Absolutely fine,' said Sandra.

'Any idea where we are?'

'Not a clue. I was trying to keep track of where we were going in the van but got totally lost after the first five minutes.'

'Me too.'

'But rather more important than *where* we are is what the hell we're doing here.'

'Unless it's just a straightforward kidnapping, my guess would be Barkas.'

'Seems more likely somehow. But it's nearly two in the morning, so we've still got quite a few hours before we're supposed to pay him back his money.'

Trevor shrugged, which caused even more pain in his shoulders from having his hands tied behind his back for so long. 'Maybe he already found out about our plan going wrong and that we've lost his fifty grand.'

'I don't see how, though.'

'Dimitris? Remember what he said about—'

'Hang on. Someone's coming.'

They both fell silent and listened to the footsteps descending the stone steps and then begin to cross the floor towards them.

'Thank you for coming,' said a man's voice that Trevor was fairly certain he recognised.

There was then a short burst of shouting in Greek,

almost all of it from the same familiar voice, before Trevor felt the tie that held his hood in place being loosened, and he squinted momentarily against the sudden invasion of light as the hood was whipped off. A quick scan of his surroundings revealed that they were in some kind of concrete cellar with what appeared to be two large boilers in one corner and several rusting pipes leading up to the floor above. He could also see that one of the thug twins was removing Sandra's hood as well, but his main focus was on the man who stood looking down at them with a heavy frown.

'I apologise for these rather barbaric methods,' said Alexandros Barkas, 'but I hope you understand that there are occasions when circumstances require such an approach.'

'You could have phoned,' said Trevor. 'If you wanted to see us this badly, we could have met you on your boat like before.'

Barkas grinned. 'Not quite, my friend. You see, the reason for this meeting is rather different this time.'

'If it's about your money,' said Sandra, 'we still have until midnight tonight before we promised to get it back to you.'

Barkas's grin widened. 'No, it's not about my money, although I hope of course that this will still be returned to me as agreed.' He paused briefly and eyed each of them in turn. 'This is a matter that is almost as important as money. It is about how the police came to suspect me as Yannis Christopoulos's murderer.'

By the end of the sentence, his volume had risen rapidly to yelling level, and his entire face and bald head had turned a peculiar shade of puce.

'I hope you don't think it was *us*,' said Trevor.

'Then who else would it be?' Barkas shouted, stooping to bring his face so close to Trevor's that he felt a fine spray of spittle on his cheeks. 'You were the only people who knew about my wife's affair with Christopoulos. The only people who heard me say that I would kill the bastard.'

Trevor glanced sideways at Sandra, assuming she was thinking the same as he was. They'd half expected Barkas would jump to conclusions and believe it was them who'd grassed him up after the police had interviewed him, but they'd also hoped his wife would already have owned up that it was her. Apparently not. So, should they drop her in it and risk Barkas being even more furious with her and doing God knows what or tell him the truth and save themselves from a similar outcome?

Sandra seemed to have made the decision for them. 'May I ask what you said to your wife after we told you about her affair?'

'No, you may not. It's none of your damned business.'

'You see,' Sandra continued undaunted, 'and I'm not sure how to tell you this, but we were at the police station when Anastasia turned up and told Lieutenant Pericles that you'd threatened to kill Christopoulos and he should charge you with the murder.'

The puce drained from Barkas's face, and he pulled himself up to his full height, passing a hand over his hairless head as he began to digest this new information. He took a slim case from his inside jacket pocket and selected one of his fat cigars. He rolled it between his fingers and sniffed at it absentmindedly.

'Is this true?' he said at last, his tone having softened considerably.

Trevor and Sandra both nodded.

Barkas began to pace slowly back and forth across the concrete floor, eventually stopping in front of them and lighting his cigar.

'I can easily find out if you're lying,' he said once he

148

was satisfied that his cigar was properly alight.

'Of course,' said Sandra.

'I could even ask my Albanian friends to discover the truth for me.'

Trevor looked up at the nearest of the thug twins and gulped at the sight of the malevolent leer that crept across his face when Barkas said something to him in Greek. The man's response left little doubt as to what Barkas had in mind, and the exact details of how this pain would be inflicted soon became clear.

'In fact, this man here has an interesting *paratsoúklı...* a nickname,' Barkas said with a vague wave of his hand at the leering Albanian. 'They call him "The Dentist". Do you want to know why?'

Trevor really, really didn't, and when neither he nor Sandra responded, Barkas spoke to the Albanian again. Whatever he said was obviously a source of great delight to the man's ears, and he picked up a small canvas bag that lay at his feet. There was an ominous sound of clanking metal objects from inside the bag as he unzipped it and conducted a hurried search before producing something that looked a lot like the kind of stainless steel forceps that dentists use for extracting teeth.

Trevor pressed himself back in his chair as if to distance himself as far as possible from the sort of implement that gave him the terrors even when he knew that anaesthetic would be involved.

'Holy shit,' he muttered.

'This really isn't necessary, you know,' said Sandra, and Trevor could hear the tremor in her voice, however much she was trying to control it.

'Really?' said Barkas, exhaling a thick cloud of cigar smoke in her general direction. 'I'm afraid I shall need a little more convincing than simply accepting your word. Oh, and before we begin, I should perhaps point out that,

149

despite his nickname, The Dentist has had no training whatsoever in this field, but I can promise you that what he lacks in expertise, he most certainly makes up for in his enthusiasm for his work.'

So saying, he clicked his fingers at The Dentist, who stepped forward eagerly, brandishing the forceps in front of him.

'*O ándras próta, nomízo,*' said Barkas, and Trevor knew enough Greek to realise that he was to be the first victim.

Again he forced himself back in his chair, the sweat stinging his eyes as the Albanian stooped and shouted something at him that he didn't understand. Probably telling him to open his mouth, thought Trevor. Well, bollocks to that, and he clamped his teeth together so tightly that his lips almost completely disappeared.

Evidently frustrated – although Trevor couldn't imagine why he would have expected such docile compliance – The Dentist called out to his thug twin, presumably for some urgent assistance. The twin needed no second invitation, and he strode across the cellar floor and immediately began to try and prise Trevor's mouth open with fingers that smelt of nicotine and diesel fuel. However much he resisted, the man's fingers were far stronger than Trevor's jaw muscles, and moments later he felt the metallic taste of the forceps on his tongue. He tried to scream, but all that came out was a high pitched gurgling noise.

'Wait!' Sandra yelled. 'We're telling you the truth, for Christ's sake! You can pull out as many of Trevor's teeth as you like, but it won't make the slightest difference. The truth's the truth, and that's all there is to it.'

'You think you can persuade me with meaningless platitudes?' said Barkas. 'No, I shall be more inclined to believe you once the first tooth is removed. But who knows? Maybe it will take more than one to convince me.'

Trevor squeezed his eyes shut and braced himself for the pain as the forceps gripped the base of one of his lower incisors, pinching the gum at the same time. It hurt, but he was under no illusion that this was nothing compared to the agony of when the whole tooth came out. He jerked his head from side to side but the fingers in his mouth restricted the movement to no more than a fraction of an inch in either direction. Even so, it was just enough to dislodge the forceps and delay the inevitable, if only for a few more seconds.

'Listen to me!' Sandra was almost shrieking now. 'You go ahead with this and he could die.'

This was news to Trevor, but he guessed – prayed even – that she had something up her sleeve that might save him from further torment. If so, she'd need to get on with it pretty damn quick as The Dentist's assistant now had Trevor's head wedged tight in the crook of one arm while keeping his fingers jammed in his mouth.

'He's a haemophiliac,' Sandra gabbled.

'A what?' said Barkas.

'Haemophiliac. It's a Greek word, isn't it?'

'Yes, of course. It's from *aíma*, meaning—'

'OK, but what you might not know is that a haemophiliac's blood doesn't clot properly, and Trevor's case is extremely serious, so if you pull out his tooth, he's gonna bleed like a stuck pig and you won't be able to stop it.' Trevor felt The Dentist's forceps clamp onto his tooth once more, barely able to concentrate on Sandra's torrent of words. 'And even if we can get him to the hospital in time – which isn't at all likely, given how far away we probably are – then do you really want me to explain exactly how he came to have a tooth yanked out by some psycho with a dentistry fetish?'

The delay before Barkas replied seemed interminable

to Trevor, but finally he heard him shout what must have been an instruction in Greek because the forceps slowly released their grip on his tooth with an accompanying groan of disappointment from The Dentist. More words from Barkas and the forceps were withdrawn from his mouth along with the thug twin's foul-smelling fingers.

Trevor opened his eyes as Barkas brushed The Dentist aside and stared down at him.

'Is this true?' he said. 'That you are a haemophiliac?'

'You want to see his medical records?' Sandra answered for him. 'Unfortunately, we don't happen to have them with us.'

Barkas took a step back and flicked cigar ash onto the cellar floor, idly spreading it with the toe of his shoe. 'Very well. I am not an unreasonable man, and I believe I told you once before that I am quite skilled in knowing who I can trust and who I can't.'

'You did, yes,' said Sandra but with more than a hint of anxious anticipation in her voice.

'I cannot claim to be totally infallible in this matter, of course, and I am by no means certain that you are telling me the truth – either about him bleeding to death or that you didn't tell the police that I'd threatened to kill Christopoulos.'

Despite his aching jaws, Trevor opened his mouth to reassure him that they were fully deserving of his trust, but Barkas abruptly motioned him to silence.

'However,' he went on. 'If I find that you have indeed betrayed my trust and lied to me, you will find yourselves back here once again, and I will let these two men do whatever they wish with you. I can assure you that this will not merely involve some unnecessary and extremely painful dental intervention, and it will be of little concern to me whether you bleed to death or not.'

While Trevor and Sandra sat in silence, hardly daring to speak in case they said something that would cause him to change his mind, Barkas switched his attention to one of the Albanians and uttered a few words in Greek. Then he flashed an unconvincing smile at Trevor and Sandra and told them they would be taken home and that he'd given instructions that the journey should be rather more gentle this time.

They both muttered their thanks as the Albanians untied them and they got to their feet, but as they turned to follow the thug twins up the stone steps, Barkas called out after them, 'And do not fail to bring me my money by midnight or you will suffer the same fate as you most definitely will if I discover you have lied to me. The same will also apply if you say a single word to the police about our little meeting here tonight.'

When they'd left the building, and as soon as Trevor was sure they were out of Barkas's hearing, he asked Sandra how she knew so much about haemophilia.

'I had an uncle who had it,' she said.

'And did *he* bleed to death?'

'Don't be silly.'

26

It didn't feel quite right somehow to be this hot and sunny for the day of a funeral. Trevor had only been to four in his life, all of which had been in England, and it had been cold, wet and windy on each occasion. He couldn't even remember having seen a funeral in a movie when the weather wasn't dreadful. Still, this was August in Greece, so it was hardly a big surprise.

As was the norm in Greece, Christopoulos's funeral was taking place only a short time after his death, and the autopsy – obligatory in cases of murder – had been carried out almost immediately after his body had been discovered. The police had issued a brief statement to the effect that Christopoulos had died as the result of several stab wounds to the chest and throat, all inflicted by a metal souvlaki skewer. They also added that there had been signs of a struggle between the victim and his killer.

Neither he nor Sandra had wanted to go to the funeral at all, especially after the terrifying ordeal with Barkas in the early hours, which meant that they'd had very little sleep and were physically and mentally exhausted. The ride back to the taverna in the Albanian thugs' van had been only marginally less uncomfortable than the outward journey, and they'd picked up a few more bruises on the way, even though their hands were no longer tied and they'd been able to lessen the impact of being thrown from side to side as the van took every bend at ridiculously high speeds. It had been about four-thirty in the morning when they'd finally staggered up the stairs to their apartment, but sleep was never likely to come easily after what they'd been through. They'd needed a couple of drinks and a decent amount of time to try to wind down before they could even contemplate hitting the sack.

Naturally, this winding-down period had included a detailed discussion of their kidnapping, Barkas's interrogation and what the hell they were going to do now. The priority was of course to get his money back to him as soon as possible but certainly by midnight that night. Another encounter with the thug twins was to be avoided at all costs, particularly as Barkas had made it perfectly clear that he would be giving them a free rein to inflict God knows what on them the next time. After a couple of hours, however, they'd realised that their brains were far too addled with fatigue and alcohol to be able to come up with any kind of strategy to identify the blackmailer and retrieve Barkas's cash, so they'd grabbed what little sleep they could before their alarm clock shocked them into bleary-eyed semi-consciousness at eight in the morning.

'How do I look?' said Trevor, his head aching from lack of sleep, a mild hangover and the whack he'd received from the Albanian's gun.

Sandra was brushing her hair in front of a full length mirror and glanced at him over her shoulder. 'You'll do, I suppose.'

'Oh, thanks a lot. And I have to say that you're not exactly looking the picture of elegance yourself.'

This was true, although Trevor had to admit to himself that, considering what they'd been subjected to, she looked pretty good in a plain blue long-sleeved dress and minimal makeup.

'It's a funeral we're going to. Not a bloody fashion show,' she snapped.

Trevor waited until she'd finished brushing her hair and moved away from the mirror, then sidled over to check himself out. His own hair could have done with a bit more care and attention, but he was fully aware that whatever he did, it would soon find its way back to its natural waywardness. The open-necked white shirt and his best pair of beige cotton trousers were smart enough, he decided, but "You'll do" was probably about right for the overall appearance. He'd actually intended to borrow a dark suit and black tie from Grigoris if he had them, but Grigoris had assured him that it was usually only the family of the deceased who dressed in black, so he'd be fine as long as he looked reasonably smart and didn't look as if he'd just come from working in the garden.

This was confirmed as Trevor and Sandra parked the van and joined the steady stream of small groups and couples making their way towards the church. Nearly all of them were casually but smartly dressed, and it was only a few of the older women who were wearing black.

When they reached the gates of the graveyard that surrounded the church, they hung back to let the other mourners pass in front of them. Based on their numbers, it was unlikely that there would be room for everyone inside what was little more than a large chapel, and besides, Trevor and Sandra were only there as observers. They were still suspects for the murder of Yannis Christopoulos, and trying to identify the real murderer was one of their few hopes of proving their innocence. Attending Christopoulos's funeral was as good a place as any to start, based entirely on the fact that, in fiction at least, murderers were often unable to resist witnessing the final laying to rest of their victims.

Once the service had begun, Trevor and Sandra hovered near the open door of the church with a dozen others who there hadn't been room for and listened to the monotone chanting of the priest. From where they stood, they could just make out the open coffin mounted on wooden trestles in front of the altar and the priest in his robes of office standing behind an elaborately gilded lectern. To the left of the coffin and at right-angles to the packed congregation, was a row of two men and three women, all dressed in black and presumably close family members of the deceased. Each of them had their head bowed, but when the priest paused, they raised them again, and Trevor stifled a gasp.

'Bloody Nora,' he whispered, his eyes fixed on the man at the nearest end of the row, who had fleetingly turned his face towards the open door.

'I know,' Sandra whispered back. 'For a moment I thought it was a ghost attending his own funeral.'

The man's solid, slightly squat physique, heavy dark eyebrows, slicked back black hair and sharp nose were all almost identical to Yannis Christopoulos's.

'Must be the brother,' said Trevor, rather more loudly than he'd intended.

'Uh-huh.'

A short, grey-haired woman in front of them turned to glare at them with an emphatic 'Sssh!', and Trevor and Sandra watched the rest of the hour long service in silence. It seemed a lot longer to Trevor, which was admittedly mainly because he barely understood a word of what the priest was saying. Bored as he was, his mind inevitably wandered and he couldn't help wondering if this was all a complete waste of time. Spotting a potential murder suspect in the crowd was a long shot at best, unless in the highly unlikely event that they hadn't yet bothered to wash the blood off their hands or were wearing a T-shirt with "MURDERER" printed on it. He'd argued the point with Sandra in the early hours when they'd got back from their nightmare meeting with Barkas, pointing out that their time would be far better spent following up the possible lead that PC Dimitris might be somehow involved in the blackmail.

'We've only got a few hours to get Barkas's money back to him,' he'd said, 'and quite frankly, there's considerably less imminent danger of us being banged up for a murder that we didn't commit than being slowly tortured to death by a pair of Albanian psychopaths.'

Sandra had said that this was true, but the funeral was fairly early in the morning, so they'd still have time to track down Dimitris once it was over. Trevor had capitulated eventually, not because he agreed with her but simply because he was much too tired to continue the argument any longer.

Thinking about that moment was enough to remind him quite how exhausted he was, and his loud yawn brought an even more withering glare from the short, grey-haired woman.

He nudged Sandra gently in the ribs and beckoned her to follow him as he led the way further from the church doorway and stopped a few yards from a freshly dug grave. On the far side, two men sat with their backs against the fence, one of them smoking a cigarette and the other wiping his brow with a grubby handkerchief. On the ground in front of them lay two long-handled spades and a pickaxe.

'What's up?' said Sandra.

'Nothing,' said Trevor. 'I just didn't think we were going to learn any more other than identifying Christopoulos's brother and staring at the back of a load of people's heads. The woman with the grey hair was getting on my nerves too.'

'Fair enough. I wasn't really expecting much until they came out and started gathering round the grave. That's normally when they spot the murderer in the movies, usually watching from a bit of a distance.'

Trevor scowled, uncertain whether or not this was meant as a joke but still believing they were wasting their time.

'I'm guessing this will be Christopoulos's final resting place,' said Sandra, loosely gesturing at the open grave.

'More than likely, and we probably ought to keep a bit of a distance ourselves. Maybe there's people here who know we're suspects and would think it was bad taste.'

'What, and make us look even more like the murderers, skulking in the background?'

'No, but—'

'I'm kidding,' said Sandra and punched him playfully in the upper arm.

'I don't know what you've got to be so jolly about.'

'Call it panic driven hysteria, if you like. I'm about as far from "jolly" as I could possibly be right now.'

They moved away from the graveside and took up position about thirty feet away, close to the graveyard's iron boundary fence and waited for the congregation to begin filing out of the church.

First came the now closed coffin, held aloft by six sturdy pallbearers. Next came the immediate family, followed by the other mourners. There was some more chanting from the priest as the coffin was lowered into the ground.

There were several faces among the small crowd that Trevor recognised, some of whom were fairly regular customers at the taverna, but no-one who seemed particularly suspicious. Apart from themselves and the two gravediggers, there was nobody lurking in the background.

'I told you this would be a waste of time,' he said. 'I reckon we should get going and see what we can find out about PC Dimitris and the blackmail.'

'Give it a few more minutes,' said Sandra. 'Have you noticed how the guy who's probably Christopoulos's brother keeps glancing in our direction?'

'Well, yes, but it's not that surprising, is it? We must look pretty shifty stood over here in the shadows, and maybe he even knows we're on Pericles's so-called list of suspects.'

They continued watching as the chief mourners stepped forward and each tossed a flower and a handful of dirt into the grave before slowly making their way towards the churchyard gate. Christopoulos's brother was now staring directly at them, and all of a sudden, he broke away from the rest of the family and walked right up to them.

'I believe you are the English people who have the taverna down by the harbour,' he said, his face completely without expression.

'That's right, yes,' said Sandra.

'Good. There is something I wish to talk to you about.'

27

'There he is,' said Sandra. 'Put your foot down.'

Thirty yards up ahead on the right side of the main road leading out of the town was a stationary police car, and leaning nonchalantly against its side was the unmistakable figure of Constable Dimitris, who was pointing a speed gun at every approaching vehicle.

Trevor floored the accelerator pedal, but the elderly camper van was built for comfort rather than speed and was only doing a few kilometres over the limit by the time it passed him. It was enough to pique the cop's interest, however, as they both realised when Sandra swivelled round in the passenger seat and Trevor checked the rear-view mirror. PC Dimitris flung open the door of his car and jumped in behind the steering wheel. The blaring siren and flashing blue lights came on less than a second later.

'Don't forget to give the brakes a dab when he gets closer,' said Sandra.

'I'll have to anyway in a sec,' said Trevor. 'He's flashing his headlights now.'

No sooner were the words out of his mouth than he slowed the van, pulled over onto the hard shoulder and switched off the engine. Milly, who had been sound asleep on the back seat, leapt to attention and stared out of the rear window to ascertain what was causing the almighty racket that had woken her.

Moments later, PC Dimitris parked a few feet from the back of the van and silenced the siren. He took his time before stepping out of the car and even longer putting on his cap and adjusting it to his satisfaction in the reflection of one of the side windows. Then he took a leisurely stroll up to the driver's door of the van and peered in through the open window, his almost permanent smirk broadening into a vindictive grin.

'You again, is it?' he said.

'It would appear so,' said Sandra, leaning over slightly from the passenger seat.

'Do you know what speed you were driving?'

'When?' said Trevor.

'Just now when you passed me.'

'Passed you?'

'Yes.'

'What speed were we doing?'

'Yes.'

Trevor scratched his head and pointlessly looked at the motionless speedometer on the dashboard. 'Not exactly, no, but I dare say you're about to tell us.'

'Fifty seven kilometres per hour,' said Dimitris and proudly showed Trevor the LED display on his speed gun.

'How interesting,' said Trevor.

'Interesting, is it? Well, I tell you how interesting it is, shall I?'

'Please do.'

'Seven kilometres per hour more than legal speed limit. That is how interesting it is.'

'Gosh, you're right, Constable. That really is absolutely fascinating, and we'd love to stay and chat, but we're really in rather a hurry, so if you'll excuse us...' Trevor let the sentence hang and fired up the engine.

PC Dimitris's grin instantly evaporated. 'Wait. You're not going anywhere. Turn off engine immediately.'

Trevor was thoroughly enjoying winding Dimitris up but did as he was told, just as Milly bounded from the back seat, jumped onto his lap and panted her hot breath directly into the cop's face. His head recoiled so abruptly from the open window that he might almost have given himself whiplash.

'Get that dog away from me!' he yelled and frantically wiped his mouth with the back of his hand, presumably as a precaution against any of Milly's slobber that may have landed there, and took a step backwards.

Trevor made a halfhearted attempt to push Milly off his lap, then let her stay where she was.

'I suppose this means a speeding fine?' he said, refocusing the constable's attention to the matter at hand and forcing an expression of resigned indignation.

PC Dimitris gazed down at his feet for several seconds while he considered his response, and when he looked up again, he was wearing the thinnest of smiles. 'Today you are lucky. Today I shall give you only the warning.'

'What?'

'Today I am in the good mood,' said Dimitris.

Trevor couldn't believe what he was hearing. This wasn't part of the plan at all. Constable Dimitris was *never* in a good mood unless he was maliciously persecuting anyone he deemed to have committed even the most trivial of misdemeanours. Drastic measures were called for.

'Incidentally, Constable,' he said, 'do you mind if I ask you a personal question?'

'Excuse me?'

'It's just that I was wondering how often you brush your teeth.'

'My teeth?'

'Yes, because I don't know if you're aware of this,

but your breath smells like some small animal or other climbed inside your mouth and took a massive shit.'

Trevor heard Sandra's muffled snort of laughter from behind him and watched Dimitris's features pass quickly through a range of contortions before settling on one that was clearly intended to convey blind fury.

'Very well,' he spluttered. 'I was going to let you go with only a warning but— '

Seemingly unable to finish the sentence, PC Dimitris opened the notepad he already had in his hand and took out a pen from one of the top pockets of his uniform shirt. 'As well as too fast driving, I shall also write you a ticket for having a brake light that isn't working.'

'Not working?' said Sandra. 'Well, thank you for telling us, officer. We had absolutely no idea.'

This was in fact a complete lie, since they had deliberately removed one of the bulbs before setting out to find Dimitris.

'I shall also need to inspect all lights to see if there are others that are not working.'

'Be my guest,' said Trevor and obediently switched on the indicators, headlights and sidelights.

Dimitris slowly circumnavigated the van, intermittently breathing into his cupped hand and sniffing.

Apparently satisfied that no further offences had been committed, he scribbled in his notepad, tore the sheet from it and handed it to Trevor at arm's length.

'You must pay the fine at a bank or post office within the next ten days,' he said, snapping his notepad closed.

'Thank you, Constable,' said Sandra. 'You have a nice day, yeah?'

PC Dimitris opened his mouth to speak but seemed to think better of it and sauntered back to his car.

The moment he'd gone, Sandra opened the glove box and took out the sheet of paper Wendy Gifford had given them and compared the handwriting at the bottom of the incriminating script with the ticket that PC Dimitris had written.

* * *

As the chief mourner at his brother's funeral, Tassos Christopoulos's duties had meant that he hadn't had time to expand on what he wanted to talk to Trevor and Sandra about, so he'd arranged to meet them at his office in town as soon as he was free. He'd only been able to give them a very rough idea of when that might be, and they'd already been waiting half an hour, sitting outside a café opposite a cobbled alleyway that led from the main thoroughfare to his office. On the table in front of them they'd laid out the script they'd got from Wendy Gifford alongside the ticket PC Dimitris had given them.

'It's not so easy to tell when the writing's in English on the script and Greek on the ticket,' said Trevor and sucked on the straw of his iced coffee.

'There's definite similarities, though,' said Sandra. 'I mean, look at the E's and the A's.'

She pointed to a couple of examples on each piece of paper, and Trevor leaned forward to take a closer look.

'Maybe,' he said, 'but that might just be wishful thinking.'

Sandra chewed at her bottom lip. 'We could really do with somebody who's an expert in this kind of thing.'

'Not likely we'll find anyone round here. Athens, probably, but we don't have the time. As it is, we've got less than ten hours till we have to get Barkas's money back to him. I only hope this chat with Tassos Christopoulos doesn't take too long, whatever the hell it's about.'

Trevor and Sandra had already speculated at length about why Christopoulos wanted to speak to them but were at a complete loss. All they could imagine was that it had something to do with his brother's murder, but this was highly disturbing in itself since he must have known by now that they were on the list of suspects.

'I need a pee,' said Sandra and disappeared inside the café.

No sooner had she gone than Trevor spotted Tassos Christopoulos approaching from the far end of the street.

'Here we go then, Milly,' he said. 'Let's hope he likes dogs.'

Milly, who had for once been lying quietly beneath the table with the end of her lead firmly trapped under Trevor's foot, pricked up her ears at the sound of her name and began sniffing the air for anything that might be of interest.

Trevor grabbed hold of her lead and got to his feet as Tassos turned into the cobbled alleyway towards his office and vanished from view. He was about to glance over his shoulder to see if there was any sign of Sandra when he recognised the two men who were moving rapidly up the pavement in the same direction as Tassos a few moments earlier. When they reached the entrance to the alleyway, they stopped and, after exchanging a few words, looked up and down the street and then at the café opposite. One of them touched the other on the arm and said something to his Albanian twin, who took a couple of seconds to register Trevor's presence.

Trevor swallowed hard and his heart began beating heavily against his ribcage, soaring into overdrive when the marginally shorter of the two men pointed directly at him and used the same finger to ostentatiously tap his watch and then make a slashing motion across his own throat. Trevor slumped back down in his chair and kept a wary eye on the pair of them as they continued on their way to the far end of the street, laughing all the way.

'What's up?' said Sandra. 'You look like you're about to throw up.'

28

'Does it bite?' Tassos Christopoulos said when he opened the door to his office and looked down in mild surprise at the wildly panting Milly in front of him.

'She doesn't usually, no,' Trevor said, his heartbeat having calmed down sufficiently by then to enable him to communicate coherently. 'I hope you don't mind us bringing her, but there was no way we could leave her in the van in this heat.'

'I quite understand,' Tassos said and bent down to give Milly a cursory pat on the head. 'In fact, I'm rather fond of dogs. I would like to have one myself, but I'm away so much on business...'

He ended the sentence with a shrug, apologised for keeping them waiting and ushered them inside.

The office occupied most of the first floor of one of the older buildings in the town, and as he pointed out, was much more modest than his office in Athens. Even so, it was tastefully and expensively furnished and seemed perfectly adequate for the needs of a bigshot lawyer who spent the majority of his time in the capital city. At the far end of the open-plan room in front of three tall windows was a large glass-topped desk mounted on a stainless steel frame and behind it a generously padded swivel chair in black leather. The walls on either side of the desk were lined with floor to ceiling shelf units that were crammed with colour-coordinated sets of legal reference books.

At the nearer end of the office, a matching pair of

two-seater settees in a dark grey material faced each other across a low coffee table of the same design as the desk and smelt faintly of fabric conditioner. They were also remarkably uncomfortable, as Trevor quickly discovered when Tassos had pointed him and Sandra towards the one closest to the wall while he seated himself on the other.

'I may as well get straight to the point,' he said after they'd turned down his offer of coffee. 'I understand that you are private detectives.'

'That's right,' said Sandra.

'And as far as I'm aware, you are the only private detectives in the area.'

'I think so, yes.'

'In that case, I wish to hire you to find out who murdered my brother.'

Without looking at her, Trevor assumed that Sandra was as stunned as he was. What the...? Why on Earth would he want to use *them* to investigate the murder when they were already suspects themselves? Doesn't he *know*? He can't do, surely. Lieutenant Pericles must have taken discretion to another level.

'So, what do you say?' Tassos prompted when his proposal was greeted with total silence.

'Well, I er... We, that is,' Sandra stammered with a brief sideways glance at Trevor. 'I'm sure we're very flattered that you should er... want to hire us to er...'

Sandra was very rarely stuck for words, but on this occasion Trevor realised she needed bailing out, and the best he could do was to answer Tassos's question with one of his own. 'Are you not happy with what the police are doing, then?'

Tassos pursed his lips for a few moments while he considered his response.

'As you know,' he said, 'this is a small town in a mostly quiet rural area, so the police here are not used to dealing with anything as big as murder. Traffic offences, disputes over land, the occasional burglary. These are the kind of issues that they are most familiar with. Don't misunderstand me, though. I believe that Lieutenant Pericles Tomaras is a good man and is doing the best job he can, given the limited resources he has at his disposal. But from what he has told me, it seems that little progress has been made towards identifying the murderer, and I am anxious to discover the truth as quickly as possible.'

'I see,' said Trevor and decided to press him on one of the main points that was bothering him. 'Are there any suspects at all?'

'A few, apparently, but there is very little real evidence against them.'

'Did Pericles – Lieutenant Tomaras – tell you who these suspects were, by any chance?'

Tassos shook his head. 'He is a good man, as I said, and takes his job very seriously, so he told me that this was confidential police information and that my knowing the identities of the suspects would not help the investigation, even though I am the victim's brother.' He gave a wry smile. 'Perhaps the opposite was true and he was worried that – *as* Yannis's brother – I would be tempted to... take matters into my own hands, so to speak.'

Trevor disguised his sigh of relief with a cough. Well, that cleared that up, then. He was about to ask another question when Sandra got in before him, having had time to recover her composure. 'I'd need to discuss this with my colleague, of course, but I'm sure we'd like to help in whatever way we can.'

'Excellent,' said Tassos, slapping his palms down onto his thighs. 'This is what I hoped you—'

'However,' Sandra interrupted, 'the problem is that we have a particularly urgent case we're dealing with at the moment, so we wouldn't be able to look into your brother's murder until that one's been resolved.'

Tassos raised a heavy, dark eyebrow, and his delight of a second ago evaporated instantly. 'Oh?'

Trevor was in complete agreement that they should be upfront about their blackmail case having to take priority but wasn't convinced that Sandra should have gone into quite so much detail when she provided Tassos with an explanation that he felt he deserved.

While she was speaking, Tassos listened patiently, occasionally tutting or shaking his head in disapproval as various aspects of the blackmail unfolded, and when she had finished, he clasped his hands together and the smile returned.

'But this is not a problem at all,' he said. 'At least, not in the immediate future.'

Trevor and Sandra exchanged puzzled glances.

'Well, it'll be a pretty big problem for us if we don't get Barkas's money back to him by midnight tonight,' said Trevor.

Tassos's smile widened. 'Alexandros Barkas is a friend of mine – well, more of an acquaintance really – and I know him well enough to know that his main obsession in life is money. As long as he gets it back, no harm will come to you.'

'Yes, but—'

Tassos pre-empted Trevor's objection with a dismissive wave of the hand. 'I shall lend you the money you owe him, and you can pay me back when you can – minus your fee for investigating my brother's murder, of course.'

This guy is full of surprises, thought Trevor, and both he and Sandra lapsed into another stunned silence while they assimilate this latest bombshell.

'Naturally,' Tassos continued, spreading his palms wide, 'this will not help you to find out *who* your blackmailer is, but it will at least buy you the time to do so. In the meantime, I would expect that you will make it a priority to investigate my brother's murder. And once that is satisfactorily concluded, I may even be able to offer you some assistance with your blackmail case.'

'That's very generous of you, Mr Christopoulos,' said Sandra, 'although—'

'I do not have immediate access to fifty thousand euros, of course, and this being a Saturday, all the banks will be closed. However, I know Barkas, as I said, so I shall phone him and tell him my intention. I'm sure that will be acceptable to him.'

Trevor hoped he was right about that. Otherwise, the consequences were too horrific to contemplate.

'So,' said Tassos, once again slapping his palms down onto his thighs, 'that's settled then. You'll take the case.'

There was only the faintest hint of a question in his tone, and since Trevor and Sandra had already decided to investigate the murder in order to try and clear their own names, they might as well get paid for doing so. At least, that's what Trevor thought, and he assumed that Sandra would be of much the same opinion, although she was not quite ready to jump in with both feet just yet.

'I think we'll need a little more information from you before we commit ourselves,' she said. 'As it stands, we know very little about your brother's murder, and even though the police wouldn't tell you who their suspects were, I'd guess they must have given you a lot more of the details than *we're* aware of.'

'Yes indeed,' said Tassos, 'but I also have some theories of my own – or one anyway.'

'Oh?'

He leaned forward and lowered his voice as if afraid he might be overheard. 'I believe very strongly – in fact, I'm almost convinced – that Yannis's murder was simply

172

a case of mistaken identity.'

'Oh?' Sandra repeated.

'Yes. You see, I— By the way, I think you might want to let your dog off her lead. I can't see she can do any damage, and it's really rather distracting.'

Trevor's almost constant fidgeting since he'd first sat down on the bone hard settee was partly due to his physical discomfort but also to the necessity of having to restrain Milly's relentless lunging against her lead in her desperation to explore the rest of the office in detail. Trevor wouldn't have put bets on Milly not doing any damage but realised he didn't have much choice in the matter, so he unclipped her lead from her collar and watched with mounting anxiety as she careered around the office like a faulty heat-seeking missile. Tassos was also keeping a close eye on her as she darted this way and that and very possibly regretted his instruction to give Milly her freedom.

'You were saying about mistaken identity, Mr Christopoulos,' Sandra prompted. 'You mean that whoever murdered your brother believed he was someone else?'

'Yes. Me. They thought they were killing *me*.'

29

Tassos Christopoulos's theory that whoever murdered his brother believed that they were killing *him* was met with a few seconds' silence while Trevor and Sandra considered the possibility. The two brothers were certainly almost identical in appearance, so it wasn't hard to imagine that the killer mistook Yannis for Tassos, especially if they didn't know either of them well. The inevitable question sprang to Trevor's mind, but Sandra beat him to it.

'But if that's true,' she said, 'why would someone want to murder *you*?'

Tassos gave a faint smile. 'You may have heard the old joke about what do you call a dozen lawyers chained together at the bottom of the ocean?'

'A good start?' said Trevor.

'Precisely. We lawyers are not a very popular breed as you probably know. The second most despised professions after realtors – estate agents – I believe. I myself have been a lawyer now for more than twenty years, and if I may say so, quite a successful one. But during that time, there have been a number of clients who have not been entirely happy with my services.'

'Unhappy enough to want to murder you?'

Tassos examined his immaculately manicured fingernails. 'Very few, I think. People make threats, of course, but they are often in the heat of the moment and have no real substance. These are clients who expected a positive outcome and are in a state of shock when their

174

case goes against them. They need somebody to blame, and usually that's me.'

'You said that "very few" of your clients would blame you enough to want to kill you,' said Sandra. 'Do you have specific examples?'

'Certainly, although the most recent is probably of particular significance with regard to my brother's murder.'

'Go on.'

'It was one of the biggest fraud trials in Greek legal history and went on for months, as this kind of trial often does. I shan't bore you with all the details, but it involved some high-ranking state officials who were accused of taking bribes from a German multinational company to secure government contracts. Also on trial were a small group of wealthy Greek businessmen who stood to benefit massively when the contracts were awarded, and it was one of these that I was defending. The court reached its decision three weeks ago, and every one of the defendants was convicted. My own client was sentenced to ten years in prison, and as he was led away, he yelled all kinds of abuse at me, blaming me for his conviction and leaving me in no doubt as to how he intended to get his revenge.'

'By murdering you?' said Trevor.

'It was rather more explicit than that, but yes, that was the gist of it. I didn't take it too seriously at the time because, as I told you, I have had threats before, but since Yannis's death, I've begun to suspect that he meant what he said.'

'But if this man's in prison, how could he possibly—?'

'Stefanos Karabellas has some very strong connections in the criminal underworld. He is also extremely rich.'

'Another one, eh?' Trevor muttered.

175

'I beg your pardon?'

'Er... nothing. Just thinking aloud, that's all.'

'So,' said Sandra, closing her eyes to help her concentration, 'you think this Stefanos whatshisface paid somebody to murder you, but whoever he paid got it wrong and murdered your brother instead?'

Tassos paused briefly before answering. 'Believe me, I have given the matter a great deal of thought and consider this to be the most likely explanation.'

'And you don't know of anyone who might have wanted *Yannis* dead? That the killer might have got the right man after all?'

'Nobody comes to mind, no.'

Trevor avoided looking at Sandra. She was presumably thinking the same thing as he was. Not only did Tassos not know that they themselves were suspects, but he must also be completely unaware of his brother's affair with Alexandros Barkas's wife. Best keep it that way, Trevor decided. For now, anyway.

'It all fits together in my mind,' Tassos went on. 'The murderer must have followed Yannis, believing him to be me, and stabbed him to death right here in this very office. With a metal souvlaki skewer, according to Lieutenant Tomaras. Rather a strange choice of weapon, wouldn't you say?'

Strange, yes, thought Trevor, but more than likely to implicate him and Sandra. Although if Tassos's theory had any merit, that would mean that the killer – a supposedly professional hitman hired by some rich bloke without any local connection – also knew about their feud with Yannis Christopoulos and decided to frame them for the murder. It really didn't make any sense.

Trevor's confused pondering was cut short by Sandra asking Tassos what Yannis was doing in his office.

'Did he often come here?' she said.

'Not that I know of, although I'm very rarely here

myself. He does – did – have a key, however.'

'Oh?'

'In case there was a break-in or a fire or something. I needed somebody local who could get in when I wasn't here. I did have to change the combination on the safe, though.'

Trevor scanned the room but saw no sign of a safe.

'It's behind that picture on the wall there,' said Tassos, obviously reading Trevor's mind, and twisted round in his seat to point to a large print of some historic sea battle on the wall behind him. 'The Battle of Navarino, 1827.'

'And you changed the combination on the safe because...?' Trevor was fairly sure he knew the answer already but decided to ask it anyway.

'Yannis was never very good with money. Even when we were children, he spent all of his pocket money almost as soon as he was given it. Usually on sweets or some trashy toy instead of saving up to buy something he really wanted. Then, as an adult, he developed a taste for gambling. Not to the level of an addiction, you understand, but enough to leave him with fairly heavy debts on a few occasions. I helped him out, of course, as any brother would, but it eventually reached the point when I had to say "No more". It wasn't that I couldn't afford to lend him the money, but I believed that this was the only way to break the circle. To make him see that he had to take responsibility for his own actions and behave accordingly.'

'So that's when he stole from you?' said Sandra.

Tassos let out a long slow breath. 'Sadly, yes. This was a couple of months ago when I was away in Athens. He already knew the safe combination because up until then I had no reason not to trust him.'

'May I ask how much he took?'

'I don't keep a lot of cash in the safe, but he stole

177

about half what was in there at the time. A little over a thousand euros.'

'Did you challenge him about it?'

'What would have been the point? He must have been desperate to steal from me, so I chose to forgive him. It seemed to be the Christian thing to do.'

'But you changed the combination of the safe afterwards,' said Trevor.

'Yes. To remove the temptation.'

'And you believe that's why he was here in your office the night he was murdered?'

'I can think of no other reason, and I assume he must have been desperate once again, but what he didn't know was that I'd changed the combination.'

Yannis Christopoulos's desperate need for money would certainly have made him even more of a prime suspect as their blackmailer if he hadn't died, Trevor was thinking, when there was a sudden crashing sound over by the desk. Expecting the worst, he swivelled his head in that direction and, sure enough, Milly was staring at him with that butter-wouldn't-melt expression that she always wore when she'd done something wrong. Next to her was an overturned metal wastebin rolling back and forth across the floor, its meagre contents spread all around. The clear explanation was that she'd been rummaging inside the bin for anything vaguely edible and managed to knock it over in the process.

'Milly!' Trevor shouted and got to his feet. 'Sorry about that, Mr Christopoulos.'

'Don't worry. There's nothing broken, is there?'

'I don't think so,' said Trevor as he hurried over to the bin and added under his breath, 'Not yet anyway.'

He knelt down and set the wastebin upright, then began to gather up its spilt contents. There wasn't a great deal, and it was mostly screwed up sheets of paper and torn envelopes as well as a couple of newspapers.

'The cleaner's supposed to empty that,' said Tassos, 'but she obviously got out as quick as she could as soon as she saw Yannis's body lying on the floor in a pool of blood. That's what she told Lieutenant Tomaras anyway.'

'Which reminds me,' said Sandra. 'I don't think it would be a good idea to let the lieutenant know that we're involved in trying to find your brother's killer. It's best he's kept in the dark about that for everyone's sake.'

Tassos opened his mouth to speak – quite possibly to ask *why* they wanted their involvement to be kept secret – when they were saved from having to explain by the opening bars of *Eye of the Tiger* blasting out from Sandra's phone. She fished it out of her pocket and checked the display.

'Sorry, I'd better take this,' she said and held the phone to her ear, mouthing the word "Grigoris" at Trevor.

She listened for a few seconds and then:

'What?' ... 'Say that again slowly.' ... 'OK, OK, we'll be there.'

She ended the call and stared blankly into the middle distance, ignoring the question on Trevor's face.

'Shit,' she said. 'That's all we need.'

30

As they turned into the narrow seafront road, Trevor and Sandra could see the police car parked outside their taverna. Grigoris had been unable to provide much detail as to why the police wanted to see them other than it being urgent and something to do with an audio recording.

Pericles was sitting in the passenger seat of the car while Constable Dimitris was leaning against the bonnet, smoking a cigarette. His almost permanent smirk was even more pronounced than usual, and he gave them a sarcastically cheery wave.

'Have you paid your speeding fine yet?' he said as soon as Trevor and Sandra were out of the van with Milly on a tight leash.

'Not yet,' said Trevor.

'Good, because fine is double if you do not pay before ten days.'

Neither Trevor or Sandra bothered to respond, and they waited while Pericles opened the car door and stepped out.

'So, what's all this about?' said Sandra.

'A very serious matter,' said Pericles. 'A very serious matter indeed.'

'Something about an audio recording, Grigoris said. Is it the one we did for Wendy Gifford? The one where Trevor and I are supposed to say how unhygienic our taverna is?'

'Correct.'

'Don't tell me you've found the blackmailer,' said Trevor.

Pericles frowned. 'Blackmailer?'

'You can't have forgotten already.'

'No, I haven't forgotten,' said Pericles, 'but I haven't had time to go looking for your blackmailer – if such a person actually *exists*.'

'What are you talking about? Of course they exist.'

'I have no real evidence to support that.'

'No real evidence? So how come we've just paid out fifty thousand euros to stop the recording being made public.'

'It seems that you have wasted your money then,' said PC Dimitris with undisguised glee.

Trevor rounded on him. 'Yeah, well you'd know all about that now, wouldn't you?'

'Me? Why would I know? You're crazy.'

Sandra gave Trevor a gentle nudge in the ribs and spoke in little more than a whisper: 'Not now, Trev. Save it for later.'

'If we can get back to the point,' said Pericles, 'I have to inform you that this recording was handed in at the police station an hour ago.'

'So?' said Trevor.

'Conspiring to bribe a government health inspector is a criminal offence.'

'But you knew all this before. We showed you the bloody script, for God's sake. So what's the big deal all of a sudden?'

'The "big deal", as you put it, is that the recording has now been made public.'

'What?' Trevor and Sandra chorused.

'It has already been played twice on the local radio station.'

'Three times actually,' PC Dimitris put in, his tone annoyingly chirpy.

Trevor was too much in shock to speak and so too was Sandra apparently. Not only had they shelled out fifty grand of somebody else's money, which might still end up with them both getting all their teeth pulled out – or worse, but the bastard who was blackmailing them had gone ahead and released the recording anyway.

'And because your threat to bribe an officer of the state is now public knowledge,' Pericles went on, 'it is my duty to act accordingly.'

'What's that supposed to mean?' said Sandra.

'It means that I will have to ask you to come with me to the police station, where you will be interviewed formally and very possibly charged.'

'Charged?' Trevor repeated, unable to believe his ears. 'Jesus Christ, you haven't got time to track down a blackmailer, but you don't seem to have a problem dealing with this bullshit.'

'It's a pity we do not still have the blasphemy laws in Greece or we could charge you with that too,' said PC Dimitris.

Trevor was almost never driven to violence, but on this occasion he came within a whisker of punching Constable Dimitris very hard in his smugly grinning face.

'So,' said Pericles, 'you can either come in the car with us or in your own vehicle. It's up to you.'

There didn't seem to be much point in arguing, and Sandra told him they'd come in the van, but before any of the four of them had moved more than a couple of paces, a silver Toyota hatchback came screeching round the corner at the far end of the narrow street.

'What are *they* doing here?' said Trevor as it pulled up next to the van.

Marcus Ingleby opened the passenger door of the Toyota and took his time clambering out onto the tarmac. Despite being only a couple of years younger than Ingleby, Eric Emerson was considerably more sprightly and took only seconds to slip out from behind the steering wheel and stride towards them. An old pal of Ingleby's and erstwhile partner in crime, Eric had recently bought a villa close to Ingleby's with the proceeds of his share of the jewellery stolen by the pair of them many years before.

'Hello, Eric. What's up?' said Sandra.

Eric removed his heavy, horn-rimmed spectacles and gave them a thorough wipe with a brilliantly white handkerchief. 'Marcus heard there was something on the radio about you two and the taverna and wanted to know what all the fuss was about.'

Trevor briefly closed his eyes and shuffled his feet. It had been bad enough telling Marcus about the whole blackmail thing, but he'd have a blue fit now the recording had been made public.

No-one spoke as they all waited for Ingleby to make his way over from the car, limping slightly as he did so. In complete contrast to Eric's dapper appearance in neatly pressed shirt and beige slacks, he was wearing a faded black T-shirt that was three sizes too big for him and his customary pair of khaki knee-length shorts. Strapped to his left leg and clear for all to see was the ever-present catheter bag, which never seemed to be less than half full.

'What the fuck's all this about then?' he said, addressing the question specifically at Pericles.

The lieutenant shifted uncomfortably from one foot to the other and was about to respond when Sandra cut in before him.

'They want us to go to the police station,' she said.

'Oh yeah? What for?'

'The thing on the radio,' said Trevor. 'You heard it, did you?'

'Not me, no. The local radio's all in bloody Greek, so

183

I never listen to it. Somebody told me about it.'

'They say they might be going to charge us with—What was it again?'

Trevor turned to Pericles, who filled in the blank. 'Threatening to bribe an officer of the state.'

'Christ on a bike,' said Ingleby, eyeballing Pericles once again. 'Ain't you got anything better to do with your time?'

'Certainly,' said Pericles, shifting back to the original foot, 'but in matters such as this, I have a duty to—'

Ingleby snorted with derision. '*Duty*? Don't make me fill my bag. You've got a duty to solve a bleedin' murder. That's what you've got, my son, so why don't you get on with that instead of pissing about harassing innocent people over some petty bullshit about an officer of the sodding state?'

'Well, I—' Pericles began, but Ingleby interrupted him for a second time.

'I tell you what,' he said. 'I'll make it simple for you, shall I? Come with me and all will become clear.'

So saying, he set off towards the taverna building at a surprisingly fast pace.

Pericles and PC Dimitris exchanged a look of utter bewilderment and a few words in Greek, then followed meekly in Ingleby's wake.

'This should be interesting,' said Trevor as he, Sandra and Eric joined the procession.

'See any rats, do you?' said Ingleby as soon as they'd all assembled inside the main door. 'Any cockroaches?'

Pericles and PC Dimitris cast their eyes around the empty dining area, paying particular attention to the tiled floor.

'No?' Ingleby went on. 'Well, perhaps we'd better 'ave a look back 'ere, shall we?'

He led the way to the back of the room and into the kitchen. This being late afternoon, all of the customers had long since left, and Grigoris and Eleni were finishing off the last of the washing up.

Clearly unhappy at having her space invaded by so many people, Eleni began barking at them in Greek but abruptly stopped when she spotted the uniformed police officers.

'Go on then,' said Ingleby. 'Have a good ferret around and tell me if you find anything un-bloody-hygienic.'

With what appeared to be a distinct reluctance, especially on the part of Constable Dimitris, the two cops carried out a fairly thorough examination of the kitchen. This included searching inside cupboards, ovens, fridges, as well as behind and underneath anything that was moveable.

'So what's the verdict then?' said Ingleby as Pericles pulled himself upright and brushed some imaginary dust from the knees of his trousers. 'Clean as a bleedin' whistle, innit?'

'Whistle?' said Pericles.

'Spotless. No rat shit, no dead mice, no cockroaches. You could eat yer dinner off that floor.'

'Well, I'm not sure I'd like to—'

'So you get the point then, yeah?' Ingleby went on. 'Since there's nothing in this whole place that gives even a teensy-weensy hint of a health hazard, why the fuck would Trevor or Sandra say that there was? It doesn't make any sense, so it makes even less sense that they would talk about bribing a bloody health inspector, right?'

Pericles cleared his throat. 'Very well. It does appear that there has been an unfortunate... misunderstanding in this instance, and I—'

'Misunderstanding?' Trevor interrupted. 'It's blackmail is what it is. How many more times do we have to tell you?'

'It is therefore my opinion,' said Pericles, ignoring the remark, 'that no further action will be necessary.'

'I dunno about "no further action",' said Ingleby. 'There's one further action you can take and that's to tell the radio station to stop broadcasting the recording and dishing the dirt on my taverna or I'll be suing them for slander.'

Pericles nodded his head and grunted, presumably in agreement, then turned on his heel and hurried out of the kitchen. PC Dimitris followed, but not before fixing both Trevor and Sandra with a malevolent scowl and muttering something in Greek.

'Right then,' said Ingleby, rubbing his palms together. 'How about a bloody drink? Is this a taverna or what?'

31

'Don't be such a baby,' said Coralie as Jimmy MacFarland failed to suppress another yelp of pain.

'Aye well, it's no ye that's in agony here, is it, hen?'

'And whose fault is that?'

MacFarland grunted and screwed up his face as what felt like a red hot branding iron caught him just above his right shoulder blade.

He was lying face down on a towel in the shade of a beach parasol, each hand clutching a fistful of sand on either side of him with every bolt of agony. For a hardened gangster from Glasgow, he had a remarkably low tolerance for any kind of pain, but this was nothing compared to the smashed hand and crushed foot inflicted on him by Trevor Hawkins and Sandra Gray. Then there was the scar on his cheek. The result of a gang fight in the backstreets of his home town when some bastard had caught him with a flick-knife. Jesus, that had hurt like hell for days afterwards, but he'd got his revenge in the end.

Coralie was right, of course. He wasn't used to this kind of sun and should have taken a lot more care about getting himself a tan, and instead of looking like a bronzed Adonis, he now had far more than a passing resemblance to an overripe tomato with a serious case of eczema.

'I thought this stuff ye're daubin' me wi' was supposed to be soothing,' he said through gritted teeth.

Coralie laughed. 'Patience, *mon cher*. You have to

wait for it to do its work.'

'Oh aye? And how long will that take?'

The only answer he got was a dollop of aftersun lotion onto the middle of his back, and he bit his lip to stop himself from crying out.

Mon cher. He rather liked the sound of that, especially as it was delivered in her incredibly sexy voice. They'd only known each other for little more than a day, and yet here he was lying flat out on the sand getting a full body massage. OK, it was more on the painful side than the sensual, but it was pretty rapid progress as far as he was concerned.

He couldn't remember having enjoyed a meal more than the one they'd shared on the previous evening. Not that the food had been anything to write home about, although he'd barely even been aware of what he'd been shovelling down his neck. No, it had been Coralie's company and how they'd seemed to click right from the off that had really made it special. Sure, he'd had to make an effort to tone down the Glasgow accent a fair amount even though her English was excellent, but from then on, they'd got on like the proverbial house on fire. There'd been one or two tricky moments, particularly when she'd asked him what he did for a living, but he'd managed to palm her off with some twaddle about working for the Scottish Tourist Board. He'd toyed with the idea of telling her he was a career criminal who occasionally killed people for money just to see her reaction, but he'd quickly decided against it on the grounds that this would almost certainly have brought any prospect of a relationship to a very abrupt end before it had even started.

Thinking of the taverna reminded him of the reason he was here at all and that Donna Vincent was going to call him tomorrow for an update on whether he'd carried out what she was paying him to do. Still, tomorrow was another day. For now – and apart from the sunburn – he was having far too much fun to bother with trivial stuff like work. Not that he'd been completely idle in that respect. He'd been keeping half an eye on Trevor Hawkins and Sandra Gray and their various comings and goings. Only a couple of hours ago he'd spotted some police activity at their taverna, and although he'd been too far away to hear what was being said, he'd got the distinct impression that Hawkins and Gray were in some kind of bother. Then two old blokes had turned up, and the cops had left looking more than a little pissed off.

'*Bonjour*, Coralie. *Ça va?*'

It was a man's voice, coming from above and behind him. MacFarland rolled onto his side and squinted up at the silhouette of a figure standing with his back to the sun.

'Oh, hi, David,' said Coralie. 'Everything OK?'

MacFarland used his hand to shield his eyes from the glare and immediately recognised the young guy who'd been running the turtle kiosk with Coralie the day before. The shite excuse for a beard hasnae got any better, he thought.

'Looks like somebody's enjoying themselves,' said the guy with a grin.

'Sunburn,' said Coralie.

'You should be more careful,' said David. 'You don't want to get skin cancer after all.'

'Aye, ye're right enough. That'd be a real bummer,' said MacFarland, hoping that the patronising little prick wasn't going to hang around much longer.

'I thought you were on duty this afternoon,' said Coralie.

David shook his head. 'I swapped with Helga. I'm doing the night shift instead.'

'Me too,' said Coralie.

'I know,' said David with rather too much emphasis

for MacFarland's liking. 'I've got hours to kill yet. Mind if I join you?'

'Help yourself,' said Coralie, vaguely indicating a patch of sand in the shade of the parasol.

Oh, fucking great, thought MacFarland, but forced himself into something approximating a welcoming smile.

David settled himself down, cross-legged on the sand and pointed at MacFarland's chest. 'You're not wearing your Archelon T-shirt.'

'Ma wha'?'

'Archelon. One of the T-shirts you bought from the kiosk yesterday.'

'Aye, well, if ye werenae such a fuckin' numpty, you'd realise I wisnae wearin' a T-shirt at all,' MacFarland wanted to say but decided to err on the side of politeness and went with: 'Aye, well, I'm keeping those fir best.'

'Good plan. They're not exactly cheap, I know, so you wouldn't want to mess them up. I'm surprised you bought two, to be honest, what with you being Scottish, yeah?'

David laughed like a loon, Coralie looked puzzled, apparently failing to understand "the joke", and MacFarland suppressed the urge to headbutt the little shit.

Time tae leave before I commit a murder I'm no even being paid for, he thought, and got to his feet.

'You're not going, are you?' said Coralie with an expression of genuine disappointment.

'Not on my account, I hope,' said David with an expression of thinly disguised delight.

'Things I need tae do,' said MacFarland, picking up his towel and shaking it with deliberate attention to the direction of the sea breeze.

'Hey, watch out,' said David, screwing up his eyes

and flapping his hands at the shower of sand.

MacFarland stifled a grin. 'Sorry aboot that, pal.'

Coralie stood up and kissed him lightly on the cheek. 'I will see you later, though, yes?'

'Nothin' more certain, hen,' said MacFarland and returned the kiss.

He ignored David's cheery shout of 'See you, mate' as he headed up the beach towards the road where he'd parked his car.

Halfway there, a black and tan mongrel dog came bounding up to him, a large piece of driftwood clenched between its teeth.

'Hey there, pooch. You wanna play, dae ye?'

He bent down and eased the stick from the dog's mouth, then threw it as hard as he could further along the beach. He watched as the dog hurtled to retrieve it before racing back towards him. When it was within a few yards, he realised that this was not just any old dog. This was a dog he recognised all too well.

'Interesting,' he said to himself and hurled the stick in the opposite direction while he considered the possibilities.

32

'Have you seen Milly?' Trevor asked.

Marcus Ingleby and Eric Emerson were still sitting at the same table where he and Sandra had left them an hour ago to take Milly for a walk on the beach. She hadn't had much exercise that day, and besides, it had been a good enough excuse to leave Marcus and Eric to their reminiscing. The more they'd had to drink, the more maudlin they'd become about the good old days of bank robberies and jewel thefts. They were all stories that Trevor and Sandra had heard many times before.

'Milly?' said Ingleby. 'Can't say I have. You lost her then?'

'No,' said Trevor. 'It's just that she ran off chasing a bird and disappeared into the distance.'

'I'm sure she'll be back when it's feeding time,' said Sandra. 'She always is.'

'Yeah, I suppose so.'

'Anyway, it'll be feeding time for the punters soon. We'd better get a move on.'

Trevor shrugged. 'I can't see we're going to be exactly trampled in the rush after that recording was broadcast.'

As it turned out, though, it was only marginally less than business as usual for a Saturday night. Most of the customers were non-Greek tourists, and it was highly unlikely that they would have been tuned in to a Greek radio station. Pericles had apparently followed up on Ingleby's demand that the station should stop playing the

192

recording, but the damage had already been done. Sooner or later, word would probably spread amongst the tourists as well as the locals, so they weren't out of the woods yet by any means.

Trevor's order-taking was even more calamitous than usual, much to the annoyance of several of the customers and Eleni in particular. Each time he went onto the terrace to take an order, he found it impossible to concentrate, constantly scanning the beach for any sign of the errant Milly. By the time all but a few stragglers had paid up and left, she still hadn't returned.

'This isn't like her at all,' said Trevor. 'I don't remember her ever having missed a mealtime.'

'I know,' said Sandra. 'Maybe we should go down to the beach and try and find her. We're pretty much finished here.'

'I just hope to God nothing's happened to her.'

'Like what?'

'I dunno. Perhaps she's been poisoned or something.'

'Poisoned?'

'It does happen round here, you know.'

'It's far more likely she's still chasing birds or whatever.'

'At this time of night?'

Sandra took him gently by the arm. 'Come on. We're not going to get anywhere stood here talking about it.'

They'd almost reached the end of the terrace and the short flight of wooden steps that led down to the quayside when Grigoris called out from behind them. He'd come out to clear more of the debris from the vacated tables and seemed anxious to catch them before they disappeared.

'Sorry,' he said, 'but I just want to remind you about tomorrow.'

'Tomorrow?' said Sandra. 'Why, what's happening tomorrow?'

'The football?'

'Oh,' said Trevor. 'Who's playing?'

'Me. I am. For the local team.'

Trevor was aware that Grigoris played football most Sundays but couldn't recall him having said there was anything special about tomorrow's game.

'You'll be able to work lunchtime, though, will you?' he said.

'For sure,' said Grigoris, 'but tomorrow is kickoff later than usual in afternoon. It is possible I am a little late here for the evening. Should be OK, but it depends.'

'On?'

'That *malákas* Dimitris is referee, and sometimes he adds time till he gets result he wants.'

'How do you mean?'

'He makes bet on result when he is referee.' Grigoris feigned a spit on the ground. 'What happens you can't even trust a cop.'

'A cop?' said Sandra. 'You wouldn't be talking about *Constable* Dimitris, would you?'

'The one he was here this afternoon. Yes.'

'Interesting,' said Trevor.

'Very,' said Sandra.

She then told Grigoris that it shouldn't be a problem if he was a little late for work tomorrow evening but to do his best to get there as soon as possible. He thanked her and went back to clearing tables while Trevor and Sandra stepped down onto the quayside.

'Are you thinking what I'm thinking?' said Sandra.

Trevor gave her a hint of a smirk. 'Very possibly.'

'If what Grigoris says is true – that PC Dimitris is fixing matches – this could be the perfect opportunity to nail the bastard.'

'We'd have to prove it, though. It's only hearsay at the moment.'

'Shouldn't be too difficult. All we need to do is—

Hello. What's this then?'

Sandra interrupted herself, and they both stopped in their tracks at the sight of a familiar looking dog racing towards them along the quayside.

'Where have *you* been?' said Trevor, struggling to maintain his balance as Milly leapt up at him with her front paws on his chest.

She was wagging her tail and panting with such evident excitement it was as if she hadn't seen him in months.

'All right, girl. Calm down, eh?' he said and gently took hold of her front legs and manoeuvred them back onto the ground.

He stooped to stroke her head, telling her how worried they'd been and firing questions at her about where she'd been for all this time. It was then that he noticed the scrap of paper attached to her collar with a rubber band. Once Milly stayed still long enough for him to remove it, he unfolded what appeared to have been torn from a table napkin and read the simple message that had been written in shaky block capitals: "I'VE BEEN FED".

33

For such a relatively small town, three veterinary clinics might have seemed excessive, but all appeared to do a reasonable trade, partly due to the abundance of farm animals in the area. Soon after they'd arrived in Greece, Trevor and Sandra had chosen one at random, but since then, Leonidas Stathakos had proved himself to be an excellent vet, a regular customer at their taverna and a good friend.

'She's fine,' he said, removing the stethoscope from his ears and straightening up from the stainless steel examination table.

This table was the only place on the entire planet where Milly behaved impeccably, or rather, froze completely, her eyes wide and her tail firmly between her legs.

'It's not poison then?' said Trevor, still needing further reassurance even after Leonidas's categorical diagnosis.

The vet smiled as he removed his disposable latex gloves. 'Thankfully not.'

'You're absolutely certain?'

'Trevor,' said Sandra in the tone she often used when she was about to give him a mild slap on the wrist. 'Which part of "she's fine" did you not understand?'

'I just wanted to—'

Leonidas interrupted him by placing a hand on his shoulder and said, 'If she'd been poisoned, you'd know about it soon enough. I've lost count of the number of cases I've seen over the years, and the symptoms are obvious. Foaming at the mouth, convulsions, and very often an appalling smell. It's a terrible way to die if I can't treat them in time. And by the way, if you ever suspect that Milly *has* been poisoned, call me immediately whatever the time of day or night.'

'So who does it?' said Trevor. 'Puts down poison, I mean.'

'In the town it's usually somebody who's been kept awake by their neighbour's dog barking. Otherwise, it's farmers trying to protect their chickens from foxes. Hunters do it too. They don't want foxes killing the hares or whatever that they want to kill themselves.'

'Seriously?'

'With the farmers, it's mostly the older generation that do it, so as soon as they die off, the better.'

Over the time that they'd known him, it had become increasingly clear that Leonidas had a far higher opinion of animals than he did of quite a few humans.

'So what caused Milly to throw up, do you think?'

'Probably just something she ate that upset her stomach. Do you know if she's eaten anything different in the past twelve hours or so?'

Trevor had already explained how Milly had gone missing the night before and how she'd been sick three or four times less than an hour after she reappeared but hadn't mentioned the "I'VE BEEN FED" note on her collar until now.

'That could be the reason then,' said Leonidas. 'Unless she picked up some rotten fish from the quayside, it's likely that whoever fed her gave something she wasn't used to. That could quite possibly make her sick if she's got a delicate stomach.'

"Delicate" wasn't a word that Trevor would have applied to Milly in any respect, either physical or psychological, and he said so.

Leonidas laughed. 'Oh well, at least there's no real harm done, but maybe give her something light to eat for the next couple of days. A little chicken and rice. That kind of thing.'

Trevor thanked him, especially for coming out on a Sunday, and lifted the still rigid Milly down from the examination table. As soon as her paws hit the floor, however, she made a dash for the open doorway, and Sandra just managed to grab hold of her lead before she could make her escape.

'And while we're on the subject of upset stomachs,' said the vet, 'I heard you two on the radio yesterday. Maybe I won't be such a regular customer at your taverna from now on.'

Trevor and Sandra both started gabbling their protestations, which would have been utterly incomprehensible even to a native English speaker, but they stopped abruptly when Leonidas raised his palms in an appeal for calm. His previously stony expression transformed itself into a wide grin.

'*Pláka káno*,' he said. 'I'm joking with you. I can't imagine for a moment that what you said was true, and especially the part about bribing a health inspector.'

Composing themselves sufficiently to produce something approaching coherent speech, Trevor and Sandra then took turns to tell Leonidas about how they'd been duped into making the recording, how they'd been blackmailed and how they'd lost the fifty thousand euros that Alexandros Barkas had lent them to pay the blackmailer.

Leonidas exhaled heavily when they'd finished. 'And they still made the recording public even after you'd paid up? Somebody doesn't like you very much, do they?'

'Apparently not,' said Sandra.

'Interesting that you mention Barkas, though. I was at

198

his house a couple of days ago to give his two German Shepherds their annual checkup and injections. Like a lot of rich people, he treats everyone else like his personal servants. Too grand to come to the clinic himself, he has me go to *him*. Still, I charge him extra for the house call, so what do I care?'

'Fair enough, I'd say,' said Trevor.

'Anyway,' Leonidas went on. 'I might as well have been the plumber come to fix the boiler for the amount of attention he and his wife paid me while I was working on their dogs. That's probably why they didn't give a damn if I overheard the blazing row they were having in the next room.'

'Oh?' said Sandra. 'What was that about?'

'To be honest, I was busy with the dogs and really couldn't be bothered to listen that closely, but there were a couple of bits and pieces I could hardly miss, given how loud they were yelling at each other.'

'Such as?'

'It was something Alexandros said – or rather, shouted – a couple of times. "The bastard had it coming" was how it translates.'

'Do you know who he was talking about?' said Trevor.

'Well, I couldn't swear to it, but I've got a pretty good idea it was Yannis Christopoulos.'

'That's hardly surprising,' said Sandra. 'He'd just found out that his wife was having an affair with Christopoulos.'

Trevor winced slightly at this blatant breach of confidentiality, but in a town where gossip was a way of life, this was probably old news by now anyway.

'There was something else, though,' said Leonidas. 'Anastasia came right out and accused him of Christopoulos's murder.'

'Also not surprising,' said Sandra.

'But it was Alexandros's response that made me take notice. He lowered his voice at this point, so I couldn't hear him clearly, but I'm almost certain he said "So what if I did?".'

'Those were his exact words?'

'Well, in Greek of course, but that's what it meant.'

* * *

'I'm confused,' said Trevor as Milly almost tore his shoulder out of its socket in her desperation to scramble into the van.

He let go of her lead and she leapt onto the back seat, her normal manic self again and no longer the catatonic frozen statue she'd been just a few minutes earlier.

'Join the club,' said Sandra. 'What Leonidas told us doesn't *necessarily* mean that Barkas was confessing to the murder.'

'Maybe he was just goading Anastasia. Winding her up, sort of thing. And don't forget that Pericles said he had a cast iron alibi for the night of the murder.'

'*He* might have done, but that's not to say he didn't pay somebody else to do it.'

'Like the two Albanians, for instance.'

'Seems more than possible to me.'

'They certainly seemed to be following Tassos Christopoulos when we went to meet him yesterday. Perhaps that's what they were up to. Planning to murder Tassos when they found out that they'd killed his brother by mistake.'

'But that doesn't make any sense,' said Sandra. 'If Barkas really *was* admitting that he murdered Yannis – or at least *had* him murdered – then that completely sinks Tassos's theory that it was a case of mistaken identity. With Yannis dead, it was job done as far as Barkas was concerned. And the fact that the Albanians happened to be on the same street at the same time as Tassos might simply have been a coincidence, and they weren't following him at all.'

'They were definitely looking shifty, though.'

Sandra laughed. 'Come off it, Trev. With those two, I'm not sure they can do anything else *but* look shifty.'

Not for the first time in the past few days, Trevor's brain cells were performing somersaults. He checked his watch. 'I suppose it's a bit early for a drink, is it?'

Sandra glanced at her own watch. 'Make mine a double.'

34

As with the previous evening, there wasn't a noticeable drop in the number of customers for Sunday lunch at the taverna. Word had obviously failed to spread as rapidly as Trevor and Sandra had feared among the local non-Greek community, which was a double-edged sword as far as Trevor was concerned. He was busier than ever, racing between kitchen and terrace with his higher than usual quota of erroneous orders since Sandra was otherwise occupied with Leonidas the vet in the back office.

Following their discussion about Yannis Christopoulos's murder at his clinic earlier that day, they'd also told Leonidas that they suspected Constable Dimitris was involved in blackmailing them over the recording that had been played on the radio. Leonidas hadn't taken much convincing, given his clear dislike of the man, who he described as a "slimy little bastard that was a disgrace to his uniform", and said he'd be more than happy to do whatever he could to help bring him down.

'Well, there is something you might be able to do for us,' Sandra had said, and she proceeded to tell Leonidas about Dimitris's less than honourable reputation as a football referee.

And this was why their friendly neighbourhood vet was now sitting in a chair in the back office of the taverna with his shirt wide open and displaying a veritable Black Forest of chest hair. Sandra hesitated as she stood over him, a tiny microphone with a thin wire in one hand and a short length of adhesive tape in the other.

'Is there a problem?' Leonidas asked.

'Er, not exactly,' said Sandra, staring at the kind of chest a gorilla would have been proud of. 'It's just that, er... I'm not sure where I'm going to fix this where it will actually stick or won't cause you quite a lot of pain when I remove it later. Well, probably not that much but— Oh, hang on a minute. I've got a better idea.' She then rummaged through the jumble of items in the small suitcase that was open on the desk in front of Leonidas and took out a disposable cigarette lighter. 'There you go.'

'A cigarette lighter?'

'Ah, that's what you're supposed to think. But inside this little beauty is an incredibly sophisticated recording device that's voice activated and picks up any sound up to about five metres away. It's got a twenty-five day standby time and can hold up to two hundred and fifty hours of recording. Then, when you're done, you just plug it into a computer and download whatever it is you've recorded. Simple.'

Judging by the expression on Leonidas's face, he wasn't quite as impressed by Sandra's sales pitch as she might have expected, but he took the lighter from her and examined it closely for several seconds.

'But I don't smoke,' he said at last.

'Oh shit. Of course you don't,' said Sandra, her tone noticeably lacking any hint of her previous enthusiasm. 'Still, it's the best I can do, and it doesn't really matter that you don't smoke because it doesn't work as a proper lighter anyway.'

Leonidas looked unconvinced.

'I've got a fountain pen recorder as well that might be more appropriate, but I didn't find it too reliable the last time I used it, to be honest.'

'Where did you get all this stuff?' he said, nodding at the open suitcase and its tangle of wires and jumble of plastic gadgets of various shapes and sizes.

'I bought most of it when I first set up as a private detective back in the UK. I didn't bring all of my gear to Greece, though. Just the few bits and pieces that I thought might come in useful.'

'I see.'

'So you're happy to use the lighter then?'

Leonidas opened his mouth to speak, but before he could utter a word, Trevor came bursting into the office, panting like he'd just run a half marathon.

'Bloody hell,' he gasped. 'They're *all* here.'

'Who are?' said Sandra. 'Not the police again?'

'No, not this time. – What's he doing with his shirt half off?'

In his state of high anxiety, Trevor had initially failed to notice that Leonidas was sitting with his shirt wide open and revealing an extraordinarily hairy chest.

'I was trying to fit him with a wire,' Sandra snapped, 'but never mind that. If it's not the police, who *is* here?'

'The Scottish bloke and his girlfriend, or whoever she is, and those two Albanian Neanderthals.'

'What? All of them together?'

Trevor shook his head and fought to get his breathing under control. 'Separate tables. MacFarland and the woman on one and the Albanians on another.'

'So what are they doing?'

'MacFarland looks like he's come for lunch. The other two turned up about ten minutes earlier and ordered a half litre of red wine. I reckon they'd been on the piss even before they got here, though. Shouting and laughing a lot and doing that throat cutting mime thing every time I walk past their table.'

'Probably just getting their kicks trying to wind us up,' said Sandra.

'I only hope they know that Tassos has talked to Barkas about paying him the money we owe him.'

'They must do. It's way past the deadline now, so if they hadn't been told, we'd have been carted off in their van hours ago.'

'And what about MacFarland? I really don't like the way he keeps turning up like this.'

'You want to tell me what's going on?' said Leonidas, buttoning his shirt. 'Like, who is this MacFarland?'

'Long story,' said Sandra. 'We'll tell you later, but right now we need to get you sorted out for your meeting with Constable Dimitris. Grigoris says he always goes for a coffee at the same bar in town before he referees a game, so you shouldn't have any problem tracking him down.'

'I certainly won't have any trouble recognising him, the number of times the little shit has stopped me on the road for some petty offence or other.'

'You're sure you're OK with doing this? I mean, what if it all goes wrong and he actually busts you for trying to bribe him?'

'He's far too greedy for that,' said Leonidas and then laughed. 'Besides, in the unlikely event of that happening, the local chief of police is a very good friend of mine.'

35

Jimmy MacFarland took a long slug from his ice cold beer and wiped the back of his hand across his mouth.

'How is the sunburn today?' Coralie asked, leaning towards him across the table.

'No so bad, thanks. They breed us tough where I come from.'

Coralie chuckled. 'Oh, sure.'

'And what's that supposed tae mean?'

'The fuss you made yesterday when I was putting the lotion on you. *Tel un lâche*.'

'A wha'?'

'*Tel un lâche*. Such a coward.'

There weren't many people in the world who could get away with calling MacFarland a coward, and Coralie may well have been unique in that respect. Besides, he knew she was teasing him, and he actually quite enjoyed it, especially the little smile that went with the gentle mockery. He could of course have come clean and defended himself by recounting numerous stories about his far from cowardly experiences as a career criminal but quickly decided to keep going with the banter instead.

'That wasnae me bein' a coward,' he said. 'That wuz you and yer horrible, rough, scaly hands.'

Coralie sat back in her chair, no trace of a smile now as her blue-grey eyes narrowed menacingly.

MacFarland was fairly sure she was faking it. Fairly sure but not completely.

'Hey, I'm just kidding ye,' he said. 'You've got fuckin' gorgeous hands. They're no too far from bein' yer best feature in fact.'

There was a disturbingly lengthy pause before Coralie's features melted back into the familiar smile, and she reached across the table to take MacFarland's hand in hers. 'So, which is my *best* feature then?'

MacFarland exhaled slowly and pursed his lips. 'Hard to say, hen. I mean ye've got so many, it's no an easy job to pick just the wan. But I guess if I really had tae choose, it'd probably be yer—'

It was almost a relief to be interrupted by his phone ringing, given that he genuinely couldn't decide between several of her physical attributes and was about to plump for "yer personality", which (a) might have sounded totally naff and (b) may well have pissed her off because he hadn't gone with her eyes, complexion, hair, legs or whatever.

He checked the display on his phone. 'Ah, shit. Sorry aboot this, darlin', but I really do havtae take this. Go ahead and order if ye're hungry. I'll no be long.'

Coralie said she was happy to wait and blew him a kiss.

Halfway between their table and the steps at the end of the terrace that led down to the quayside, MacFarland hit the answer button. 'Aye?'

He'd been expecting Donna Vincent's call round about this time and was reasonably well prepared with what he was going to tell her.

'Well?'

'I'm nae so bad, thanks. How about you?'

'Don't fuck with me, MacFarland. Is it done or not?'

'Of course.'

'Both of them?'

'Both, aye.'

'How?'

207

'Pardon me?'

'How did you do it?'

'Quietly and quickly.'

'I mean did you shoot them or what?'

'Shot 'em both, aye. Wan in the chest and wan in the heid. I'm a professional. Oh, and just tae be clear and so there's nae misunderstanding, *each* o' them got wan in the chest and wan in the heid. Not like the woman got wan in the chest and the guy got wan in the heid – or the other way round for that matter.'

'How interesting.'

'"Interesting" isnae the word I woulda used, but each to their own, I guess.'

'No, what I mean is that I'm curious to know where you got the gun. You see, I've been in touch with my contact there – the one you were supposed to pick up the gun from – and he tells me he's not seen hide nor hair of you.'

'That's because I prefer not tae involve anyone else on a job like this if I can help it. The fewer the people who know what I'm up tae, the less chance of a fuckup or somebody opening their gobs in the wrong place at the wrong time.'

'So where did you get the gun?'

'I'd rather not say over the phone.'

MacFarland was fully aware that confessing to a double murder using his own phone instead of a burner wouldn't have been a great idea in normal circumstances, but since there hadn't actually *been* any murders, it hardly mattered.

'And you think I'm gonna just take your word for it that the job's been done, do you?'

'Aye, well, there's such a thing as trust y'know,' said MacFarland, hoping his smirk didn't come across in his voice.

'Trust *you*? Are you serious? Harry always said he

wouldn't trust you as far as he could throw you.'

MacFarland stifled another smirk. 'God rest the poor man's soul.'

'Don't piss me about, MacFarland.' Donna's volume was building to a crescendo. 'Unless I get proof, you can kiss goodbye to the second half of your money.'

'Proof? What sorta proof? Ye want me to send ye their heids in the post or wha'?'

'Fucking comedian, aren't you, eh? Well, maybe you won't find it quite so funny when I call my local contact and discover that Trevor Hawkins and Sandra Gray are still upright and walking around without a care in the world.'

MacFarland barely managed to get out the words 'Aye, good plan' before the line went dead.

As he made his way back to join Coralie at the taverna, he doubted the "without a care in the world" part of what Donna had said, but it wouldn't be long before she found out that Trevor Hawkins and Sandra Gray were still very much in the land of the living.

When she'd first got in contact with him, he'd been tempted to turn the job down flat. Anything to avoid getting on a bloody aeroplane. But after he'd thought it over, he realised that actually getting paid to do something he'd gladly have done for free was far too good an opportunity to miss. He had plenty of reasons for wanting to wreak some serious revenge on the two bastards who'd caused him major physical damage, not to mention being directly responsible for Harry Vincent coming within a gnat's whisker of depriving him of his genitalia. They certainly had it coming to them, but the more he thought about it, the more he began to wonder whether death might be a bit excessive as a means of revenge. Further along the line of this thought process, it had started to dawn on him that the one person who deserved retribution far more than Trevor Hawkins and

Sandra Gray was Harry Vincent. That fucker had treated him like shit through all the years he'd worked for him, and MacFarland had lost count of the number of times he'd had to resist an overwhelming urge to slit the bastard's throat. But Harry was already dead, of course. His widow wasn't, though, so how about that for a plan? Screw as much cash out of her as possible and then totally piss her off by doing sod all about what she'd paid him to do.

He climbed the wooden steps up to the terrace of the taverna and smiled to himself. All in all, the plan had worked out pretty well. Donna Vincent would be wetting herself with rage as soon as she found out the truth, and he was damn sure he'd scared the crap out of Hawkins and Gray simply by turning up on their doorstep, so his need for revenge was at least partially satisfied.

The downside, of course, was that he'd miss out on the second half of his not insubstantial fee, but that couldn't be helped. He'd have to trade the Jeep in for something a lot less expensive at the hire place and move out of the fancy hotel to— To where exactly? He wondered how Coralie might feel about him moving into her tent with her at the turtle volunteers' camp. Jesus. A tent? He'd never been camping in his entire life and nor had he ever had the slightest desire to do so. On the other hand, he'd never had the prospect of sharing a tent with someone like Coralie before now, so maybe that would compensate for the complete lack of anything that resembled creature comforts.

And speaking of Coralie, what the fuck were those two goons doing at her table?

'That's ma chair yer sittin' on, pal,' he said to one of the two men.

The second was standing on the other side of Coralie, who was not looking at all happy about how close they were or their obviously lecherous attention.

'They're Albanian,' she said.

'Are they indeed? Well, I dinnae see that's much o' an excuse fir bein' a pain in the arse.' MacFarland turned to the one that was sitting in his chair. 'Right, pal, ye've had yer fun, so why don't you and yer chum fuck off outta here before I beat the livin' shit outta the pair o' youse.'

The man in the chair stared up at him with a leering grin that displayed the absence of several teeth but said nothing.

'Oh, I get it. Ye dinnae speak English, right? Well, looks like I'll havtae give ye a wee bit o' a clue.'

So saying, MacFarland grabbed hold of the man's upper arm and was about to pull him upright when the leering grin vanished instantly and he jumped to his feet, hurling the chair backwards in the process. He yelled something in a language MacFarland didn't understand, which wasn't that surprising, but the intent was perfectly clear.

'So ye wanna play rough, dae ye? OK then, but I havtae warn ye that yer makin' a big fuckin' mistake which ye may or may not live tae regret.'

MacFarland was more than prepared for the punch to the face, and since it was more of a roundhouse than a straight jab, he dodged it easily and brought his knee up sharply into the man's groin. Also as predicted, the second guy was quick to come to his mate's aid. He was probably under the impression that rushing MacFarland from behind would give him the advantage of surprise, but the impact of elbow against teeth was a clear enough indication of his mistake. He reeled backwards, spitting out blood and a couple of pieces of tooth.

By now, his mate had sufficiently recovered from the damage to his wedding tackle to launch another attack, albeit in a crouching position that was no doubt the result of the still excruciating pain. His hand whipped round to his back pocket, and MacFarland had had enough experience of Glasgow street fights in his youth to know what was coming next, and it wasn't going to be his comb. There was a faint click, and the sun glinted off the blade of the flick-knife for a moment, but before the man could make his lunge, MacFarland smashed a beer bottle against the edge of the table.

The Albanian hesitated, his eyes fixed on the threat of the jagged glass rim. It was all the split second MacFarland needed to take aim and thrust the broken base of the beer bottle over the knife. Not quite enough time, though, to make sure his hand was out of the way when the tip of the blade cleared the neck of the bottle by half an inch and scored a direct hit close to the edge of his palm. But it was little more than a nick and nowhere near as bad as the wound his attacker had suffered. The Albanian instantly let go of the knife handle and glanced at the gouges the broken teeth of glass had made in the knuckles of his right hand, the blood quickly skipping through the oozing and trickling stages to a steady flow from each cut. Making full use of this second momentary distraction, MacFarland followed up with a hard slap with the flat of his hand to the guy's ear and sent him sprawling. From personal experience, MacFarland knew that this would not only cause a considerable degree of pain but also temporary, if not permanent, deafness in the stricken ear.

There was nothing wrong with his own hearing, however, and he wheeled round to face the onrushing sound of heavy footsteps from behind him, but had managed less than ten degrees before something very hard caught him a brain-rattling blow across the back of the skull.

36

Moments after Leonidas had left for his meeting with PC Dimitris, Trevor and Sandra rushed out onto the terrace to see what all the commotion was about. The noise level was well above the normal lunchtime hubbub, which didn't usually include quite the same amount of shouting, overturned furniture or breaking glass.

Several of the customers who were nearest to the epicentre of the disturbance were on their feet and edging away from what quickly became apparent to be a major brawl between the Scottish bloke and the two Albanian thugs. Despite being outnumbered, MacFarland seemed to have been getting the upper hand, judging by one of his opponents being flat out on the ground and the other with blood streaming down his chin. A second later, however, MacFarland was hit from behind with what looked like some kind of cosh. His knees crumpled and he fell forward, his upper body glancing off the edge of a table and twisting him round so that he ended up on his back, totally motionless and with his eyes closed.

The Albanians clearly hadn't finished with him yet, though, as the guy who was on the ground clutching his ear suddenly jumped up and landed a couple of hefty kicks in the region of MacFarland's ribcage.

'Hey, pack that in!' Trevor shouted, more out of spontaneity than any real sense of bravery.

Even so, he began to move forward but was brushed aside by the familiarly short but stocky shape of Eleni the cook, who was wielding a meat cleaver with an immensely large and very shiny blade. She strode towards the two Albanians, swishing the meat cleaver back and forth in front of her and yelling at the top of her voice.

The pair of them yelled back at her with plenty of gesticulating but probably realised that this crazed Greek woman meant business and started to back away. To reinforce her point, Eleni raised the cleaver high above her head as if about to launch it flying through the air at whichever of them happened to be nearest, and after the briefest of glances at each other, the two Albanians turned and raced towards the steps at the end of the terrace.

Her mission accomplished, Eleni stomped back to her kitchen, muttering to herself and rhythmically slapping the back edge of the cleaver onto the palm of her hand. As Sandra did her best to calm the other customers with offers of free wine, the young woman that MacFarland was with knelt down beside him and began gently stroking his hair.

'Is he all right?' said Trevor.

'He is unconscious,' said the woman, rather snappily in Trevor's opinion.

'He's not... dead then?'

MacFarland's eyelids flickered.

'What the fuck?' he said, and his eyes opened wide, darting from side to side.

'One of the men,' said the woman. 'They hit you on the head.'

'What with? A fuckin' sledgehammer?' He started to sit up, massaging the back of his skull, but almost immediately lay back down again. 'Jesus. Feels like ma heid's gonna explode. Who were they two bastards anyway?'

'Albanians,' said Trevor. 'Right pair of thugs, they

214

are.'

'Aye well, I kinda gathered that.'

'Do you think we should fetch a doctor?'

'Nah. Couple o' paracetamol and a large Scotch might help, though. You got any?'

'Scotch?'

'Paracetamol. This bein' a bar an' all, I figure you maybe have the Scotch.'

'I think we've got some in the office. Paracetamol, that is.'

'Perhaps we should get you inside,' said Sandra, who had managed to get all the customers settled by now. 'You'd be a lot more comfortable than lying here on the floor.'

'Aye, that sounds like a plan,' said MacFarland, wincing as he tried to sit up again. 'I may need a wee bit o' help gettin' there, though.'

Trevor and the young woman each took an arm and eased him slowly to his feet, then followed Sandra across the road and into the taverna.

Once inside the back office, they lowered him down onto an old armchair that should have been consigned to the tip at least a decade ago. Sandra went back out to fetch some whisky from the bar while Trevor rummaged for the paracetamol in what passed for a first aid box.

'Ah, here we are,' he said and handed MacFarland the pack. 'You want some water with that?'

'Nae, I'll wait for the Scotch to wash 'em doon.'

Trevor wasn't sure whether you were supposed to mix alcohol and paracetamol but decided not to mention it.

'Finest single malt in the house,' said Sandra as she breezed back into the office bearing a small tumbler half filled with whisky.

MacFarland took the glass from her and eyed it suspiciously. 'What's this then? Scotch rationed round here, is it?'

'Perhaps you shouldn't have too much,' said the young woman who was perched on the arm of the chair and still stroking his hair. 'Not after you've had concussion.'

'Away, hen. Best medicine in the world, this.' So saying, he popped a couple of paracetamol into his mouth and drained the glass of whisky in one, then smacked his lips. 'Aye, not bad. Not bad at all. A wee refill would be good when ye're ready.'

Sandra clearly wasn't ready as she took no notice of the empty glass that MacFarland held out to her and fixed her attention on the young woman instead.

'I don't think we've met before,' she said. 'I'm Sandra and this is Trevor.'

'Coralie,' said the woman with a fleeting smile. 'Coralie Cormier.'

'Well, isn't this all very cosy and civilised,' said MacFarland. 'And since we're all at the introductions stage, I'm Jimmy MacFarland.'

'We know,' said Trevor.

'Aye, course you do. I wasnae sure if you'd remember me or no.'

'How could we forget?' said Sandra.

'And I certainly have plenty o' reasons to remember youse two. I mean ye did more damage tae me than those Armenian bastards just now.'

'Albanian,' Trevor corrected lamely.

'Whatever,' said MacFarland. 'Do youse know how long it took for ma hand and foot to get back to normal? How much pain I went through?'

'So that's why you're here, is it?' said Sandra. 'To get your revenge? Bit ironic, don't you think? I mean, here's us feeding you paracetamol and Scotch while you're trying to decide whether to just break our legs or murder us in our beds.'

216

MacFarland shifted uncomfortably in his chair. 'Well, I— Maybe we can talk about this some other time, what with me feelin' a wee bit muzzy-headed right now.'

He rubbed the back of his skull for emphasis, and Coralie stopped stroking his hair.

'I don't understand,' she said. 'What is this about breaking legs and murder?'

'Long story, hen,' said MacFarland, taking her hand in his. 'We're only messin', that's all.'

The narrow-eyed stare that he then fixed on Trevor and Sandra in turn was easy enough to interpret. Whatever he'd told Coralie about himself, it was a fair bet that words like "gangster" or "murder" hadn't entered into it.

'That's right. Just messin',' said Trevor, recognising that the safest response was to play along.

He forced a grin at Coralie, and MacFarland responded with a barely perceptible nod and a subtle wink of approval.

'So, how's about that wee refill then?' he said, once again holding out his empty whisky glass to Sandra.

'I'll go,' said Trevor, grabbing the glass and heading for the office door, glad to get away if only for a few minutes. Even when MacFarland was "playing nice", the guy still scared the absolute shit out of him.

37

It had taken Trevor and Sandra even longer than usual to clear up after the last of the lunchtime customers had left, partly because Grigoris had had to head off early to get to his football match and partly because of the additional debris from MacFarland's dustup with the Albanians. By the time they'd finished, it was almost too late for a siesta, and MacFarland's continued presence in the back office made the prospect of even a short rest less likely still.

Coralie – the woman they supposed to be his girlfriend – had already gone to carry out some volunteer duty or other, but MacFarland seemed perfectly happy to stay where he was, slumped in the armchair and necking whisky. It was also fairly clear that he'd been waiting to say something now that Coralie was out of the way.

'Not that I owe youse two a damn thing – least of all an explanation,' he said, 'but I just wanted tae let yer know how bloody lucky ye've been.'

'Oh yeah? So how's that then?' said Trevor, thinking that he did in theory owe them a fair bit for the single malt he'd been putting away, not to mention the small matter of Eleni saving him from an even more severe beating.

'Ye said before that youse were brickin' it that I'd come here to break yer legs or murder yer.'

'And?'

'Well, I have to tell yer it was the latter of the two.'

'But you changed your mind?' said Trevor, more in

hope than expectation that this was indeed the case.

'I dare say ye've heard o' a wee lassie by the name o' Donna Vincent?'

Trevor and Sandra nodded in unison, and MacFarland launched into a detailed account of how Donna had hired him to kill them both and the numerous ways her husband Harry had mistreated him over the years.

'Naturally, I had ma ain reasons for wanting to croak the pair o' yer, but at the end o' the day I decided that pissing off Donna Vincent and takin' a shitload o' her money at the same time was worth more to me than sending youse two to a well deserved early grave. Of course, there's still the option of breakin' yer legs.'

There was a brief pause as MacFarland eyeballed them both with the cold hard stare of a professional killer, then suddenly burst out laughing and slapped the arm of his chair.

'Relax,' he said. 'I'm only kiddin'. It'd hardly be worth the effort and may even be a wee bit tricky in ma current condition. And speakin' o' which, I'm bloody starvin'. Any chance o' some grub to soak up some o' this here whisky?'

* * *

By the time MacFarland had finished eating and decided he needed to go back to his own place for a lie down, Trevor and Sandra had already begun setting up for the evening session at the taverna. They were halfway through laying the tables out on the terrace, when Leonidas the vet appeared, waving the cigarette lighter Sandra had given him.

'Got the bastard,' he said, grinning triumphantly.

'He fell for it?' said Sandra. 'He took the bribe?'

'Absolutely. Not at first, though. He was obviously suspicious, so I had to work quite hard to persuade him.'

'And you managed to record it all?'

'As far as I know, but I haven't been able to play it back on this to check.'

'No, I'll have to plug it into the laptop,' said Sandra, taking the lighter from him. 'Let's go and see, shall we?'

Trevor and Leonidas followed Sandra into the back office and watched as she slid the plastic cover from the lighter and plugged the recording device into the USB slot on her laptop. Seconds later, they were all listening to the remarkably clear voices of Leonidas and PC Dimitris with the expected background sounds of a busy café. The conversation between the two men was all in Greek of course, so Leonidas translated as they went along.

DIMITRIS: You said you wanted to see me about a matter of some importance.

LEONIDAS: That's right.

DIMITRIS: Well?

LEONIDAS: I was wondering about the football match this afternoon.

DIMITRIS: What about it?

LEONIDAS: You're refereeing it, aren't you?

DIMITRIS: Uh-huh.

LEONIDAS: Do you actually get paid, or do you just do it for the love of the game?

DIMITRIS: I get paid, sure.

LEONIDAS: Can't be much, though, can it? Not for amateur football, I mean.

DIMITRIS: Every little helps.

At this point, Leonidas stopped translating and suggested that Sandra fast forward the recording. 'There's several more minutes of this sort of thing until we got to the part you'll be most interested in.'

Sandra did as she was told and then resumed the

playback. The rather stilted conversation continued in Greek, and Trevor and Sandra looked to Leonidas to carry on with his translation. Instead, he told them that this was a particularly awkward moment which could easily have blown the whole plan.

'Dimitris had taken out a cigarette, but his lighter had run out of gas, so he reached across for mine, which was sitting on the table in front of me. I guess I panicked because I snatched it up before he could get to it and told him mine didn't work either. "I didn't think you even smoked," he said, so I told him I used to smoke, but I gave up a few years ago. "So why do you have it?" he said. I gave him some nonsense about the lighter having sentimental value, that it used to belong to my father.'

'A cheap plastic disposable lighter?' said Trevor.

Leonidas shrugged. 'Like I said, I panicked, and it was the best I could come up with on the spur of the moment.'

'And he believed you?'

'I doubt it, no, but I quickly changed the subject and got him to lose interest in the lighter by starting to talk directly about the bribe for the first time. That should be coming up any second now.'

Leonidas picked up on the translating once again but stopped almost immediately as Grigoris came through the office doorway, breathing heavily.

'Sorry I'm late,' he panted. 'Dimitris added ten minutes to the end of game.'

'So who won?' said Trevor, expecting that he already knew the answer.

'We did. Four-two, but two of our goals were penalties – both in the last ten minutes – and I'm sure were wrong referee decisions. I think maybe Dimitris has been taking the bribes again.'

38

Constable Dimitris's car was parked up in exactly the same spot as it had been two days ago, and once again he was pointing his speed camera at every passing vehicle. The traffic on the main road out of town was fairly light for a Monday morning, so Trevor had plenty of space to wind the van up to maximum speed by the time they passed him.

As on the previous occasion, Trevor checked the rear-view mirror to see PC Dimitris fling open the door of his car and jump in behind the steering wheel. The blaring siren and flashing blue lights came on less than a second later. Then came the flashing headlights as he sped up behind them, and Trevor pulled the van over onto the hard shoulder.

'Oh, I'm so looking forward to this,' said Sandra as they waited for Dimitris to adjust his cap and saunter up to the driver's door of the van.

'You do not learn your lesson, eh?' he said, peering in through Trevor's open window and already reaching for the notepad in the back pocket of his trousers.

'Is there a problem, officer?' said Trevor, scarcely able to suppress a grin.

'You know very well what is the problem. You were going even faster than you were on Saturday. This time you are in very serious trouble. Very serious indeed.'

Sandra leaned across from the passenger seat as Dimitris took out his pen and flipped open his notepad.

'I'd say the boot was rather on the other foot,' she

said, and unlike Trevor, made no attempt to hide her amusement.

Dimitris went into suspended animation, except for his mouth. 'Boot and foot? What are you talking about?'

'Good game yesterday, was it?'

This time, the suspended animation included his mouth.

'Must have been good,' said Trevor. 'Four-two, I heard, and two penalties. Mind you, ten minutes added on at the end seemed quite a lot, though.'

'This is none of your business,' said Dimitris, his hand trembling slightly as he began to write in his notepad.

'Oh, but I think it is,' said Sandra. 'You haven't got a light, have you? This one seems to have run out of gas.'

By glacial degrees, Dimitris raised his eyes to take in the disposable cigarette lighter that Sandra was holding out in front of her.

'Although it's not really a lighter at all,' she said and slipped off the plastic cover to reveal the recording mechanism inside.

The colour drained from Dimitris's cheeks, and he stared at it as if it were some kind of explosive device that was about to go off in his face.

'What... is that?' he said at last.

'Go on. Take a wild guess.'

'This is from yesterday? From when I talked with Leonidas Stathakos?'

'It is indeed,' said Sandra, 'although unfortunately this little gizmo doesn't have a playback mode, but I can assure you we've listened to every word back at the office. Of course, you'd be more than welcome to come back with us and give it a listen yourself, but I don't suppose you need reminding of what was actually said.'

Dimitris slowly returned the notepad to his back pocket. 'OK, you may leave now. This time I let you off with a warning.'

Trevor wondered whether Dimitris really was that stupid or he was simply clutching at even the flimsiest of straws.

'I don't think you've fully grasped what's going on here, have you?' he said. 'I mean, do you seriously believe that we would go to all that trouble to get evidence that you take bribes just so we could keep it as insurance in case we needed it to get out of a speeding ticket?'

Dimitris took his time as he appeared to be processing the logic of what Trevor had asked him. When he spoke, it was little above a whisper: 'So what is it you want?'

'Information,' said Sandra.

'Information? About what?'

'Well, to start with, there's the matter of your involvement in the attempt to blackmail us.'

Dimitris's laugh was thin and unconvincing. 'You crazy? I know nothing about no blackmail.'

Sandra held up the recording device as a none too gentle reminder. 'Of course, if you'd rather we just passed this on to Lieutenant Pericles...'

She let the threat hang in the air while Dimitris muttered something in Greek and bit his lip, his gaze fixed on the ground between his feet.

'Fine,' said Sandra after no response was forthcoming. 'Next stop, the police station then, Trev.'

'Seems that way,' said Trevor and fired up the van's engine.

'Wait. Wait,' said Dimitris, his eyes flitting back and forth between Trevor and Sandra. 'I am not the man who does the blackmail, but I will tell you what I know.'

'Good decision,' said Sandra. 'So if you'd like to step inside the van—'

'No, not now,' Dimitris interrupted. 'I am still on duty. You must wait till I finish my shift and then we meet. But not in public. I will call and tell you where.'

Trevor wasn't convinced that letting Dimitris choose the venue for the meeting was such a great idea or why it shouldn't be in public, but they agreed anyway and set off back to the taverna. As they drove away, Trevor checked his rear-view mirror to see Dimitris take off his cap and then hurl it to the ground before stomping on it several times with both feet.

39

The road zig-zagged up the steep hill between houses that had been built long before those in the lower town and eventually levelled out over a distance of about two hundred metres. In this part of the "old town", almost every building was a bar or taverna with the occasional small shop interspersed here and there. Tables and chairs spilled out onto the road on either side, every one of them occupied by casually dressed diners of every age group. White-shirted sweating waiters weaved their way between the tables, expertly avoiding small children and any outstretched legs, carrying enormous, heavily laden trays at head height on the palm of one hand.

'Monday evening, and it's still heaving,' said Trevor and wound up his window against the all pervading aroma of roasting pork.

'Always is in the summer,' said Sandra. 'Hardly surprising though, is it? I mean, the view from up here is stunning.'

Trevor couldn't disagree. During the daytime, almost the whole of the bay was visible and sometimes even the islands of Zakynthos and Kefalonia in the distance, and at night the panorama was just as spectacular with the twinkling lights of the lower town and the harbour beyond.

He drove to the far end of the level area and eventually found a space that was marginally wide enough to park the van. He switched off the engine, yawned and stretched. It had been a long day. In fact, it had been a bloody long week altogether.

'What time is it?' he said, the words barely distinguishable through a second yawn.

'Quarter to ten,' said Sandra. 'We're a bit early, but we may as well wait for him at the top.'

She opened the passenger door and was about to jump out when Milly came hurtling forward from the back seat. Trevor managed to grab her by the collar before she could make her escape.

'Sorry, Mills. Not this time,' he said. 'Hopefully we won't be too long, and it's cooled down a bit now, so you'll be OK if we leave some of the windows open.'

Milly looked at him with a slight tilt of her head from side to side. Trevor repeated his apology and wound down his window by a couple of inches, and Sandra did the same with hers.

'See you later, Milly,' she said and slammed the door shut before the dog could make a second break for freedom.

Like the road that led up from the lower town, the pathway zig-zagged up an equally steep hill. Trevor stared up at the tastefully illuminated castle ruins at the top, about half of its walls and turrets remarkably intact after eight hundred years.

'Why here, though?' he said, bracing himself for the climb and almost wishing they'd brought Milly along to help haul him up the hill.

Sandra shrugged. 'He's obviously paranoid about being seen talking to us when he's off duty, so he insisted it had to be after dark, and you probably couldn't get anywhere much less public than up there at this time of night.'

'There's also the other possibility that he's planning on killing us.'

'Unlikely. We already told him that Leonidas has a copy of the recording and will go straight to the police if anything happens to us.'

Trevor responded with a grunt and set off up the path. 'Well, it had better be worth it, that's all I can say.'

If anything, Sandra was even less fit than he was, and by the time they'd reached what remained of the castle's gatehouse at the top of the hill she was gasping for breath.

'Bloody hell,' she rasped. 'Like you said... This had... better be... worth it.'

As soon as she'd recovered her breathing enough to be able to walk again, she followed Trevor through the gatehouse archway and into a large flat area, the floor of which was paved with grey stone slabs and most of them obscured by grass and weeds. Around the perimeter were half a dozen smaller archways in various states of disrepair.

'May as well have a look round while we wait,' said Trevor and stepped through the nearest of the archways into what must have been some kind of chamber, but little more than the foundations of the walls still remained.

He backed out of the chamber and was about to explore what the next archway had to offer when he spotted that Sandra was sitting on an enormous block of flat stone at the far end of the open area.

'I thought we were going to check the place out,' he said and wandered over to join her.

'Some other time,' she said. 'I'm not really in the right frame of mind to play tourist right now.'

'I wasn't exactly talking about sightseeing. I just thought it might be worth having a look round to make sure that—'

He broke off, distracted by Sandra suddenly flicking her eyes past him and towards the gatehouse.

'He's here,' she said.

Trevor turned to see PC Dimitris standing framed in

the gatehouse archway. The moon was almost full, and he could see that he was out of uniform now and dressed in a pastel yellow polo shirt and cream coloured cotton trousers. Taking a last draw on his cigarette, he crushed the butt under his heel and began walking towards them.

'You are recording this?' he said as he came within earshot and scarcely out of breath at all after the climb up the hill.

'Of course,' said Sandra with the beaming smile of someone who knew they were totally in control of a situation.

Dimitris gave a slight nod of resignation and sat down on a second block of stone that was roughly at right-angles to the one that Sandra was sitting on.

'So what is it you want to know?' he said.

'Oh, pretty much everything you've got,' said Sandra, 'but let's start with why you've been blackmailing us, shall we?'

Dimitris snorted and took a packet of cigarettes from his trouser pocket. 'Not *my* idea. I was just working for... someone else.'

'Oh yes?' said Trevor, suspecting a lie. 'So who would that be, then?'

'I didn't make phone calls. I only organised getting the paper to the English teacher woman and then got some kid to pick up the money at the water park. That is all.'

'You didn't answer my question.'

Dimitris avoided Trevor's eye contact and took a cigarette from the packet. 'Didn't I?'

Trevor detected a definite smirk in the constable's tone which he didn't much care for, and apparently neither did Sandra.

'You do realise what's at stake here, don't you?' she said, clearly bristling with irritation. 'If we hand over the recording of you taking a bribe, you can kiss goodbye to your career and probably look forward to some fairly serious prison time.'

Dimitris lit his cigarette and shrugged. 'But at least I will still be alive.'

'What do you mean?'

'What you think I mean? He finds out I've even been *talking* to you, then...' He made the internationally recognised mime of quickly crossing his throat with his finger. 'This is a very dangerous man. You understand? Family don't matter. He still kill me anyway.'

'Family? Are you saying he's a relative of yours?'

Dimitris took a deep drag on his cigarette and looked down at the ground without responding. Evidently, he'd said more than he'd intended.

'So what is he?' said Sandra. 'Brother? Uncle? Cousin? *What?*'

'I say nothing more,' said Dimitris without looking up and exhaled a cloud of smoke.

'From where I'm sitting, you really don't have a lot of choice.'

This time, Dimitris met Sandra's gaze, his eyes blazing with fury. 'I have choice. I just told you.'

'And what if we put it about that you *have* been talking to us about the blackmail? Whoever it is is bound to find out sooner or later and then...'

She repeated his throat slashing gesture, and Dimitris swallowed hard.

Sandra let the idea sink in for several seconds before continuing. 'OK, let's leave the "who" for now and get onto the "why".'

'The what?'

'No, the "why". Why did this unknown man decide to blackmail us in the first place? We're pretty sure he wanted to get our taverna closed down, so what reason did he have?'

There was another lengthy pause while Dimitris

appeared to be considering his options, although Sandra's ultimatum must have been uppermost in his mind. Losing his job and probably being handed a prison sentence for taking bribes were nothing compared to the likely consequences if she carried out her threat to expose him publicly.

'OK,' said Dimitris, 'but you promise not to say who told you this?'

'Not so long as you tell us the truth,' said Trevor. 'Unless what you've told us already about your part in the blackmail is a pack of lies, you're just the monkey. What we want is the organ grinder himself.'

'Excuse me?'

'Never mind,' said Sandra. 'You have our word, OK? So what were you going to say?'

Dimitris opened his mouth to speak, but the only sound anyone heard was a loud bang, and out of the corner of his eye Trevor caught a flash of fire against the night sky from somewhere at the top of the castle's one remaining tower.

His mouth still open, Dimitris's eyes popped wide momentarily, and he then slid sideways off his stone seat and lay flat on his back on the ground.

'Jesus,' said Trevor as he and Sandra both jumped to his side. 'He's been shot.'

'No shit,' said Sandra. 'Did you see where it came from?'

'Up there on the tower, I think.'

'We need to get under cover in case they start shooting again.'

Another loud bang and a second bullet pinged off a flagstone less than a foot from where Trevor was kneeling.

'They just have!' he shouted.

Both crouching low, Trevor and Sandra each took one of Dimitris's arms. Two more shots ricocheted off the stone slabs close by as they scrambled across the uneven ground to drag him into the lee of a wall that was out of the direct line of fire from the tower.

They laid him down gently with his head supported on a small clump of grass and saw that a patch of crimson was already spreading rapidly across the chest of his pale yellow shirt as he fought to get air into his lungs. A fit of heavy coughing and spluttering followed, and blood began to ooze from the corner of his mouth. He muttered something inaudible, so Trevor and Sandra bent closer to hear what he was saying.

'*Xenotho...*'

'*Xenotho*? What's that?' said Trevor. 'Greek for "foreigner", isn't it? Is that what you're trying to tell us? The man who blackmailed us is a foreigner?'

The shake of Dimitris's head was barely perceptible. '*Xenotho... cheío.*'

'*Xenothocheío*? Hospital? You want us to get you to a hospital?'

'No, it's not hospital. It's hotel,' said Sandra.

'Hotel. Yes.'

The effort of speaking brought on another coughing fit and blood spattered onto the front of his shirt.

'What's a hotel got to do with it?' said Trevor.

Dimitris's voice was now so faint that whatever he replied was lost, however close they leaned into him.

Callous though he knew it was, Trevor realised that he had no more than moments to live and that this might be their only chance to find the answer to the biggest question of all. 'So can you tell us the name of the blackmailer now?'

He held his ear within a couple of inches of Dimitris's mouth, but all he heard was a deep gurgling sound.

'He's gone,' said Sandra, and Trevor sat up to take in the staring, sightless eyes and the heaving, blood-smeared chest that was now completely motionless.

40

Temporary floodlights had been set up around Constable Dimitris's body, and there were a couple more up on the castle tower. As well as the people in white forensic suits, uniformed police were everywhere, two of them stationed down at the bottom of the hill to prevent gawpers and the press from getting to the crime scene. Trevor guessed that the whole of the local force had been called in, regardless of whether they were supposed to be on duty or not. PC Dimitris was, after all, "one of their own".

Lieutenant Pericles had already ushered Trevor and Sandra to one side to ask the inevitable questions while another officer took notes.

'You didn't see who fired the shots?'

'Just heard a bang and saw a flash from up on the tower,' said Trevor. 'Then there were another two or three shots, presumably from the same place.'

'And you saw nobody come down from there? You saw nobody leave?'

Trevor shook his head. 'We were too busy getting Dimitris and ourselves out of the firing line, and we weren't exactly going to chase after them.'

'Of course not,' said Pericles, although Trevor felt there was something about his tone that suggested he maybe thought they should have done.

Sandra must have picked up on it too.

'And what if we *had* gone after them?' she said. 'More than likely you'd have ended up with three bodies instead of just one, and surely it was far more important to try and save Dimitris's life?'

'Indeed,' said Pericles, again without much conviction.

Perhaps it was his personal brand of paranoia, but another possibility suddenly popped into Trevor's mind. 'Jesus, don't tell me you suspect it was us that killed him?'

Pericles ignored the question and asked one of his own. 'You said the reason you were up here at the castle was because you had arranged a meeting with Dimitris, so what was the purpose of this meeting?'

When Sandra began to explain how they'd managed to get evidence of Dimitris accepting a bribe to fix a football match, Pericles motioned to the other officer to stop taking notes, then sent him away altogether after she'd started to talk about his involvement in the blackmail.

'But,' she concluded, 'he died before he could tell us who he was working for – who the real blackmailer is.'

Pericles slowly removed his cap and scratched the back of his head, his features contorted as he processed what he'd been told.

'This is all very interesting,' he said at last, 'but it is not the first occasion that I have had to point out to you that my resources are limited and that solving a murder – two murders – is far more important than spending police time on investigating an alleged blackmail attempt.'

'It's not bloody "alleged",' said Trevor, aware that he was trembling with anger. 'How much more evidence do you need that it's the real thing, for Christ's sake?'

'I think you need to calm down,' said Pericles, replacing his cap.

'Calm down? Calm down? How the hell do you—?'

Sandra placed a firm hand on Trevor's arm to shut

him up.

'What you don't seem to understand,' she said quietly, 'is that the blackmail and Dimitris's murder are both part of the same thing. They're inextricably linked. I mean, why else would somebody want to kill him? He told us himself that if the blackmailer found out that he'd even been *talking* to us, he'd be a dead man.'

Pericles took even longer than before to take in this new information. 'Is this true?'

'Absolutely.'

'Very well then, I shall—'

But before Pericles could get any further with what he was about to say, he was interrupted by the return of the note-taking officer who said a few words in Greek and then disappeared again.

'My apologies,' said Pericles, 'but I am needed elsewhere.'

'So is that it then?' said Trevor, his anger resurfacing in the belief that they were being fobbed off once more.

'It?'

'You're just going to ignore everything we've been telling you?'

'Not at all. But as you can see, I'm extremely busy right now, and it would be much better if you could come to see me at the police station tomorrow morning so that we can discuss this matter further.'

Trevor almost choked. Finally they seemed to be getting somewhere.

Pericles had already hurried away without waiting for a response, and without stopping, he called out over his shoulder, 'And make sure you have your hands swabbed for gunshot residue before you leave.'

'Oh, bloody Nora,' said Trevor. 'He *does* suspect us.'

'Just a formality, I guess,' said Sandra, 'and they won't find any, so we'll be in the clear.'

'Yeah, I s'pose.'

'Anyway, I'm knackered and in serious need of a very large and very strong drink.'

'Sounds good to me,' said Trevor, and they headed off to find someone who'd cross their palms with whatever they used to detect gunshot residue.

41

It was well after two in the morning when Trevor and Sandra had finally climbed into bed, utterly exhausted from the traumatic events of the evening and not entirely sober. Both had fallen asleep within seconds, only to be woken by Milly's loud and frantic barking.

Trevor barely had the energy even to mutter at her to be quiet, a command that she either didn't hear or chose to ignore, so he rolled onto his front and covered his head with his pillow in an attempt to block out the noise. It didn't work.

'What's all that racket about?' he said, casting the pillow aside and sitting up, almost wide awake now and not in the best of moods.

Milly was standing in the open doorway of the bedroom with her attention fixed on the staircase that led down into the taverna's kitchen. Even when Trevor shouted at her to be quiet, there was not a moment's pause in her barking, so he leapt from the bed and strode towards her. Sorely tempted though he was, he'd never so much as laid a hand on Milly in anger, and he didn't intend to start now, but some kind of physical intervention was required if he was ever to get any sleep. As he began to reach for her collar, however, the thought flashed through his mind that maybe Milly was alerting them to the presence of an intruder downstairs. But no sooner had this possibility occurred to him than he smelt the smoke. A moment later, he saw the flames that were already racing up the wooden staircase.

He opened his mouth to call out to Sandra, but all that came out was a hoarse whisper. He moistened his lips with his tongue and tried again, amazed at the level of noise she was able to sleep through.

'What is it?' she said blearily and without even lifting her head from her pillow.

'We're on fire,' said Trevor, unable to raise his voice above a croak.

Sandra yawned heavily. 'Who is?'

'*We* are. The taverna is. It's on fire.'

Four strides across the bedroom floor and she was by his side. 'Oh my God.'

'We need to get out. Quick,' said Trevor, beginning to choke from the acrid fumes of the smoke.

He grabbed Milly by the collar but needed little effort to lead her to the double wood-framed window at the rear of the bedroom. Sandra was right behind them and took hold of the metal handle to open it.

'Shit. Bloody thing's stuck.'

'What?'

'It won't budge,' Sandra grunted, the veins standing out on her forehead as she applied every ounce of strength she possessed to get it to shift. 'I don't remember ever opening this window since we moved in.'

'Here, let me have a go,' said Trevor, despite a fleeting realisation that she was almost certainly stronger than he was.

Sandra took over holding Milly's collar, which was probably unnecessary now as her frantic barking had given way to a low whimpering and she was exhibiting not the slightest inclination to return to the top of the stairs.

Despite the panic-induced burst of adrenaline giving a much needed boost to his muscle power, it became abundantly clear to Trevor that there was no way he was going to shift the latch.

'Bloody thing's got about six layers of paint over it,' he said, his eyes rapidly scanning the room for anything he could use as some kind of tool.

The first thing he spotted was the lamp on the nearest bedside table, and he yanked the cable from the wall without wasting time to unplug it. He swung the lamp's heavy brass pedestal up against the underside of the window latch, twice missing it entirely but eventually scoring a couple of direct hits. One more and the latch flew up out of its socket. It still needed several blows with the palm of his hand to get both sides of the window to open, and they gave way with the sound of splintering wood.

'You go first, and I'll pass Milly down to you,' he said, hearing a whooshing noise as the outside air hit the rapidly ascending flames on the staircase.

Although they were on the upper floor, the back of the taverna building was built into a rocky slope, so the drop was no more than nine or ten feet.

Sandra climbed onto the low sill of the window, then turned and gripped it with both hands before lowering herself down and jumping the last couple of feet to the ground. Trevor picked Milly up with his arms under her belly, and she mercifully kept her struggling to a minimum as he leaned halfway out of the window. Sandra was on tiptoe and had to stretch her arms to their fullest extent above her head to reach her but managed to make sufficient contact for Trevor to let go. She almost toppled backwards as she took Milly's full weight in her hands but steadied herself before delivering her safely onto the rocky slope.

Seconds later, Trevor stood beside them and stared back up at the open window and the swiftly intensifying red and orange glow. A loud crashing sound – presumably the entire staircase collapsing – jolted his brain into the necessity for urgent action.

'Fire brigade,' he said and reached for his phone in the back pocket of his jeans only to realise that all he was wearing was a pair of boxer shorts. 'Shit.'

He turned to Sandra, but apart from a T-shirt, she was as scantily dressed as he was.

'I haven't got mine either,' she said.

Trevor's mind raced. The sooner the fire brigade got there, the more likelihood there was that the rest of the taverna might be saved. 'I'll have to go back in.'

Sandra began to protest, but Trevor shouted at her about not losing valuable time and told her to cup her hands together to give him a leg-up.

Without any further argument, she braced herself to take the strain with her legs planted firmly apart and her fingers interlaced. Trevor put his hands on her shoulders and with one foot on her upturned palms, launched himself upwards. Making sure he had a solid grip on the sill and using the soles of his feet against the wall, he clambered up until his waist was level with the bottom of the window frame. The ferocious blast of heat that hit him was almost enough to make him lose his purchase on the sill, but he clenched his teeth and swung both feet into the room. The flames were already advancing rapidly across the wooden floorboards, and the swirling black smoke made his eyes sting.

Trying to inhale as little as possible, he snatched up the mobile phone from the bedside table where the lamp had been, then hurried back to the window. He tossed the phone down to Sandra before climbing out and dropping down to the ground with considerably less care than previously. He landed awkwardly and fell sideways, a sudden shaft of pain shooting up his left leg and his lungs heaving with the effort of coughing and attempting to take in gulp after gulp of fresh air.

At this time of year – during the hottest months of the

summer – the fire brigade was on constant standby because of the risk of wildfires, and in no more than five minutes after Sandra made the call, blaring sirens could be heard approaching rapidly from the centre of town. In even less time, a fire truck and a pickup roared up the narrow road in front of the taverna.

Unable to put any weight on what he suspected was a sprained ankle, Trevor hopped around the side of the building with his arm across Sandra's shoulders. The fire crew were already unravelling hoses, and one of them shouted at Trevor and Sandra in Greek. Rudimentary as their knowledge of the language was, they gathered he was asking if there was anyone else inside the building.

'*Óchi, móno emeís,*' said Sandra as powerful jets of water began to target the upper floor and a couple of other firefighters smashed their way through the front door at ground level.

42

Being woken by Sandra's phone call in the ridiculously early hours of the morning was guaranteed to put Marcus Ingleby in the foulest of moods, but that was before she'd even told him about the fire. After a good couple of minutes of expletive-ridden shouting and questioning, however, he'd calmed down enough to ask if anyone was hurt. Reassured that the only human and canine damage was Trevor's suspected sprained ankle, Ingleby rang Eric to get him to drive him to the taverna.

By now, the fire was almost completely under control, although smouldering timbers filled the air with an acrid stench, and firefighters were still pumping gallons of water into the building. Once he had made sure for himself that Trevor, Sandra and Milly were at least physically unscathed apart from Trevor's ankle, he had to be forcibly restrained by the fire crew from entering the taverna to inspect the damage. Ultimately having had to admit defeat and accepting Eric's reasoning that it was not only far too dangerous but he'd also be getting in the way of the firefighters doing their job, Ingleby allowed himself to be driven back to his villa with Trevor, Sandra and Milly as his guests for as long as they needed.

Back in the relative calm of his living room, Ingleby was smoking a cigarette with one hand and feeding pieces of biscuit to Milly with the other. She at least seemed to have recovered from the ordeal of the fire, while Trevor and Sandra were understandably still in shock. They were already on their third mug of tea, each of which had been "livened up", as Ingleby put it, with a hefty measure of whisky.

'And you've no idea how the fire started?' Ingleby asked for about the fourth time. 'You or Eleni hadn't left one of the gas rings on in the kitchen or something?'

'No,' said Sandra. 'We always check that sort of thing before we go to bed every night.'

'Yeah, but you'd only just witnessed a murder. Maybe you forgot this time.'

Sandra shook her head. 'Locking up and making a last check round is like an automatic ritual even when we're fit to drop.'

Ingleby took a deep draw on his cigarette. 'Well, if it's not that or some bloody electrical fault, it seems to me we're looking at it being started deliberately.'

'Arson?' said Trevor, whose brain had taken far too much of a battering that night to cope with any kind of logic.

'I believe that is the dictionary definition, yes.'

'You mean somebody was trying to kill us?'

'Not necessarily, although they might have considered you to be what's called collateral damage.'

'But who'd want to burn down the taverna?'

'I've got a pretty good idea,' said Sandra before Ingleby could answer. 'The same person who's been blackmailing us but still failed to get us closed down even after the recording went public.'

In that moment, Trevor realised quite how much of a mess his head was in. In normal circumstances, he told himself, he would have quickly come to the same conclusion, but being within feet of a fatal shooting and narrowly escaping being burned alive all in one night could hardly be considered normal circumstances.

'This PC Dimwit,' said Ingleby, apparently caring little for the accepted etiquette of not speaking ill of the dead. 'Tell me again exactly what he said and especially the last part. Something about a hotel, wasn't it?'

'I'm sorry, Marcus,' Sandra said with a heavy sigh. 'We're obviously as gutted as you are about the taverna, but I really think Trev and I could do with a bit of a kip for a few hours – or try to anyway. We'd probably make more sense once we've had a rest for a while.'

'Yeah, I guess "gutted" isn't the best word you might've used, and I really do understand what you're sayin', but I reckon it's better if you told it all now while everything's still fresh in yer minds. Maybe there's some little detail you might have missed when you told me before.'

'I'm not sure there's anything else we—'

Sandra's objection was interrupted by a heavy knocking on the front door of the villa.

'Fuck's sake, what's wrong with the bloody bell?' Ingleby snapped, stubbing his cigarette out in the ashtray on the table next to him and beginning to ease himself up out of his armchair.

'Don't worry, Marcus. I'll get it,' said Eric, who had been sitting quietly sipping whisky as Trevor and Sandra's story had unfolded.

'Bit bloody early for a social call,' said Ingleby, taking advantage of the fact that he was already leaning forward to check whether his catheter bag needed emptying.

Trevor had a clear view of the bag and could see that it was almost brim full, but Ingleby merely sat back in his chair and lit another cigarette.

'It's the police,' said Eric, leading the way back into the living room with Lieutenant Pericles following close behind.

Pericles removed his cap and tucked it under his arm. '*Kalıméra.*'

'Not much of a good bloody morning if you ask me,'

said Ingleby.

'No, I understand, but perhaps the situation is not quite as bad as it might have been.'

'Oh? You mean it was all a terrible dream and my taverna hasn't been burned to the ground after all?'

Pericles frowned, seemingly failing to grasp the sarcasm of Ingleby's remark. 'No, *kýrie*, it was not a dream. Your taverna really was on fire.'

'So how come it's not as bad as it might have been?'

'Because the *pyrosvestikí* – the fire brigade – came so quickly, the damage was mainly just to the kitchen and the apartment upstairs. The fire chief told me that it was very lucky that none of the gas bottles in the kitchen exploded or most of the building would have been destroyed.'

'Well, hoo-fucking-ray for that. So when are we likely to be able to re-open again?'

'This is not for me to say, but I believe there will be much to repair in the kitchen area, and the whole building will have to be made safe. May I ask if you are insured?'

'As far as I know,' said Ingleby with a slight shrug. 'I leave all that sort of stuff to my broker in the town. Mind you, he's a useless waste of space most of the time, so in answer to your question: fuck knows.'

'Is there any idea yet how the fire started?' said Sandra.

'That is one of the reasons I came to visit you now. To ask you the same thing.'

'We've been over that already, and we can't see any other alternative than it was started deliberately.'

'It is too early to be certain, but from his first examination, this is also what the fire chief believes.'

Trevor couldn't put his finger on exactly what it was about Pericles's tone and the raised eyebrow, but there was more than a hint of accusation in the statement.

'Wait a minute. Wait a minute,' he said. 'Is that why you asked whether the taverna was insured? You think we set fire to the place so we could claim the insurance money?'

'In a case like this, and at such an early stage in the investigation, we cannot rule out any possibilities.'

'Well, you can fucking rule that one out for a start,' said Ingleby, ferociously stubbing his half-smoked cigarette out in the ashtray. 'That makes no bloody sense at all.'

'All the same—'

'Bollocks to "all the same". I just told you I don't even know if I'm insured, for Christ's sake. So instead of pissing about with a total non-starter like that, why don't you join up a few dots and start giving some thought to how this fire – a deliberately started fire – might connect up with all the blackmail stuff?'

'As I have said many times before, finding Yannis Christopoulos's killer must be the priority, and now I have a second murder to investigate. The murder of a fellow police officer.'

'OK, it looks like you're gonna need some help with the dot joining,' said Ingleby forcing himself up out of his chair. 'Trevor and Sandra will fill you in while I go and empty this bastard.'

Tapping the bulging catheter bag on his leg, he hobbled off towards the bathroom with Milly trotting along at his heels.

Pericles declined Sandra's offer of tea or coffee and also her invitation to sit down.

'I have many things to attend to,' he said, 'so please be brief.'

'Fair enough,' said Sandra, 'but it's starting to seem fairly clear that whoever was trying to blackmail us must have started the fire at the taverna. Their motive right from the beginning was pretty obviously to get us closed down, so when the audio recording failed to do the trick, what was the only option left open to him?'

'This is possible, I agree, but I do not see how this is relevant to the shooting of my constable – or Christopoulos's murder for that matter.'

'OK, forget Christopoulos for now, but there's a definite connection between the blackmail and Dimitris's death. We've already told you about his involvement in the blackmail and that he was terrified what would happen to him if he spoke to anyone about who was really behind it. *That's* why he was murdered. Find the blackmailer, and you find Dimitris's killer.'

'Ah, if only it was so simple.'

'Look, there's something else we didn't get the chance to tell you up at the castle. Although Dimitris refused to name the blackmailer specifically, he did let slip that it was some relative of his. It's more than likely that he's local, so maybe you could check out whichever of his relations happen to live round here.'

Pericles pursed his lips and spread his palms outward. 'Like most Greeks in an area like this, he has many relatives, so I don't see how this would be of much help.'

'Well, how about this then?' said Trevor. 'It was hard to make it out, but literally with his dying breath, we're almost sure he was trying to tell us something about a hotel.'

'Hotel?'

'Yes.'

'Which one?'

'Dunno. It was just the one word. That's all he said.'

'*Xenothocheío*,' Sandra added.

Pericles scratched the back of his head and pondered for several seconds.

'I suppose there is one person I can think of who is related to Dimitris and has a connection with hotels,' he said at last, and Trevor and Sandra both sat forward, eagerly awaiting a name to fall from his lips.

43

If it hadn't been for the gentle breeze wafting across the terrace at the back of Ingleby's villa, the heat would have been stifling. Trevor and Sandra had forced themselves out of bed to grab a late lunch and were now lying on adjacent sun loungers under a parasol by the side of the pool and watching Milly cavorting about in the water. As for Ingleby himself, he rarely surfaced before midday anyway, but given that none of them had hit the hay before seven in the morning, he was unlikely to make an appearance before early evening.

After Pericles had left, Eric had followed suit and gone back to his own villa a short walk away, leaving the others deep in discussion about the latest revelation. In their minds, there could now be little doubt that Alexandros Barkas was the chief instigator in the blackmail attempt and hence, very probably, the arson attack as well as PC Dimitris's murder. As a first cousin of Dimitris and whose main business was developing his chain of hotels, Pericles could think of no-one else who matched the information that Trevor and Sandra had gleaned from the recently deceased constable. Pericles had warned them, however, that it was too soon to jump to conclusions as such evidence was purely circumstantial, but he promised to bring Barkas in for questioning later in the day.

Trevor took a sip from his glass of iced coffee on the low table between the two sun loungers. Even though they'd already gone over Barkas's probable motivation in some detail, there were still some aspects that bothered him. Yes, it made perfect sense that the taverna's location was a prime site to build a new hotel and could be bought at a much reduced price if it had been closed down and very probably for little more than a pittance if it had been razed to the ground. But why all the blackmail stuff, which in all likelihood led to him having PC Dimitris killed to keep his mouth shut? Why not just get the dodgy recording of Trevor and Sandra dishing the dirt - quite literally – on the taverna's hygiene standards and make it public like he did anyway? OK, it didn't get the result he wanted, but it still didn't explain why he'd gone through the whole rigmarole of threatening phone calls and all the rest of it. According to Ingleby, who seemed to be fairly clued up about Barkas and his reputation, the guy probably wanted the blackmail money as a nice bit of icing on his cake and that: 'I've come across greedy bastards like him before that would sell their own grandmother's spleen if they thought there was a few quid in it.'

Trevor twisted his head to the left to check if Sandra was awake. She had her eyes firmly closed, but that didn't necessarily mean anything.

'Sand?' he said. 'You asleep?'

'Yes,' said Sandra without opening her eyes.

Trevor turned on his side to face her. 'I just about get why Barkas would try and blackmail us on top of getting the taverna closed down, but why the hell would he actually *lend* us the money to pay off the supposed blackmailer? I mean, all he'd be doing would be getting his own money back, so what was the point?'

'Because he knew he *would* get it back, I suppose.'

'Or maybe he thought it would take suspicion away from him – that he was the blackmailer himself – and divert attention from his real motive.'

'Could be,' said Sandra, although Trevor suspected

251

that her mind wasn't fully engaged with the conversation.

Seconds later, however, she was abruptly snapped out of her trance-like state when Milly decided she'd cooled off enough and clambered out of the pool, partially drenching Sandra as she shook off the excess water from her fur.

'Bloody hell, Milly,' said Sandra, sitting up with her eyes now fully open. 'I was almost dropping off then.'

Normally, Trevor would have raised at least a chuckle, but his mind was far too occupied with puzzling over the various inconsistencies in the Barkas conundrum.

'I knew you weren't listening,' he said.

'I was. I was. It's just that we've been over most of this stuff already, and I'm too knackered to think about it any more right now.'

'Most of it, yeah, but not all. For instance, when Barkas let us go after his Albanian goons had kidnapped us, why did he threaten us with all sorts of shit if we didn't get his money back to him? Presumably he'd already been given it by whoever it was at the water park.'

'Well, if you're right about the whole blackmail thing being a smokescreen to hide his real motive, perhaps he wanted to reinforce the idea that he wasn't the blackmailer himself. Telling us what he'd do to us if we didn't pay up was just part of the act.'

'Yeah, I see that,' he said, 'but then he goes and accepts Tassos Christopoulos's offer of covering the loan.'

'Why wouldn't he? Like Marcus said, the guy's a greedy bastard, so he must have been over the moon. Not only had he got his own money back, but he'd also got an unexpected fifty grand bonus which Tassos was never going to see again.'

It was Trevor's turn to not be giving the conversation his full attention. As soon as the name Tassos Christopoulos had left his lips, his already overstretched brain cells were thrown into even greater turmoil.

'Shit,' he said, only vaguely aware that he'd spoken out loud.

'What now?'

'Tassos Christopoulos. He's paying us to find out who killed his brother and so far we've done almost bugger all about it.'

'We can't prove it yet, I know, but I thought we'd decided it had to be Barkas. From what Leonidas told us, he damn near admitted it. And since it's highly likely he had Dimitris killed, it's not as if he hasn't got form.'

'But that's exactly my point. We can't *prove* any of it. We can hardly go to Tassos and tell him we *think* it was Barkas that murdered his brother.'

Sandra picked up her glass of iced coffee. 'Course not, but Pericles said he was going to bring Barkas in for questioning some time today, so maybe that'll get some results. But until then, there's not a lot we can do about it, so in the meantime...'

Instead of finishing the sentence, Sandra lay back on the sun lounger, closed her eyes and clasped her hands across her stomach, while Trevor's brain continued its uphill battle to try and turn its internal chaos into something approaching some kind of order.

44

As soon as he'd left Trevor and Sandra's taverna following his "wee argument" with the two Albanians, Jimmy MacFarland had returned to his hotel and told the receptionist that he wanted to settle his bill to date and include two more nights that he'd be staying. Since his phone conversation with Donna Vincent earlier that day, he was currently unemployed, and checking out of the five star hotel was something of a priority before she froze the credit card she'd given him.

His mission successfully accomplished, he'd gone up to his room, hung a "Do Not Disturb" sign on the door, and after a quick shower, had climbed into the luxuriously massive bed. He slept soundly through the night and then intermittently for the whole of the following day, nursing his injuries and never once leaving the room.

On the second night, he switched off the bedside lamp and closed his eyes with absolute certainty that it was likely to be a very long time – if ever – before he slept in such a bed again. He was determined to make the most of it, which he assumed he had done because the next thing he knew, there was a firm but polite knock on his door.

Through a haze of semi-consciousness, he gradually remembered having ordered breakfast to be delivered to his room on his final morning at the hotel. It was absurdly expensive, but Donna Vincent would be picking up the tab, so what the hell? Might as well go out in a blaze of extravagance. He'd eaten nothing for almost thirty-six hours, and his stomach was complaining loudly at its shameful neglect, but the breakfast was hardly what might be described as a gut buster and as far away from a full Scottish as Hamilton Academicals were from winning the league. And who decided it was OK to have cheese for breakfast, for Christ's sake? Still, after he'd scoffed every last morsel of cereal, bread, croissant and all the rest of it, including the cheese and even the yoghurt, MacFarland guessed it would probably be enough to keep him going till lunch, which of course he'd have to pay for himself from now on.

Freshly showered and dressed, he packed up his meagre belongings and bid farewell to his brief flirtation with the life of luxury. The first item on today's agenda was to find alternative accommodation that was at least within sniffing distance of his own personal budget. He still had plenty of the fee that Donna had already paid him but was fully aware that this might have to last him for quite a while until his next job came along.

Targeting the back streets of the town and the most tawdry of the "Rooms to Let" signs, he spent the entire morning traipsing around with nothing to show for it. This being the middle of August and the height of the tourist season, there wasn't a single vacancy in even the shittiest places he enquired at.

Thoroughly pissed off and his T-shirt wringing with sweat, he decided it was well past time for a couple of cold beers and a bite to eat, so he headed down to the harbour and Trevor and Sandra's taverna. Now that they were best pals – or more accurately that they knew he wasn't intending to kill them or even break their legs – maybe they might be able to help him find some cheap digs somewhere.

'Fuck me,' he said, coming to an abrupt halt as the

blackened outside of the upper storey came into view. 'Looks like some numpty's been playin' wi' matches.'

Recovering from the shock, he moved closer and stopped at the length of red and white tape that cordoned off the front of the building. The main door of the taverna had been boarded up, but water managed to seep out from underneath like an only marginally cleaner oil slick.

'This isnae turnin' oot tae be ma lucky day, is it?' he said. 'Nor theirs neither, I guess.'

'First sign of madness, talking to yourself.'

He instantly recognised the heavily accented voice and spun round. 'Hey, darlin'. How ye doin'?'

'I'm fine,' said Coralie. 'It's your mental health I'm worried about.'

MacFarland laughed. 'Nae lasting damage from the concussion as far as I know.'

'Glad to hear it or I might have to find myself another boyfriend.'

'Ach, youse women are so fickle,' he said, then pointed his thumb back over his shoulder at the taverna. 'Any idea what happened here?'

'I don't know, but there's a rumour going round that it may have been... Oh, what's the word when it's deliberate?'

'Arson?'

'Arson, yes.'

'No shit. That's a bummer. Anyone know who started it?'

Coralie shook her head. 'Listen, I've just finished my shift at the kiosk, and I'm starving. Any idea where I might find someone who's gentleman enough to offer to buy me lunch?'

'Sorry, hen, but I might be able to stretch to a souvlaki or two if I'll dae instead.'

* * *

In MacFarland's line of work, premature death was always a distinct possibility, but he'd never seen the point of making a will because he had nobody to leave anything to and nothing to leave them even if he had. Equally, he found the whole idea of a bucket list utterly absurd, but if he had one, it was an absolute certainty that it would never in a million years include the phrase "Go camping".

'You never know, you might even enjoy it,' Coralie had said over lunch at a quayside taverna after MacFarland had explained his reason for being in urgent need of cheap accommodation – but without any mention of his deal with Donna Vincent. Instead, he'd given her some story about how he'd overspent on his holiday budget but wanted to stay on for a while longer.

'It's no gonna happen, hen,' he'd said and used his fingers to count off the many negative aspects of sleeping under canvas, including the hard ground, snakes, scorpions and far too much fresh air. 'I'd never get a wink o' kip.'

Coralie, however, had worn him down eventually, and he'd had to admit to himself that he didn't exactly have a lot of options open to him, and besides, snuggling up with Coralie night after night held an appeal that outweighed most of the downsides of camping except perhaps for the snakes and scorpions. He'd agreed to at least give it a try, which was why he was now lying flat on his back inside Coralie's two-person tent while she crouched, watching him from just outside the open flap.

'Well?' she said.

MacFarland shifted his position slightly and winced. 'There's some pointy wee rock right in the middle o' ma back for starters. Can we no get wan o' they blowup mattress jobbies or somethin'?'

'No, we can't, and you'll get used to it in no time, I'm sure.'

'The rock?'

'And I thought you were such a tough guy.'

'Aye well, appearances can be deceptive, as the saying goes.' He forced himself into a sitting position and massaged his ribs, still sore – but hopefully not broken – from the kicking he'd had a couple of days ago. 'It's like a fuckin' oven in here an' all.'

'Perhaps I should turn on the air conditioning then.'

'Oh, ha bloody ha.'

'Anyway, it's the middle of the afternoon. It'll be quite a bit cooler at night.'

'Yeah? So how does "quite a bit cooler" convert intae Fahrenheit?'

'Fahra what?'

'Oh shit. Sorry. I wuz forgettin' ye're wan o' they metric types.'

Coralie laughed and extended her hand to help MacFarland scramble out of the tent. 'Come on. I'll show you round the rest of the camp.'

The grand tour took no more than five minutes. The turtle volunteers' camp was in the lower part of a private campsite, and the owners had given the group a heavily discounted rate. Apart from forty or so tents, which ranged from shabby not-at-all-chic to the almost luxurious, there was a temporary shower and toilet block and an open fronted wooden construction that housed a reasonably well equipped kitchen. MacFarland was hardly the fussy type, but he wasn't sure he'd be too keen to eat anything that was cooked up in here, and although he was gagging for one, even refused the coffee that Coralie offered to make him.

'Welcome to your new home,' said Coralie and kissed him on the cheek.

'Aye well, let's see how I feel after I've spent a night

wi' a rock stickin' in ma back. Right now, though, I've something I need tae do.'

45

It was early evening when Trevor and Sandra walked into the local police station, having been summoned by Lieutenant Pericles to "further assist with my enquiries". The timing would not have been ideal in normal circumstances as they would have been busy getting ready for the evening trade at the taverna right about now, but the fire had rendered this unnecessary. When it would be able to re-open was anyone's guess, particularly after Ingleby discovered that his "useless fucking prick of a broker" had failed to renew the insurance policy for the past two years, having presumably pocketed the premiums himself. Unsurprisingly, Ingleby had screamed down the phone at him for several minutes, threatening him with everything from a lawsuit to cutting off his balls and making him eat them in a pie.

'Have you talked to Barkas yet?' Trevor asked as soon as they entered Pericles's office.

Pericles was sitting behind his desk, the grey tinge to his face and the drooping eyelids suggesting he hadn't slept in quite some time.

'Not yet,' he said. 'I sent a couple of officers to his house earlier, but it seems that no-one was at home. I've put out an alert, though, so it shouldn't be long.'

'Maybe he's done a runner,' said Sandra. 'He couldn't know how much Dimitris told us about the blackmail before he died and decided to hedge his bets.'

'Excuse me?'

'Sorry. It's just an expression. What I mean is that if he thought you might be onto him for the blackmail – and, more importantly, Dimitris's murder – he's not going to hang around waiting for you to arrest him.'

Pericles spread his palms on top of the desk. 'But I have no real evidence to charge him with anything yet. I simply need to question him first.'

'But he doesn't know that, does he?'

'And what about the Albanians?' Trevor chipped in.

'Albanians?'

'The two that kidnapped Sandra and me.'

'You were kidnapped? But you haven't told me of this before.'

'Because Barkas went into quite a lot of detail about what he'd do to us if we did, but we're way beyond that now anyway. The point is that these two Albanians were working for him when they kidnapped us, and you can bet your life that Barkas wouldn't have wanted to get his hands dirty and killed Dimitris himself. He'd've got *them* to do it.'

'Once again, I must remind you that theories are not evidence, and as I already told you earlier today, we cannot jump to conclusions about *kýrios* Barkas's involvement either in the alleged blackmail or Dimitris's murder.'

Trevor slapped his palm to his forehead. 'Oh God, here we go again with the "alleged". We've got a bloody recording of Dimitris *admitting* to the blackmail and putting the finger on him.'

'Very well. I agree that the blackmail attempt was probably genuine—'

'Thank you,' Trevor interrupted with more than a hint of sarcasm.

'But,' Pericles continued, 'all the recording tells us is that the blackmailer was a relative of Dimitris and that he may or may not have said something about a hotel.'

'If I might make a suggestion,' said Sandra, playing the good cop to Trevor's bad cop, which was rather ironic given who they were talking to. 'Since you've been unable to track down Barkas so far, wouldn't it be an idea to have a word with these two Albanian guys? You never know what they might cough up.'

Pericles visibly bristled. 'I would prefer it if you did not try to teach me my job, and although I have only heard these people mentioned for the first time less than two minutes ago, I had already decided to make this my next course of action. Do you happen to know where they might be found?'

Sandra shook her head. 'Not a clue, but they surely can't be that hard to find in a place this size.'

'It is not always as simple as you—' Pericles began but broke off when the door of his office flew back on its hinges and in marched Anastasia Barkas.

Her eyes were fixed on Pericles, but her focus shifted instantly when she spotted Trevor and Sandra sitting across the desk from him.

'So you two are here again, are you?' she snarled. 'In that case, I will say what I have to say in English as you are probably too stupid to understand Greek, and I expect this will be of interest to you too since you are at least partly responsible for what has happened.'

Pericles had half risen from his chair, but Anastasia gestured to him to remain seated with an imperious flap of her hand.

'*Kyría*,' he said, 'I am in the middle of a meeting, but if you would care to wait outside for a few minutes, I will—'

'I think that what I have to tell you is much more important than whatever you three are gossiping about.'

'Well, I—'

Before Pericles could continue, Anastasia pushed her way between Trevor and Sandra's chairs, planted her hands wide apart on the desk and leaned forward, pinning her gaze on the police lieutenant's eyes.

'I wish to report a murder.'

Pericles raised an eyebrow. 'Oh?'

'A murder, yes.'

'Whose murder?'

'My husband's.'

Pericles's other eyebrow shot up to join its partner. '*Kýrios* Barkas?'

Anastasia muttered something in Greek and glanced up at the ceiling. 'I only have one husband, and yes, his name is *kýrios* Barkas, which is why *my* name is *kyría* Barkas.'

'Yes, of course,' said Pericles, then paused as if struggling to decide what question to ask next. 'And how— *when* did this murder take place?'

Anastasia checked the tiny but expensive looking watch on her wrist. 'Seven and a half hours ago.'

'And where was this?'

'At our house.'

'You were there at the time?'

'Yes.'

'That must have been very distressing for you,' said Pericles and added almost as an afterthought, 'And you're absolutely certain it was murder.'

'Oh, absolutely.'

'So did you see who the killer was?'

'Not as such, no.'

'But do you have any idea who it might have been?'

'More than an idea. I know exactly who it was.'

'You do?'

Anastasia pulled herself upright and folded her arms across her chest. 'Of course I do. Why wouldn't I?' she said with a hint of a smirk. 'I can't remember quite how many times I stabbed him, but it was more than enough to make sure the bastard wouldn't be taking another breath until he ended up in Hell like he deserved.'

46

By the time Trevor and Sandra had got back to Ingleby's villa for their second night, the old guy had apparently decided to call it a day and was already in bed. The following morning, however, he was up and about even before they were, which was definitely a first. As they reached the bottom of the marble staircase, their astonishment stopped them in their tracks, and they were further amazed to see that he was sitting at the breakfast bar that separated the kitchen area from the living room, reading a newspaper and actually *eating*.

'Well I never,' said Trevor.

'Problem?' said Ingleby without looking up from his paper and through a mouthful of cereal.

'Just surprised to see you out of your bed quite so early.'

'I couldn't be arsed to wait around for you to get in last night, but I'm a bit keen to know how you got on at the cop shop. In particular, who the bastard was that set fire to my fucking taverna.'

'Alexandros Barkas. Except it wasn't him personally.'

Ingleby froze the loaded cereal spoon halfway to his mouth. 'What the fuck does that mean?'

'He got his two Albanian goons to do it.'

'And you know this how?'

'Mrs Barkas told us. Well, she told Pericles actually, but we just happened to be there at the time.'

'Barkas's missus ratted him out?'

'After she'd killed him, yes.'

Ingleby's spoon fell from his hand and clattered into the cereal bowl, sending splatters of milk over the marble-topped breakfast bar. 'Whoa there. Hang on a minute. She *killed* him?'

'Said she couldn't remember quite how many times she'd stabbed him.'

'Hell hath no fury like a woman scorned, eh?'

'Except it was more the other way round really,' said Sandra. 'On account of it being her that was having the affair.'

'So why'd she do it then?'

Trevor and Sandra then took it in turns to summarise everything that Anastasia Barkas had said, and there was plenty to get through. Pericles had obviously asked her why she'd murdered her husband, and she'd told him that she was convinced it was him that had killed her lover Yannis Christopoulos, even though he'd repeatedly denied it. Since he'd found out for certain she was having an affair – and who with – Barkas had become increasingly abusive towards her, both verbally and physically, and it was the final straw when they were having yet another major row and he punched her in the stomach. They were in the kitchen at the time, and she retaliated with the first thing that came to hand, which happened to be a very large knife.

'Jesus,' said Ingleby, lighting a cigarette and taking a deep draw. 'So how come she owned up to it?'

'Seems she was seriously in love with Christopoulos and couldn't imagine life without him,' said Sandra. 'So, as far as she was concerned, it didn't matter much whether she spent the next chunk of it behind bars or as a free woman. She also said that it wouldn't take the cops long to figure out who'd done Barkas in, so she may as well get it over with.'

'Might get her a reduced sentence too, I guess.'

'I don't think she was bothered about that at all, or when Pericles told her that there were mitigating circumstances and she could very probably plead self defence.'

Ingleby flicked ash from his cigarette into the half full cereal bowl. 'So what about torching my taverna? He'd actually admitted that to her, had he?'

'And a lot more besides,' said Trevor. 'I mean, she was in full flow and nothing was gonna stop her. It was like she wanted to dish every bit of dirt on her dead hubby that she knew about. Like the fact that, although he denied having anything to do with Christopoulos's murder, he'd admitted to her that he'd got the two Albanians to rub out PC Dimitris.'

'Because he thought Dimitris was gonna blab to you about the blackmail.'

'Mrs B also confirmed what we'd suspected. He'd decided that the taverna would be a prime site for a hotel, and his plan was not only to get us closed down but make a nice bit of cash on the side. Of course, that part of the blackmail didn't work out when it was his own money we borrowed, but then along came Tassos and coughed up another fifty grand, so Barkas was well chuffed.'

This time, the ash from Ingleby's cigarette missed the cereal bowl completely and ended up on the top of the breakfast bar. 'Not that I really give a shit, but I'm curious why PC Dimwit got involved in all this.'

'Well, according to Pericles,' said Sandra, 'he was seriously pissed off about being passed over for promotion so often, and when Barkas asked for his help, he jumped at the chance of earning a nice little payout for very little work. Barkas didn't particularly need him, but if anything had gone wrong, he was going to make him the fall guy. I suppose he also saw the advantage of having a cop on the inside so he could keep a step ahead of any investigation. Oh, and Constable Dimitris also hated Trevor and me – and you too, come to that.'

'Good to know our efforts to wind the prick up hadn't gone unrewarded. So what now?'

It was a good question, thought Trevor. Now that the mystery of the blackmail had been solved and the perpetrator was dead, the only outstanding issue – apart from getting the taverna up and running again – was finding out who killed Yannis Christopoulos.

'Tassos Christopoulos is paying us to find out who murdered his brother,' he said, 'but it seems pretty clear that Barkas had nothing to do with it, or why else would he admit to having Dimitris killed but deny murdering Christopoulos?'

'Back to square one,' said Sandra.

'Yeah, well, good luck with that then,' said Ingleby and picked up his spoon.

He was about to dip it into the cereal bowl when he spotted the cigarette ash floating on top of the milk and decided against it. Instead, he went back to the newspaper he'd been reading when Trevor and Sandra had made their appearance at the bottom of the stairs and opened it to a random page about halfway through. Trevor saw that it was the *Daily Mirror*, which Ingleby bought fairly regularly from a shop in town that stocked a small selection of English newspapers two or three days after being published. They'd given up telling him that he could get much more up to date news online even though they knew he never went near the internet on the grounds that "I don't want every Tom, Dick and GCH-fucking-Q keeping tabs on everything I do."

'Anything interesting?' Trevor asked casually, despite knowing full well that picking up the newspaper was Ingleby's version of hanging a "Do Not Disturb" sign on his nose.

'I thought you had a murder to solve,' Ingleby said and turned a page.

Trevor wandered over to the sliding glass patio doors and looked out just as Milly was clambering out of the swimming pool. He turned back to Ingleby. 'Er, do you mind if we leave Milly here for now? It's only that she's been in the pool and I don't want her dripping all over the inside of the van.'

'No problem,' said Ingleby, turning another page. 'It'd be good to have some intelligent company for a change.'

Trevor and Sandra left the villa by the front door and climbed into the van.

'So where do we go from square one?' said Sandra.

'What about that guy who got done for fraud?' said Trevor. 'The one that threatened Tassos when he was convicted and might have had Yannis killed by mistake. Stefanos something-or-other.'

'Karabellas.'

'That's the one, yeah. Worth looking into, don't you think?'

Sandra briefly chewed at her bottom lip before answering. 'I'm still not sure I buy that whole mistaken identity theory. There's the murder weapon for a start. The souvlaki skewer. Very possibly a fairly limp attempt to implicate us, so what would some fat cat fraudster with zero connection to us or the taverna have to gain from putting us in the frame?'

Trevor very much doubted that killing Yannis with a souvlaki skewer was intended to point the finger at him and Sandra for the murder and was about to say so when the image of Ingleby's newspaper flashed into his mind. There was something about it that brought back a fuzzy memory of another newspaper that he'd seen somewhere else. He couldn't remember where exactly or why it suddenly seemed to be significant, but his brain was nagging at him that it might well be an important clue in figuring out the identity of Yannis Christopoulos's killer.

47

Trevor and Sandra hadn't been back to the taverna since the night of the fire, but they could avoid it no longer as they had an appointment to meet up with a structural engineer who would make an initial assessment of the damage. Ingleby had been asking around and had got a couple of recommendations for this particular guy, and he'd been especially swayed by the knowledge that he wasn't a ripoff merchant.

While they were waiting for the engineer, they stood in silence in front of the building, gazing up at the blackened walls of the upper floor for a good minute or so until Sandra said, 'Can't see from here, but hopefully the roof's OK.'

'Should be,' said Trevor in a kind of dazed monotone. 'Flat concrete, so the fire probably didn't affect it.'

'*Kalıméra.*'

They both turned at the sound of the cheery greeting to see a man who was taller than most Greeks and had grey, thinning hair combed backwards from the forehead. He wore rimless glasses and carried a clipboard in one hand and what appeared to be a small plastic toolbox in the other.

'*Kalıméra*,' said Sandra. 'You must be *kýrıos* Nikolaidis, the structural engineer?'

'Correct,' he said, 'but please call me Elias.'

Introductions and handshakes completed, the engineer expressed his sympathy for what had happened, which Trevor found rather incongruous since it was precisely this sort of thing that kept him in business. Even so, he seemed pleasant enough, and he and Sandra watched as he took a screwdriver from his toolbox and removed the plywood sheet that had been used to cover the front door.

Most of the water from the fire hoses had now seeped away, but there was an all pervading smell of charred wood and damp. The engineer wrote some notes on his clipboard and then led the way into the kitchen where the stench was far worse, and everything that hadn't been completely or partially destroyed by the fire was coated in a thick layer of black grime.

'I understand that this is where the fire started,' said Elias.

'So we've been told,' said Sandra.

The engineer began scribbling on his clipboard once again, so Trevor and Sandra left him to it and stepped out of the kitchen to breathe some considerably less acrid air.

'It's gonna cost an absolute fortune to put this lot right,' said Trevor, 'and God knows what it's like upstairs.'

Sandra shrugged. 'And it's all having to come out of Marcus's own pocket. I only hope he can afford it and doesn't decide to cut his losses and close the place down after all, which would be bloody ironic after everything that's happened.'

'Plus we'd be out of a job.'

'Not at all. We'd be OK. We could always go back to the UK and get the detective agency up and running again, but this taverna is Marcus's pride and joy, and he wouldn't want to give Barkas the satisfaction.'

'From beyond the grave?'

'I guess it's more a case of Barkas having beaten him, and you know how much Marcus doesn't like to be beaten.'

Trevor was about to agree and add something about the old bugger being stubborn as a mule when Elias came out of the kitchen and pointed to what little remained of the staircase that led to the upstairs apartment.

'Sorry,' he said, 'but there's no way I can get up there without breaking my neck. I'll have to come back later with a ladder.'

'Fair enough,' said Sandra. 'Do you need us to be here as well?'

'No, don't worry. I can manage on my own, and I'll let you have my report when I've finished.'

Trevor and Sandra thanked him and he left with a cheery wave of his clipboard.

The moment he'd disappeared from view, Sandra's phone rang. It was Tassos Christopoulos.

Not surprisingly, he wanted to know if they'd made any progress in finding out who killed his brother, so Sandra gave him some guff about how they were following up on a couple of promising leads but that it was too early to make any definite conclusions just yet. They continued the conversation for a few more minutes, and when she came off the phone, Trevor asked her what the rest of it was about.

'He'd heard about Mrs Barkas murdering her hubby and that he was the blackmailer,' she said, 'and he was asking if there was any chance of seeing his fifty grand again.'

'Yeah, I heard you say we were looking into it. One more lie doesn't hurt, I suppose, but I guess we really ought to have a word with Pericles about that.'

'We can try, but I've no idea how these things work. It's also occurred to me that our fee for finding Yannis's killer was supposed to be coming out of that.'

'Not that we've done much to earn it yet. Is he in town at the moment?'

Sandra shook her head. 'Athens. But he said he'd be coming down tomorrow or the next day and wants to meet up.'

'Oh shit.'

'Exactly.'

'And he'll no doubt want to hear all about these great leads we've been following.'

'Uh-huh.'

While they'd been talking, they'd made their way back to the van, and they drove back to Ingleby's villa in silence, both of them wrapped up in their own thoughts as to what the hell to do next about the Yannis Christopoulos murder. In Trevor's case, he was still obsessing about Ingleby's newspaper and growing increasingly frustrated that he couldn't put his finger on why it seemed to be quite so important. It was only as they parked up at the villa and he switched off the engine that inspiration struck – a light bulb moment that was hardly bright but certainly flickered.

'Tassos is in Athens, yeah?' he said.

'I told you already,' said Sandra.

'And if I remember rightly, that's where he was when Yannis was murdered.'

'I think so, but I don't see why that's—'

'Right then,' Trevor interrupted and slapped both palms down onto the steering wheel before turning to Sandra with a broad grin. 'We have a little job to do tonight, so make sure you bring your lock-picking doodahs.'

48

Trevor and Sandra kept their heads down as they made their way along the well lit alleyway leading to Tassos Christopoulos's office building. The single CCTV camera that covered the alleyway hadn't been working when the police checked it after Yannis's murder, but they weren't taking any chances that it had been fixed in the meantime.

'This breaking and entering lark is becoming a bit of a habit,' said Trevor.

'Yeah, well,' said Sandra. 'This one was your idea, don't forget. And you still haven't told me what the hell we're doing this for.'

'I want to make sure I'm right first.'

Sandra grunted and stooped to examine the lock on the heavy wooden door at the end of the alleyway. Then she fished her lock-picking tools out of her pocket and set to work.

'Easy peasy,' she said as Trevor heard a loud click and the door swung open.

Stepping into the short hallway, they both switched on their pen torches and slowly mounted the stairs. Picking the lock to Tassos's office door took even less time than the one at ground level.

'You're getting good at this,' said Trevor.

'I've had a lot of practice lately.'

Trevor understood exactly why Sandra was being tetchy. Being dragged out at two in the morning so that most, if not all, of the nearby bars and restaurants would have shut up shop for the night to break into a client's office without knowing why was bound to annoy the hell out of her. Sandra was one of those people who hated doing anything unless there was a perfectly good reason, but more than that, Trevor keeping her in the dark was guaranteed to send her blood pressure soaring. But it was true what he'd told her. He hadn't wanted to get her hopes up in advance, particularly as he was highly doubtful that his theory would bear any fruit. It was certainly a long shot, and his biggest fear was that Tassos's office had been cleaned since their last visit.

Apparently it hadn't, as Trevor soon realised when he shone his torch at the wastebin next to the desk at the far end of the office. Maybe the regular cleaner had refused to set foot in here again after she'd discovered Christopoulos's body and the accompanying gore, or perhaps the office *had* been cleaned, but nobody had bothered to empty the wastebin. Whatever the reason, its contents were still there, so at least Trevor's theory could now be put to the test.

He almost ran across the office floor and dropped to his knees in front of the wastebin as if he was about to offer up a prayer to this unlikely shrine. Clamping his pen torch between his teeth, he took out the first of two folded newspapers and opened it up to the front page.

'Nope,' he said to himself, then repeated the action with the second newspaper.

'D'you want to tell me now quite why we've broken into this guy's office just so you can rummage through his wastebin?'

Trevor turned towards where Sandra was standing near the middle of the floor, aware that a huge grin had already spread across his face.

'This,' he said, brandishing the newspaper at her.

'It's a newspaper. So?'

'Come here and take a look.'

276

Sandra hesitated for a moment before ambling over to where he was still kneeling beside the bin, her frown the exact opposite of Trevor's triumphantly beaming grin. He focused his torch on the paper's header, and she bent at the waist to look over his shoulder.

'OK,' she said. 'It's a Greek newspaper. And I ask again, so what?'

'Check out the date, though.'

Sandra stooped lower and took her time reading the words aloud: '*Tetárti*... seventh... *Avgoústou*.'

'Wednesday the seventh of August,' Trevor translated, unable to contain his excitement.

'Yes, thanks, Trev. My Greek may not be that great, but I can understand *that*.'

'Wednesday the seventh of August,' Trevor repeated. 'Yannis Christopoulos was murdered that same night or in the early hours of Thursday morning.'

Sandra straightened and exhaled a long deep breath. 'No, you've lost me, I'm afraid.'

'Tassos Christopoulos said he was in Athens when his brother was murdered.'

Trevor studied her face as the frown began to lift, millimetre by millimetre.

'Yeah, I see what you're getting at,' she said at last, 'but I'm not sure quite what that proves.'

Trevor launched himself upright. 'It proves that he *lied*, Sand. That's what it *proves*.'

'It might not be his paper of course.'

'Whose else is it gonna be? He doesn't share the office with anyone, and it's hardly likely that Yannis would have taken a newspaper with him when he was going to rob the place.'

'The cleaner?'

'She only comes in twice a week. Tuesdays and Thursdays, and it was the Thursday morning that she discovered the body.'

'Maybe Tassos brought it with him when he came down from Athens the day *after* the murder.'

'It's a possibility, but I don't really see a hotshot lawyer like Tassos carting around a day old newspaper.'

'So, if he *did* lie about being here on the Wednesday, what are you suggesting? That he killed his own brother?'

'It's happened before,' said Trevor, scouring his memory for a specific example, but the best he could manage was: 'Cain and Abel, for instance.'

'But why would he hire us to investigate the murder if it was him that did it?'

'I know. It doesn't make any sense, but don't you think it's a bit odd that he doesn't seem too bothered that he might still be in danger himself, given that he believes the killer might have got the wrong man and he was the real target?'

'Yeah, I've wondered about that. It certainly doesn't look like he's been taking much in the way of precautions, but a cavalier attitude to his own safety and a newspaper in a bin don't exactly add up to hard evidence. That's what Pericles would say.'

'But what if we could get more real proof that he lied about being here on the day of Yannis's murder? Surely he'd have to take us seriously then.'

'And how do we do that?'

'I dunno. In the movies, the cops usually check out a suspect's bank account and whatnot to see if they've used their credit card in a certain place to track their movements. That kind of thing.'

'The cops do.'

'Yeah.'

'And you think Pericles is likely to play ball based on what little evidence we've got? For a start, I'm pretty sure they'd need a warrant for snooping into somebody's personal finances. And here's another thing. How do we tell him about the newspaper without admitting to breaking in to Tassos's office?'

'Oh, I'm sure you'll think of something,' said Trevor and kissed her lightly on the cheek.

49

Pericles's office was becoming like a second home for Trevor and Sandra – or a third since they'd had to move out of their own apartment and into the relative luxury of Ingleby's villa – and not for the first time, Pericles looked none too pleased to see them. Given the number of times he'd had to repeat himself, he might as well have had a leaflet printed up about how busy he was and how under-resourced. His expression soured even further when they told him of their suspicions about Tassos Christopoulos.

'Please don't tell me you broke into *kýrios* Christopoulos's office,' he said, placing a hand to his face and peering at them through his fingers.

Trevor decided to treat this as an instruction rather than a request for confirmation that they hadn't acted illegally so simply said, 'OK,' and then quickly added, 'But don't you see that it proves Tassos was here on the day of the murder? That he was lying?'

'It proves nothing at all.'

'Well, you could always just ask him about it.'

Pericles sat back in his chair and stared up at the ceiling. 'Yes, of course. "Hello, Mr Hotshot Lawyer. It appears that a newspaper which was found in your office wastebin – very likely by illicit means – would seem to indicate that you lied about your whereabouts on the day of your brother's murder. Oh yes, and that you probably murdered him as well".'

'I didn't know you did sarcasm quite so well,' said

Sandra.

Pericles brought his gaze back to eye level. 'That was *not* sarcasm. I am merely trying to get you to understand that... What is the expression? I wouldn't have a foot to stand on.'

Sandra then broached the subject of looking into Tassos's bank statements to at least try and get better proof that he was lying. This raised a sardonic chuckle from Pericles, who wasn't normally given to displays of amusement of any description, and he wearily explained about the strict criteria for obtaining a warrant and how this might be perfectly simple in a Hollywood movie, but this was by no means the case in real life.

'So the answer's "no" then,' said Trevor.

Pericles's only response was to sigh heavily, pick up his pen and return his attention to the paperwork he'd been engrossed in when they'd first entered his office.

Sandra gave Trevor a "told you so" look and headed for the door. Disappointed that Sandra hadn't come up with something that might persuade Pericles to be more cooperative, Trevor was about to follow when he remembered a question they'd forgotten to ask.

'Any luck finding the Albanians?'

'Yes and no,' Pericles mumbled.

'Sorry?'

Another heavy sigh as Pericles dropped his pen and looked up from his paperwork. 'They were in the hospital.'

'Oh? How come?'

'They had been very severely beaten.'

'Yeah?'

'Apparently by a man who was possibly English but spoke with a very strange accent. That is all they would say.'

'So did you ask them about working for Barkas, killing Dimitris and all that stuff?'

'I didn't get the chance. By the time I arrived at the hospital – after my officers had told me where they were – they had discharged themselves and haven't been seen since. I would imagine that they have returned to their own country to avoid prosecution.'

'Shit.'

'As you say. Shit.'

'Can't you get them back? I mean, doesn't Greece have a whatchermacallit... extradition treaty with Albania?'

For the second time in a matter of minutes, Pericles laughed but did not bother to reply. Instead, he lowered his head and returned to his paperwork, muttering something to himself in Greek.

* * *

Trevor and Sandra took the short walk to the square in the centre of the town and found a table outside one of the many bars and restaurants that surrounded it. It wasn't the bar that they would normally have chosen whenever they ventured into town – mainly because it was one of the most expensive – but this being mid morning at the height of the tourist season, everywhere else was heaving.

Trevor ordered an iced coffee and Sandra an ouzo.

'Bit early, isn't it?' said Trevor when the waiter returned with the drinks and Sandra added several ice cubes to her ouzo, bringing the level up almost to the top of the glass.

'As Ingleby would say, the sun must be over the yardarm somewhere in the world,' she said and swirled the ice around in the tumbler, watching the transparent liquid turn cloudy.

'Please don't tell me you're celebrating because you were right about Pericles turning us down.'

Sandra almost choked on the first sip of her ouzo. 'Celebrating? God, Trev, do you really think I'm that petty?'

'No, but—'

'Rather more important than me being right is the fact that, once again, we've hit a brick wall in finding out who killed Yannis Christopoulos.'

'His brother, you mean.'

'Very possibly, but where the hell's the evidence?'

Trevor had lost count of the number of times they'd asked themselves the same question ever since they'd received the USB stick and the incriminating recording. As on almost every other occasion, however, it was a question that neither of them could answer, so they sat in silence for several minutes, sipping their drinks and lost in their own thoughts.

'What we need is a hacker,' said Sandra, breaking into Trevor's mental gymnastics.

'A what?'

'A hacker. One of those computer nerds who—'

'Yes, I know what a hacker is.'

'Get them to have a look at Tassos's bank records and stuff.'

Trevor immediately saw the logic of what Sandra was suggesting except for one potential flaw. 'Do you know any hackers then?'

'Not exactly.'

'Not exactly?'

'Well, no, I don't, but it shouldn't be that hard to find one.'

Trevor failed to suppress a smirk. 'What, we just put an ad in the paper, do we?'

'Oh, very funny.'

'Jesus, Sand, if it was quite so easy to track these people down, fighting cybercrime wouldn't be much more than a cottage industry.'

Sandra took a mouthful of ouzo and crunched down hard on the ice cube that came with it. 'Don't take the piss.'

'I'm not, I'm not,' Trevor lied. 'All I'm saying is that—'

'Mind if I join youse?'

The accent was unmistakable, as was the ponytail and the deep scar on MacFarland's right cheek.

'Er...' said Trevor, which MacFarland took to be invitation enough, and he flopped down in one of the two vacant wicker chairs at their table.

Trevor's hesitation had nothing to do with trying to decide whether to say "yes" or "no", since "no" was always going to be the wrong answer with someone like MacFarland. It was more that he was taken aback by the man's sudden appearance, and despite his previous assurances that he wasn't going to break their legs or slit their throats, the guy still made him decidedly uneasy.

'Fuckin' hot or what?' said MacFarland, mopping his brow with a remarkably clean white handkerchief. Then he caught the eye of a passing waiter and ordered a beer. 'An' unless it's colder than a December night in Achiltibuie, ye can bring us some ice an' all, yeah?'

'*Polý krýo*,' Sandra translated for the benefit of the utterly bemused waiter.

'So, what's up wi' youse two,' said MacFarland, stuffing his handkerchief back into his trouser pocket. 'Youse look like ye've lost a shillin' an' found sixpence. Although, since we're here, I guess that should be lost a euro and found fifty cents.'

Trevor and Sandra looked at each other, neither knowing quite how to respond.

'Oh, you know,' said Trevor after an embarrassingly long pause. 'Same old, same old.'

'Aye well, that fire at your place was a real pisser. Bound tae put anyone in a mood. So how'd it happen?'

'Arson, probably.'

'Ah, Christ, that's a bastard. Any idea who done it?'

'Cops are pretty sure it was a couple of Albanians working for a guy called Barkas. The same two you had your... disagreement with at the taverna.'

'Oh aye?'

MacFarland lowered his gaze to the glass top of the coffee table between them and lightly drummed the fingers of his right hand. As he did so, Trevor noticed the cuts and grazes on almost every knuckle and had a pretty good idea how he'd come by them but decided to say nothing and change the subject to something that had nothing at all to do with Albanians.

'I don't suppose you know any computer hackers, do you?' he said.

50

In answer to Trevor's question, Jimmy MacFarland's list of contacts didn't include a single computer hacker.

'It's no really ma field,' he'd said and winked as he added, 'I'm more in the gangster and thuggery line o' business.'

Drawing a blank with MacFarland, Sandra had then had a flash of inspiration.

'What about Vangelis?' she'd said. 'Our local Mr Fixit.'

'I think he's probably a bit too old to know much about computers,' Trevor had said, 'let alone how to hack into somebody's bank account.'

'No, not Vangelis himself, but I bet he knows somebody who can.'

Sandra was right. Since the night of the fire, Vangelis had no longer been able to occupy his usual table on the terrace and had temporarily transferred his custom to another taverna further along the quayside.

'*Yeia sas,*' he said as soon as he spotted them approaching and greeted them like along lost brother and sister. '*Kathíste. Kathíste.*'

Trevor and Sandra did as they were bid and joined him at his table, excusing themselves for interrupting his lunch, which appeared to be a large bowl of tuna salad and half a litre of red wine.

'No problem if you don't mind watching me eat,' he said, then leaned forward and almost whispered, 'The *mayionéza* here is shit. They must use the cheap stuff.

Not like at your place.'

Despite his disapproval of the mayonnaise dressing, he shovelled in a large forkful of tuna and shredded lettuce, a good deal of the offending mayonnaise clinging to his enormous grey moustache.

Well into his seventies – although nobody knew quite how far – he wore his matching grey hair long and unkempt, and the deeply etched lines and leathery skin of his face bore testament to his decades spent fishing for whatever he could catch in the bay. As for how a "simple fisherman" had learned to speak such good English, this, like his age, was also unknown, although there was a rumour that he'd been to university in the UK as a young man but had dropped out early on. Now long retired, he still managed to eat out twice a day except on Sundays, and as with his age and command of English, it was also a mystery how he could afford it on what was presumably a tiny pension. Nor did anyone ever bother to ask.

What people – a *lot* of people *–did* ask him for was his help and advice on anything and everything from whether it would rain in three days' time to... well, if he knew anybody that was a computer hacker.

'Yes, of course,' he said nonchalantly as if he'd just been asked if Olympiakos would win the football league next season. 'One of my great-granddaughters is an expert with computers. I'm sure she will be able to help you.'

'That's brilliant,' said Trevor. 'What's her name?'

'Ah, now you're asking,' said Vangelis, wiping his bowl clean with a piece of bread. 'I have so many, it's difficult to remember. Maria, maybe? Kristina?' He shook his head. 'No, that's her mother's name. Don't worry, though. I know where she lives. I was there for her fifteenth birthday last November.'

* * *

The great-granddaughter's name turned out to be Anna, which Vangelis remembered the moment they intercepted her on her way home from fetching groceries for her mother. This was a fortunate chance encounter according to Vangelis as he'd already made it clear to Trevor and Sandra that if they were asking her to get involved in something that was even remotely illegal, it was essential that her mother should know nothing about it at all.

'She's one of those hardline Greek Orthodox types and thinks breaking any of the Ten Commandments should be punishable by lengthy prison sentences,' Vangelis had told them. 'I've also heard her say that the only reason God didn't give Moses a lot more commandments was because the stone tablet wasn't big enough and should have included things like double parking and belching loudly in public.'

He'd also been quick to inform them that Anna's mother was not of his blood and only related by marriage.

Anna, on the other hand, seemed totally unfazed when Sandra asked her if she would be able to hack into somebody's bank account.

'Sure. Why not?' she said. 'It'll be fun.'

Since her mother would have grounded her for life – or more than likely reported her to the police – if she'd known what Anna was up to, it was decided that the girl would come back to Ingleby's villa with them to work her techno magic in peace. So, after she'd nipped back to her house to fetch her laptop and told her mother that she was going out again to see a schoolfriend who was ill in bed, off they all went in Trevor and Sandra's van.

As expected, Ingleby himself was upstairs taking his siesta, which left only Milly to greet them as they went in via the sliding glass door at the back of the villa. Instantly recognising that there were two new people entering her domain, her greeting was even more manically enthusiastic than normal, and she repeatedly ignored Trevor's command to "Get down!" when she had her front paws planted on Anna's chest and was straining to reach a lickable part of her face.

'It's OK. I love dogs,' said Anna. 'Mama won't let us have any kind of pets at home.'

While the mutual love fest was going on, Sandra set up Anna's laptop on the large oval dining table between the living room and the kitchen area.

'All ready,' she said, and after Trevor managed to extricate Anna from Milly's overly exuberant attentions, the girl sat herself down and began feverishly tapping at the keyboard.

'And all you have is the man's name?' she said.

'I'm afraid so, yes,' said Sandra.

'Not even the bank he uses?'

'No, but I think he said once that it's one of those on the town square.'

Anna sniffed. 'Well, that narrows it down to four, I suppose.'

'Sorry. It's the best we can do, I'm afraid.'

'No problem. It might take me a bit longer, that's all.'

'Of course.'

'Can we get you anything? A drink or something?'

'No, I'm fine, thanks, but what I *would* like is for you all to go somewhere else and leave me to work in peace.'

'Sure,' said Trevor, and with a last glance at the blur of Anna's fingers on the keyboard and the gobbledygook appearing on the computer screen, he went out onto the patio with Sandra and Vangelis following close behind.

Within minutes of stretching out on one of the sun loungers by the pool, Vangelis was fast asleep and snoring like a hippopotamus with adenoid issues. Trevor and Sandra lay in silence on a couple of the other loungers, watching Milly perform her usual totally unsynchronised swimming routine.

Also as usual lately, Trevor's brain was fighting a losing battle to make sense of everything that had happened over the last few days and what was likely to happen in the near future if Anna managed to come up with the goods. It was at about this point that his brain decided it was far too exhausted to cooperate any further and shut down completely.

He'd no idea how long he'd been asleep when he was woken by a girl's voice saying, 'Well, I hope you've all had a nice rest while I've been working my boots off.'

'Socks,' said Trevor with a yawn and pushed himself up to a sitting position, squinting up at Anna with one eye still closed.

'What?'

'Working my *socks* off is the usual expression, I think.'

Anna shrugged. 'If you say so, but I thought you'd be more interested in knowing if I found what you're looking for instead of giving me English lessons.'

'Don't mind him,' said Sandra, raising her voice to be heard over the still snoring Vangelis. 'So did you have any luck?'

Another shrug from the teenager. 'Luck's got nothing to do with it. It's all about this and these,' she said, pointing to her head and then waggling her fingers in front of her.

'So does that mean...?'

Sandra left the question unfinished as Anna was already striding back towards the patio door with a 'You'd better come and see for yourselves' flung over her shoulder.

51

Predictably enough, Pericles's first words when Trevor and Sandra showed him the relevant printout of Tassos Christopoulos's credit card statement were: 'Where the hell did you get this?'

Sandra had said something about not being able to reveal their sources, which did nothing at all to placate him. If anything, it made him even angrier.

'Are you completely crazy?' he'd shouted, slamming his fist down on the top of his desk. 'You have clearly obtained this... this *information* illegally, which means that it is utterly worthless as a piece of evidence. Worthless! Do you understand?'

Despite his euphoria that they had finally had a positive result in their investigation into Yannis Christopoulos's murder, Trevor had kept his tone as calm as he was able and pointed out that, whilst they perfectly understood the document's lack of value as hard evidence, it did at least prove beyond doubt that Tassos had lied about being out of the area at the time of his brother's murder.

'There it is in black and white – or strictly speaking, black white and yellow,' he'd said, once again drawing Pericles's attention to the highlighted item on the statement. 'A payment of fifty euros at a petrol station in this very town and dated the seventh of August.'

Pericles had unclenched his fist and jabbed his finger randomly at the sheet of paper in his other hand, repeated how worthless it was as a piece of evidence and added that – far from using it as a reason for arresting Tassos Christopoulos – he was considerably more inclined to charge Trevor and Sandra with illegally hacking into the man's private bank account.

And so the battle of wits continued for another half hour or so until, presumably worn down by Trevor and Sandra's dogged persistence, Pericles ultimately capitulated and, with vociferously articulated reluctance, was forced to agree that there were at least reasonable grounds to question Tassos about his whereabouts on the seventh of August. Naturally, he would not be able to confront him about his credit card payment on that day, nor even the newspaper found in his office, which had also been obtained by illegal means, and he was therefore highly doubtful that much good would come out of such an interview.

Not that they'd admitted it to Pericles, but Trevor and Sandra didn't hold out a lot of hope either, although getting him to actually *talk* to the guy was at least a step in the right direction.

'I guess all we can do now is wait and see,' Sandra had said, and they'd headed back to Ingleby's villa to do exactly that.

* * *

'He's a bloody top notch lawyer, this Tassos Christopoulos, isn't he?' said Ingleby. 'So he's hardly the type that's gonna be quakin' in his boots and cough the lot, is he? "Oh yes, officer, you got me bang to rights on this one. It's true I lied about where I was on the whatever of August, so it stands to reason I murdered my brother, dunnit".'

Marcus Ingleby was holding forth in his favourite armchair to his audience of Trevor, Sandra and Eric Emerson while they all sipped – or glugged – their pre-dinner drinks.

'I mean, where's the fuckin' evidence for a start?' Ingleby went on. 'You've already said that Sergeant – oh, excuse me – *Lieutenant* Periwinkle can't tell him anything about the newspaper or the credit card stuff, so what's he gonna do? Rely on the bloke's honesty and sense of fair play? He's a bloody lawyer, for fuck's sake.'

'Yes, we know all that, Marcus, but—'

'Different in our day, weren't it, Eric,' said Ingleby, cutting short Trevor's remark and jabbing a heavily nicotine-stained finger at his old partner in crime, who was sitting on one end of the L-shaped settee.

Oh blimey, here we go, thought Trevor. More bullshit about the good old days of armed robbery.

Eric nodded his unequivocal agreement. 'Certainly was, Marcus. Certainly was.'

'Christ almighty. In them days, if the Old Bill got even a sniff that you'd been a bit of a naughty boy, they'd 'ave yer down the nick in a heartbeat and batter the shit out of yer till you owned up to whatever they reckoned you'd done.'

'Yes,' said Eric, 'and more often than not, having to confess to all kinds of stuff you hadn't had the slightest involvement with.'

'Too right,' said Ingleby and drained his glass of whisky. 'Yer average crim nowadays don't know they're born, what with all the recording and videoing and all that malarkey. The filth can't lay so much as a finger on 'em without bein' busted themselves.'

Trevor failed to understand why Ingleby should be quite so wistfully nostalgic about police brutality and decided against pointing out that such incidents were by no means unheard of even now and often dependent on the colour of the victim's skin. Instead, he got up and wandered over to the kitchen area at the far end of the open-plan room to dish up the evening meal he'd been cooking – or, more accurately, microwaving.

Sandra soon joined him. 'Shit, now they've started reminiscing about all the jobs they pulled together – in excruciating detail.'

'Yeah, well, I knew that'd be coming next,' said Trevor, grabbing an oven glove and opening the door of the microwave.

'Tell you what. If they keep at it, maybe after we've eaten this we should have a swim in the pool and then get an early night.'

'Good plan. I'm knackered as hell anyway, so a decent bit of kip wouldn't go amiss.'

Trevor could feel Sandra's breath on the side of his face as she leaned towards him and whispered, 'That wasn't necessarily what I had in mind.'

'Oh right,' said Trevor, forgetting that the oven glove was on his left hand and taking hold of the red hot dish in the microwave with his right. 'Aaagh! Piss and bollocks.'

'That's one of the many things I love about you, Trev, you smooth talker, you.'

52

With the taverna still not open for business, Trevor and Sandra had little else to do but wait to hear if Pericles had interviewed Tassos Christopoulos yet, and if so, what the result had been. They'd therefore spent most of the following day lounging by the pool and occasionally lapsing into a doze or nipping into the villa to fetch another drink. Not that they were expecting Pericles to get in touch with them directly, but this didn't stop Trevor checking his phone every few minutes.

'Do you think we should call him?' he said after drawing yet another blank. 'I mean, it's been nearly twenty-four hours now.'

'No, he'd only get pissy,' said Sandra. 'And in any case, we don't even know if Tassos is back from Athens yet.'

'He told you it was gonna be either yesterday or today.'

'I don't know, Trev. Maybe he won't be back till tonight or he changed his mind altogether.'

'I guess so, but all this hanging around waiting is doing my head in. I just can't seem to settle to anything.'

'Oh yeah? Like what exactly? A spot of housework or writing your memoirs perhaps? There *is* nothing to do, so why don't you make the most of it and take it easy while we still can. Besides, I dunno what you're getting so worked up about. It's not as if we're expecting what would be a bloody miracle.'

Trevor knew she was right, of course, but her logic

did nothing to calm his jangling nerves, and for want of anything better to do, decided to get himself another iced coffee from the kitchen.

'You want one?' he said as he levered himself to his feet and picked up his empty glass.

'No thanks. Any more caffeine and I'll be seeing double.'

A blast of cool air hit him as Trevor opened the sliding patio door and stepped inside. Ingleby insisted on having the aircon turned up full blast all day and every day during the summer, arguing on several occasions that someone of his advanced years needed their creature comforts, so "Bugger the expense, and bugger global warming."

Trevor turned on the cold tap at the kitchen sink and was rinsing the foamy residue from his glass when his phone vibrated in the back pocket of his shorts. In his haste to answer it, the glass fell from his hand into the stainless steel sink and lost a sizeable chunk of its rim, but his heart-pumping excitement evaporated instantly as soon as he saw who the caller was.

Minutes later, however, he was racing out onto the patio, almost tripping over the sill of the sliding door in the process, and yelling, 'Guess what! Guess what!'

By the time he reached the edge of the swimming pool and was standing over Sandra's sun lounger, she was rousing herself from a light sleep and blearily opened her eyes.

'What's all the shouting about?'

'That was Vangelis,' said Trevor, hopping from one foot to the other like he was desperate for a pee.

'What was Vangelis?'

'On the phone. Just now.'

Sandra raised her upper body onto her elbow. 'And?'

'And they've only gone and charged Tassos with murder, haven't they? He heard it on the local radio a few minutes ago.'

'Bloody hell,' said Sandra, sitting up fully now on the edge of the lounger with her feet on the floor.

'Quite,' said Trevor and then took several deep breaths before he was able to speak coherently and summarise what Vangelis had told him, ending with: 'Oh yes, and he said something about Anna deserving a hefty bonus.'

'Too right,' said Sandra and added, 'OK, *now* I reckon we can give Pericles a call.'

* * *

Pericles was looking a lot more cheerful than he'd been for the previous several days, which may well have been the main reason he'd agreed to tell Trevor and Sandra the gist of his interview with Tassos Christopoulos earlier that day.

He sat back in his chair, his palms spread wide on his desktop. 'This is, of course, highly irregular, but since you have been of *some* assistance in solving this case – even though by questionable means – I am willing to... bend the rules a little on this occasion.' Then he leaned forward and eyeballed them each in turn. 'However, you are to tell no-one a single word of what I'm about to say. Is that perfectly clear?'

Trevor and Sandra said that it was, and Trevor decided against challenging him over the "*some* assistance" part of his statement as it was almost *entirely* because of them that Tassos was now in custody. This was not the time to antagonise the guy, so he bit his tongue and listened intently as Pericles began his fairly detailed account of his meeting with the man who was a liar at the very least and very probably a murderer too.

Tassos had been surprised that the lieutenant wanted to speak to him and asked if it was about some progress that had been made in the investigation. Pericles had responded by telling him that they were following a potentially useful new lead, at which point Tassos said that he'd be happy to come to the police station straight away as he had returned from Athens early that morning.

'He was smiling like he hadn't a care in the world when he walked through the door,' said Pericles, 'but the smile began to slip when I asked him to remind me where he was on the day of his brother's murder, and it disappeared altogether when I asked him if he could *prove* that he was in Athens that day. Any witnesses, for instance.

'This made him very angry, and he started shouting at me and banging on the desk. How dare I not accept his word? Was I accusing him of lying? All that kind of thing. So when I told him that a witness had seen him in the town on the day of the murder—'

'There was a *witness*?' Trevor interrupted, amazed that this had not been mentioned before.

Pericles dropped his gaze to the desktop and mumbled something about not being able to mention the real evidence and police interview techniques.

Trevor couldn't remember having ever seen him look quite so embarrassed but wasn't at all surprised, given that it was probably an extremely rare occurrence that Lieutenant "By the Book" Pericles would play fast and loose with the truth.

'Anyway,' Pericles continued, 'Tassos immediately stopped his shouting and went very quiet for several seconds. Then he wanted to know who the witness was, but I told him that this was confidential information. He was silent again for several more seconds and finally admitted that he'd lied about where he'd been. He claimed that the only reason for this was that he'd been having an affair with a married woman from one of the nearby villages and didn't want her to become involved in a scandal.'

'And you believed him?' said Sandra.

'Certainly not. It was a very thin excuse, and when I asked him to name the woman in question so she might be able to give him an alibi, he refused and began shouting and cursing again. He jumped to his feet, knocking his chair flying and yelling that he would report me to my superiors and have me kicked off the force or demoted to constable at the very least.'

'On what grounds?'

Pericles shrugged. 'He didn't say, but as you know, he's a top lawyer and is probably very good at twisting the evidence when it suits him.'

'And would be well aware that attack is often the best form of defence.'

'Exactly.'

'So then what happened?' said Trevor, eager to get to the part when Pericles nailed him for the murder.

'Well, I had to shout even louder than him to be heard, but I reminded him that this was a very serious matter and that lying about his whereabouts was highly suspicious. There was a brief pause while he seemed to be considering what I'd just said, and then the yelling began once again – but at an even greater volume than before:

'"How dare you! Are you seriously telling me that you think I killed my own brother? My own *brother*, for Christ's sake. What possible reason could I have? And why the hell would I hire those two Brits to find out who the murderer was if I'd done it myself? No. Whoever murdered Yannis was obviously a complete maniac. You think that's what I am, do you? The kind of crazed bastard who would not only strangle somebody but then stab them God knows how many times with a fucking souvlaki skewer?'

Pericles resumed his original position, sitting back in

his chair with his palms spread wide on the desktop, but this time with an enormous grin lighting up his face. 'And that's when I knew.'

'Knew?' said Trevor. 'Knew what?'

'That I had him, of course.'

Trevor and Sandra exchanged puzzled glances.

'Sorry, but I think you might have to be a bit more specific,' said Sandra.

Pericles sighed contentedly, apparently relishing what he was about to tell them. 'The thing is that in every serious case – and especially homicide – the police often withhold a certain amount of information from the public and even from the victim's nearest and dearest. After all, it's not at all uncommon for murders to be committed by the person's husband or wife or some other close family member. Or in this case, their brother.'

Met with Trevor and Sandra's blank expressions in response, Pericles went on with his explanation. 'According to the pathologist's report, the cause of Yannis Christopoulos's death was the multiple stab wounds to his chest and throat with a metal souvlaki skewer.'

'Yes, we know that,' said Trevor, failing to contain his impatience.

'Precisely my point,' said Pericles, 'because what no-one else knew apart from the police and the pathologist was that the killer had also attempted to *strangle* the victim, almost certainly before resorting to the souvlaki skewer.'

'Bloody hell,' said Trevor.

'Shit,' said Sandra.

'And this is why I have charged Tassos Christopoulos with Yannis's murder, and he is currently behind the bars of our modest cell here at the station, awaiting transfer to more suitable accommodation to be kept on remand until our enquiries have been completed. It is most unlikely that he will be granted bail as we have already made further progress in gathering evidence against him.'

'Oh?' said Trevor.

'Yes indeed. As soon as I had read Tassos his rights, I immediately obtained a warrant to search his house and office. I don't know what I was expecting to find, and I was astonished to hear that my officers had discovered a bundle of heavily bloodstained clothes hidden away in his garage. They have already been sent for analysis, but if, as I suspect, the blood is his brother's, we will be a long way towards securing a conviction.'

'Bit strange that, isn't it?' said Sandra. 'I would have expected that a guy who's obviously as smart as Tassos would have done a much better job of getting rid of any incriminating evidence long before now.'

'Yes, that surprised me too, but who knows? Maybe he is so arrogant that he never believed for a moment that he would become a suspect. Leaving the murder weapon behind also strikes me as foolishly careless. We're still waiting for the results of the DNA test on the souvlaki skewer that we requested straight after the murder, and there's a slight chance that traces might be found that would definitely help to prove his guilt.'

'He's not confessed yet, I suppose?' said Trevor.

Pericles shook his head. 'And not likely to either, I wouldn't think. A lawyer like him will almost certainly fight this thing to the very end, so we will have to make sure we do everything possible to get a conviction. And speaking of which, I have much work to do, so if you'll excuse me...'

He let the sentence hang, but it was clear that the conversation was over, so Trevor and Sandra got to their feet and thanked him for his time and for filling them in on all the details.

'Don't forget what I told you, though,' Pericles said

as they headed for the office door. 'All of this is strictly confidential, so if you breathe so much of a word of it, I shall have to seriously consider charging you both with the several offences that I know you've committed.'

Trevor and Sandra nodded sheepishly, then closed the door behind them and made their way across the reception area to the exit. Before they got there, however, they heard a man's voice calling out their names. They turned towards an open door at the far end of the reception area, and just beyond it a cell with floor-to-ceiling iron bars, not unlike the cell of a sheriff's office in almost every Western movie Trevor had ever seen.

'This is all because of you!' the man shouted, and although it was difficult to see clearly, the voice was unmistakably that of Tassos Christopoulos. 'But they will never convict me of this crime, and when I am acquitted, I shall come looking for you.'

It was a moment that was almost exactly the same as a year ago when Donna Vincent had yelled at them from the very same cell, threatening all kinds of revenge.

'You might have to join the queue,' Trevor shouted back, then he and Sandra stepped out into the warm evening air and straight to the nearest bar.

53

Even through the fog of a mild hangover, Trevor realised that this was the first time in almost a fortnight that he'd woken up without the all too familiar feeling of dread gnawing at his insides. Alexandros Barkas was dead, his Albanian thugs had apparently fled the country, and Tassos Christopoulos was safely behind bars and in no position to carry out his threats of revenge. Quite how he knew that it was him and Sandra that were mainly responsible for bringing him to justice was a total mystery. Pericles would never have told him about the newspaper they'd found in his office or how they'd hacked into his bank account, so maybe he'd happened to mention it to one of his officers and they'd blabbed to Tassos. Who knew? And right now, who cared?

He propped himself up on his pillow. Beside him, Sandra's eyes were still closed, but the faint smile on her lips indicated that she too was experiencing the same sense of relief, even in her sleep.

Trevor reached out for his watch on the bedside table. Almost midday. Hardly surprising since they'd been celebrating their new-found freedom from the horrors of the past two weeks well into the early hours. Unable to drive – and scarcely able to walk in a straight line – they'd taken a cab from town back to Ingleby's villa and found him still up and keen to keep the party going. Trevor had no idea how many "last little nightcaps" they'd knocked back, but his throbbing head told him it must have been quite a few.

Easing himself from underneath the thin cotton sheet so as not to wake Sandra, he padded across the floor to the en suite bathroom in search of paracetamol. He'd taken no more than three paces, however, when a bleary voice from behind him stopped him in his tracks.

'What time is it?'

'Late.'

'How late?'

'Nearly twelve.'

'I'm guessing that's midday and not midnight,' said Sandra, her forearm across her eyes to shield them from the intense sunlight that managed to seep its way through the slats in the Venetian blinds of both windows.

Trevor retraced his steps and perched himself on the edge of the bed. 'How are you feeling?'

'A bit shit, to be honest.'

'Me too. But, hey, look on the bright side. We're finally in the clear. No more blackmail. No more being kidnapped. No more death threats to worry about.'

'And no more brain cells after last night.'

'Jesus, Sand, you looked happier when you were asleep.'

Sandra lowered her forearm and sat up abruptly, wincing from the sudden movement. 'It's OK. I'm fine really. Just taking me a while to come round and get my head straight. I'll be all right after a shower and something to— Actually, though, I think I'll skip the solids for now.'

'Might do us good to go for a bit of a walk on the beach. Blow some of the cobwebs away. Maybe check out the taverna while we're there and see if they've started work on it yet.'

The suggestion was met with a low groan, and Sandra slid back down to the horizontal position. Trevor leaned across to kiss her, but she gently fended him off with the palm of her hand.

'Take my advice, Trev. You might want to hang on with that till I've at least cleaned my teeth.'

An hour later, they descended the marble staircase to find Marcus Ingleby in his usual armchair, a glass of whisky in his hand and Milly dozing peacefully at his feet.

'Good afternoon,' he said, ostentatiously looking up at the clock on the wall to reinforce the sarcasm in his tone.

Trevor was in too good a mood to even consider rising to the bait.

'We were thinking of taking Milly for a run on the beach,' he said. 'Check out if anything's happening at the taverna while we're at it.'

'Not a lot probably, but perhaps I'll join you anyway. I could do with a bit of exercise.'

Trevor couldn't remember Ingleby ever having uttered the word "exercise" before, never mind doing anything at all physical that might be described as such. It was also going to be blazing hot down on the beach, but arguing with the old man was never likely to result in a positive outcome.

* * *

As expected, work had yet to begin on repairing the fire damage at the taverna.

'Somebody's gonna get a rocket up their arses,' said Ingleby, surveying the blackened walls of the upper floor and the boarded-up windows.

'To be fair, they've only had a few days,' said Sandra. 'And we haven't even had the report from the engineer yet.'

Ingleby cleared his throat and spat a gobbet of phlegm onto the ground. Then he muttered something inaudible and limped off across the taverna's terrace, pounding the wooden flooring with his walking stick with every step he took.

Trevor clipped Milly's lead to her collar. 'This is going to be fun.'

'If we keep a few yards behind him, we won't be able to hear him whingeing,' said Sandra. 'Pretend we're on our own.'

'Good plan,' said Trevor, and they waited until Ingleby had disappeared down the steps at the far end of the terrace and onto the quayside.

Maintaining the distance between themselves and Ingleby was no easy task, however, as the old man walked so slowly that they had to stop three times before they reached the end of the promenade to avoid catching up with him. Slackening their own pace to match Ingleby's was a major effort, given Milly's constant lunging on her lead, and almost impossible when they stepped down onto the beach. The softness of the sand sapped at Ingleby's feet and reduced his forward progress to that of an unambitious snail.

Nor could Trevor set Milly free to race around like a mad thing and relieve his arm and shoulder from the unrelenting strain of trying to hold her in check. Although never crowded even at this period of the holiday season, there were far too many people soaking up the sun or playing beach games to make this a safe option. Also, of course, there was the multitude of turtle nests, which she would inevitably disturb.

Still, Trevor reminded himself, they were free at last from their recent spate of nightmarish situations, and although not perfect, all was pretty much right with the world. He took in a deep lungful of the tangy sea air, lightly tinged with the cloying aroma of suntan lotion and began to hum the opening bars of Steppenwolf's *Born to be Wild*.

'Bloody hell,' said Sandra. 'This ought to be called

On the Beach with Mr Grumpy and Mr Happy.'

'Not that long ago it would have been *On the Beach with Mr Grumpy and Mr Seriously Shitting Himself.*'

'Well, all I can say is it's a definite improvement.'

Sandra beamed a smile at him and took his one free hand in hers as they stopped to watch Ingleby clamber crablike over a stretch of rocks that acted as a natural barrier between the sandy beach and a small cove beyond.

Once they'd climbed over the rocks themselves, they saw that Ingleby had sat down with his walking stick planted vertically in the sand and close to the familiar bamboo markers and red and white tape of the only visible turtle nest on the whole stretch of beach. His legs were stretched out in front of him in a V-shape, and he was bending forward to fiddle with his catheter bag. As usual, it was almost full to the brim.

'He's not going to empty that thing, is he?' said Trevor.

'You know, I've hardly ever seen him empty it at all,' said Sandra. 'Why it never seems to overflow or even actually burst is beyond me.'

Apparently satisfied with the state of his catheter bag – and making no attempt to empty it – Ingleby sat back with his palms spread behind him to support himself and stared out to sea. He was about twenty yards from where Trevor and Sandra were standing and roughly midway between them and a second wall of rocks that formed the little cove. In complete contrast to the beach they'd just left, Ingleby was the only occupant, and given the solitary turtle nest, Trevor decided it was safe to let Milly off her lead. The moment she was free, she hurtled off across the sand, and Ingleby had to brace himself against the onslaught of her enthusiastic greeting.

'Better go and join the old bugger, I suppose,' said Trevor. 'Hopefully he'll have calmed down by now.'

By the time they got to him, Milly had raced off into the sea and was cavorting about in the gently rolling waves and barking her delight.

'She's 'avin' a good time then,' said Ingleby without taking his eyes off her.

'Aren't you?' said Sandra.

Ingleby took off his battered straw hat and fanned himself. 'Yeah, I'm all right. Nice glass of cold beer wouldn't go amiss, though.'

'One that's half full, you mean?' said Trevor.

'What?'

'He said you're a bit hopeful,' Sandra cut in and nudged Trevor gently in the ribs.

They sat down either side of Ingleby, all of them silently enjoying Milly's aquatic performance for several minutes until Trevor became aware of another presence on the otherwise deserted beach. He turned through a hundred and eighty degrees and looked up at the dune bank that rose steeply above the beach and formed the fourth side of the cove. It was about twelve feet high, and beyond it a dirt track which ran beside an area of scrub and the occasional pine tree.

Scrambling down the bank was a man who was inappropriately dressed in a long sleeved white shirt and what appeared to be dark suit trousers. When he had made it safely down from the dune, he strode across the sand towards them, his solid, rather squat physique alarmingly familiar, and in his outstretched hand something glinted in the sun. A gun that was pointed directly at them.

54

'Stay where you are!' Tassos Christopoulos shouted when Trevor made a move to stand up, and reinforced the command by aiming the gun at his chest.

Tassos moved round in front of the small group and stood with his back to the sea, wiping the sweat from his brow with the sleeve of his shirt.

'Not the ideal weather for chasing about after you two,' he said, ignoring Ingleby and pointing his semi-automatic at Trevor and Sandra in turn. 'Still, it means that I'll be able to take my revenge much sooner than I would ever have imagined possible.'

'But I thought you were—'

'In a police cell? Indeed I was, Sandra, my dear, and was about to be transferred to prison when I had a stroke of good fortune. You see, your friend the lieutenant decided it was so unlikely that I would try to escape, he sent only one officer to drive me, and it took very little effort to... disable him as soon as we were round the corner from the police station and he stopped for a red light.'

'You shot him?' said Trevor.

'No, of course not. They'd handcuffed my wrists in front of me, so I merely reached over from the back seat and throttled him till he was unconscious. Then it was a simple matter of getting the handcuffs key from his pocket and relieving him of his gun.'

'But why make a run for it?' said Trevor. 'Not to mention assaulting a cop? That's not going to do your

309

case much good, is it? Especially when you were shouting your mouth off about how you were innocent and they'd never convict you.'

Tassos scratched the back of his head with his gun-free hand and scowled. 'Ah yes, that was before the "new evidence" came to light. Somewhat foolishly, I had forgotten to dispose of the clothes I was wearing when brother Yannis met his untimely end, and the police found them when they searched my house. A souvlaki skewer in the neck produces rather a lot of blood, you know.'

'Bit fucking stupid, that,' said Ingleby, speaking for the first time.

'Overconfident, I think I'd prefer, but what's done is done, and if you'll excuse me, I am in a bit of a hurry.' He pulled back the slide on his pistol and released it with a loud click. 'I'm sure the lieutenant can't be far behind, and I have a boat to catch.'

'A boat?' said Trevor, certain that there were no ferries or island hoppers closer than about thirty miles.

'Used to belong to that arsehole Barkas. Quite a beauty she is too. That's where I was heading when I happened to spot you three on the quayside and decided on a quick detour. A second stroke of luck in such a short time, eh? The gods must be smiling on me for a change.'

'You'd better make the most of it then,' said Ingleby, ''cos they sure as hell won't be smiling on you when you end up in chokey for the rest of yer natural.'

Tassos laughed and swung the gun round to aim it at Ingleby's head. 'I've no idea what most of that means, but at least I won't have to listen to you for very much longer, and I certainly don't have time to grant any last requests, unless of course—'

'Oi! You!'

Even before they all turned towards the wall of rocks

separating the cove from the main beach, the voice was instantly recognisable from these two syllables alone.

Jimmy MacFarland was hopping down from the rocks with Coralie hot on his heels.

Tassos watched them as they hurried across the sand but kept his gun trained on Ingleby. When they'd come within half a dozen yards, he swung the muzzle round, and they skidded to a halt.

'I don't know who the hell you are, but I suggest that you leave now while you still have the chance.'

'Aye, well I suggest ye get yer damn feet off o' that wee nest there, ye fuckin' radge, ye.'

MacFarland pointed down to where Tassos was standing right in the centre of the metal grid that was used to protect turtle nests from scavengers and at the dislodged bamboo marker and broken red and white tape.

Tassos fleetingly cast an eye over the damage and snorted with derision. 'I don't know what language you're speaking or if you understand English, and you may be half blind as well, so you may not have noticed that I have a gun here and it's fully loaded.'

'And *you* may not have noticed that I'm from Glesgae, and I'm fully fuckin' annoyed.'

It flitted through Trevor's mind that he could make a lunge for Tassos and the gun while he was distracted but quickly dismissed the impulse almost as soon as it had occurred to him. Even if he succeeded in bundling him over, there was every possibility that he'd still get a shot off and hit either MacFarland or his girlfriend. But at precisely the same moment that Trevor abandoned his misguided act of heroism, Milly had apparently had enough of frolicking in the sea and pelted up the beach to rejoin her human companions. She stopped immediately behind Tassos with a flurry of scattered sand and made her first vigorous attempt to shake herself dry.

Startled by the sudden and unexpected commotion, Tassos instinctively shifted his attention away from MacFarland and fractionally lowered his gun. MacFarland needed no second invitation, and he launched himself through the air, throwing his arms around Tassos's legs above the knees and rugby-tackled him to the ground. As Tassos fell, there was a sharp explosion and a flash of flame erupted from the barrel of his semi-automatic.

With Tassos sprawled on his back, MacFarland wasted no time in picking himself up and squatting heavily on top of him with his legs planted either side of the man's chest. In the same movement, he grabbed hold of Tassos's arm and twisted it almost to the point of breaking. Tassos shrieked in pain, and his fingers released their grip on the gun, but not before a second shot rang out.

Trevor made a headlong dive across the sand and snatched up the weapon while MacFarland repeatedly pummelled his fist into Tassos's face, yelling a single word with every blow: 'Do. Not. Fuck. Wi'. The. Fuckin'. Turtles.'

There was no telling how much longer he would have gone on hammering at the man's already blood-smeared face if Coralie hadn't stepped forward and placed a firm hand on his pumping shoulder.

'That's enough, Jimmy. That's *enough*!' she shouted, and MacFarland struck twice more before sitting back on his haunches, his breath coming in short, deep bursts.

Beneath him, Tassos Christopoulos lay unconscious, his head to one side as the blood dripped steadily onto the soft white sand.

Still stretched out on his belly with the semi-automatic in his hand, Trevor remembered the two gunshots and, hauling himself onto his knees, he turned to Sandra and Ingleby. 'Everyone OK?'

'I'm all right,' said Sandra, 'but I think Marcus has been hit.'

As when they'd first arrived at the cove, Ingleby was sitting upright and bending forward to inspect his catheter bag. Instead of being almost full, however, the bag was now completely empty and flattened against his leg like a deflated balloon with a dark, wet patch on the sand immediately underneath it.

'Fuck's sake,' said Ingleby, 'and I don't even have a spare on me.'

Despite their near death experience of the last few minutes – or perhaps from the sheer relief at their narrow escape – Trevor and Sandra couldn't help but laugh.

Ingleby swore at them. 'Wait till you get to my age. Won't find it so bleedin' funny then, will yer?'

Trevor glanced over to where MacFarland had climbed off Tassos's prone body and was sitting with Coralie's arm around his shoulders, her head pressed gently against the side of his face. With her free hand, she was vainly trying to fend Milly off from her overly enthusiastic licking of MacFarland's bloodied knuckles.

'Thanks, Jimmy,' said Trevor. 'It seems we owe you our lives.'

As soon as the words had left his mouth, he realised quite how absurdly melodramatic they'd sounded. Melodramatic but entirely accurate nevertheless. The irony was not lost on him either. Saved by the very man who they'd been sure was out to kill them when he'd first shown up at the taverna.

'Nae bother,' said MacFarland. 'And in any case, I only did it fir the wee turtles.'

If it hadn't been for the faint smile and the hint of a wink, Trevor might have taken him seriously.

A series of muted groans announced that Tassos was starting to regain consciousness, but were almost drowned out by the strident blaring of rapidly approaching sirens on the dirt track above the beach.

'Sounds like the cavalry have arrived,' said Sandra.

'About bloody time,' said Ingleby, unfastening his ruined catheter bag from his leg and tossing it over his shoulder.

'I hope ye're gonna pick that up,' said MacFarland. 'D'ye have any idea how many turtles die from swallowing plastic.'

'Not a clue.'

'A fuck of a lot. That's how many – give or take.'

TWO WEEKS LATER

The taverna's terrace was packed, and Trevor suspected that at least some of the diners had been tempted by Ingleby's offer of free wine to celebrate the grand re-opening. It was hardly the most generous of gestures as the local wine, bought in bulk, cost little more than bottled water, but as Ingleby had said, 'It's the thought that counts, innit. And anyway, there ain't that many who can resist a freebie when it's offered, can they?'

He wasn't a man who was easily impressed, but he'd been full of praise for the speed and efficiency with which the builders had carried out the extensive repairs to the ground floor and kitchen of the taverna. He'd maybe had to pay over the odds to get the place up and running again in such a short time, but the extra cash hadn't seemed to bother him unduly. On the other hand, getting the upstairs apartment fit for habitation again would have to wait until he'd replenished the coffers from the taverna's takings or possibly some other source which he didn't care to discuss.

Three tables had been pushed together in pride of place at the very edge of the terrace, immediately overlooking the smooth moonlit water of the harbour, and were now almost entirely covered with what remained of the lavish feast of a meal. Naturally enough, Ingleby held court from the head of the table with Eric Emerson on his right and Trevor and Sandra on his left. Also in attendance were Jimmy MacFarland and his girlfriend Coralie, Leonidas the vet and Mr Fixit

Vangelis. Lieutenant Pericles had been invited as well but had sent his apologies, saying he was far too busy to spare the time. It may also have been that he'd preferred to keep a low profile as he was no doubt still smarting from the embarrassment of how Tassos Christopoulos had been able to escape so easily from police custody.

After a visit to the hospital to have his facial injuries patched up, the latest information on Tassos was that he'd been transferred to prison in the back of a secure police van and accompanied by four officers to ensure that there was no repeat of the previous fiasco. It would be several months before his trial came to court, and given his recent escape attempt, it was no surprise that he'd been refused bail, even though he'd hired the most expensive criminal lawyer in Greece to take his case. Since his arrest, the evidence against him had grown in strength and most crucially because the bundle of clothes found in his garage had tested positive for his brother's blood. Even so, and despite the attempted murder of Trevor, Sandra and Ingleby being added to his charge sheet, Tassos had continued to plead his innocence, so his motive for killing Yannis remained a mystery. Trevor and Sandra had speculated that the most likely explanation was an argument over money. Tassos had told them when they'd first met that Yannis was often in debt and had borrowed from his brother on several occasions until Tassos refused to lend him any more.

'Maybe what he told us was *partly* true at least,' Trevor had said. 'Yannis had gone to Tassos's office to steal from his safe like he'd done before but found that the combination had been changed. The bit that Tassos may have left out, though, was that he caught Yannis in the act and they had a massive row which turned into a punch-up. Tassos had him by the throat at one point, but perhaps Yannis had managed to break out of it and started to get the upper hand. Realising he was losing the fight, Tassos grabbed whatever was nearest and the rest we know.'

Sandra had queried why Tassos would have had a metal souvlaki skewer lying around in his office, but they'd agreed this would probably never be known. Besides, *why* it was there was irrelevant. What mattered was that it had been proven to be the murder weapon and that was that.

Something else that had bothered them both was why Tassos had hired them to find his brother's killer when he knew full well that he was the murderer. The only theory they'd come up with that made any sense at all was that he'd tried to play the same trick as Barkas, who'd lent them money to pay off their supposed blackmailer to divert suspicion from himself. What better way to throw the police off the scent than to let it be known he was actively seeking the killer's identity?

'He probably also thought you two were pretty crap at this detective lark so weren't likely to come up with the goods,' Ingleby had added unhelpfully.

Back in the present, Ingleby was now quizzing MacFarland about his life of crime and – with Eric's enthusiastic support – banging on once again about how easy it was compared to what it was like in his day.

'Don't get me wrong,' he was saying, ''cos we're obviously all grateful for you savin' our lives an' that, but I must admit you could've knocked me down with a feather when Lieutenant Periwinkle didn't even charge yer for what you done to that Tassos bloke.'

'Self defence, he reckoned,' said MacFarland.

'Self defence? That's a good'un. Bloke's face looked like it'd been through a fuckin' meat grinder by the time you'd finished with 'im.'

'Aye, well mebbe the lieutenant saw it as a bit o' revenge for mekkin' 'im look a right wee screw-up.'

'You kiddin'? The man's the straightest cop I've ever

317

met in my life, and I've come across quite a few bent ones over the years, I can tell yer.'

'I bet ye 'ave,' said MacFarland. 'But all that kinda shite's no fir me nae more.'

'What? Goin' straight, are yer?' said Ingleby and lit a cigarette.

MacFarland turned to Coralie at his side with a beaming smile and gently squeezed her hand. 'I am that, aye.'

'Makin' an honest man of yer, is she?'

'I'm going to do my best,' said Coralie, returning MacFarland's smile.

Trevor was surprised that MacFarland had presumably come clean to Coralie about his past life – although perhaps not about every detail – and that she'd apparently either forgiven his transgressions and believed that he had genuinely turned his back on his criminal ways or that she was so much in love with him that she hadn't really cared. Something else that surprised Trevor was what he came out with next.

'Since I've been here, I've got quite intae this turtle stuff, so I'm stayin' on as a volunteer fir the rest o' the season.'

More than half of Trevor's mouthful of beer sprayed across the cluttered table.

'You got a problem wi' that, pal?' said MacFarland with a narrow-eyed stare.

'Not at all,' Trevor spluttered through a fit of coughing. 'I'm just a bit—'

'Surprised? Aye, me too, but at least you and Sandra can sleep easy in yer beds now – and with both yer legs still attached.'

'That's certainly good to know,' said Sandra and pushed back her chair. 'But on that positive note, I have to say I'm feeling a little queasy after all that food, so I think I might have a bit of a stroll on the beach to walk it off.'

'You OK?' said Trevor.

'I'm fine. Just overstuffed, that's all.'

'But you hardly ate a thing.'

Sandra got to her feet and held out her hand. 'Come with me if you like.'

To a chorus of "*Yeıa mas*" and raised glasses, Trevor and Sandra walked to the end of the terrace and the short flight of steps that led down to the quayside.

'Well, that was a bit of a turn-up,' said Trevor as soon he was sure that they were out of earshot of the rest of the group. 'MacFarland, I mean.'

'From hired killer and all round gangster to turtle volunteer is quite a leap, yeah.'

They continued chatting about the events of the evening, who'd said what to who and the latest developments in the Tassos Christopoulos case until they reached the point on the quayside where the promenade turned sharply to the right towards the mouth of the harbour. They ignored the turning, however, and carried straight on, down onto the sandy beach, and headed for the gently lapping waves at the water's edge.

Trevor picked up a pebble and hurled it out to sea. During the last couple of weeks, his and Sandra's world had finally returned to something approaching normality, which was exactly the way he liked it.

He picked up another pebble and was about to throw it when he noticed that Sandra had sat down on the sand with her legs stretched out in front of her and was gently massaging her abdomen with both hands.

'Stomach playing up still?' he said.

'Kind of,' said Sandra with a half smile.

'I think Marcus usually has some Rennies with him. Shall I nip back and get some?'

'No, I'll be fine. I don't think Rennies will help right now.'

'OK, if you're sure.'

Trevor threw the pebble slightly further out to sea than the first one, trying to get it to skim, but it disappeared below the surface after only two bounces. He searched the sand around his feet for a pebble that was much flatter than the first two but could find nothing suitable for his purpose, so he picked up the largest and lobbed it into the water where it made a satisfying splash.

'Never could get the hang of this skimming business. They say it's all in the wrist, but I don't seem to have the—'

'Trev,' Sandra interrupted. 'Why don't you give it up and come and sit down.'

She patted the sand beside her, and Trevor did as she asked, putting an arm around her shoulders as he did so.

'Not getting a bit chilly, are you?' he said. 'It's just that—'

'No, I'm not at all chilly, and will you please stop fussing because I've got something important to tell you.'

Oh Jesus, thought Trevor. It's not cancer, is it?

'I thought you might have guessed by now, but knowing you, I doubt—'

Trevor gazed into her eyes and gripped her rather too firmly by the arm. 'Christ, Sand, it's not... you know... cancer, is it?'

'What?'

'Cancer. I mean, I've noticed you've been a bit on the poorly side lately and—'

'No, it's not cancer, Trev. I'm actually pregnant.'

Trevor felt his mouth open and close, unable to form words as his brain whirled with far too many potential responses to be able to choose one in particular. Eventually it settled for a stammered 'P – pregnant?'

'As in I— *we* are going to have a baby.'

320

'Seriously?'

'Well, it's not really the sort of thing I'd joke about, so yes, we're going to have a baby. Seriously.'

Trevor barely heard what she'd said, so loud was the pounding blood in his head. He stared back out to sea in a futile attempt to calm his racing thoughts.

'You are... pleased, aren't you?' said Sandra with more than a hint of hesitation.

Trevor turned towards her so quickly that he winced at the shooting pain in his neck. '*Pleased*? Bloody Nora, it's brilliant.'

He threw his arms around her and kissed her for so long that she finally had to ease him away.

'I don't think asphyxiation is a good plan at this stage,' she gasped and chuckled simultaneously.

'Sorry, sorry. It's just that... Well, I... Bloody Nora, Sand. This is incredible.'

Sandra smiled into his eyes and took his hand in both of hers. 'There is one thing, though.'

'Oh?' said Trevor, alarm bells suddenly combining with the pounding in his ears.

'And it is totally and utterly non-negotiable.'

'Oh? What's that?'

'If it turns out to be a girl, there is not a chance in hell that we'll be calling her Nora.'

THE END

DEAR READER

Authors always appreciate reviews – especially if they're good ones of course – so I'd be eternally grateful if you could spare the time to write a few words about *Dishing the Dirt* on Amazon, Goodreads or anywhere else you can think of. It really can make a difference. Reviews also help other readers decide whether to buy a book or not, so you'll be doing them a service as well.

MAILING LIST

If you'd like to be kept informed about my new books, special offers on my books and other relevant information, please click on the link below and add your details.

Don't worry, any emails I send you will be few and far between, and I certainly won't be sharing your details with any third parties. You can also easily unsubscribe at any time.

http://eepurl.com/cwvFpb

AND FINALLY...

I'm always interested to hear from my readers, so please do take a couple of minutes to contact me via my website at https://rob-johnson.org.uk/contact/

ABOUT THE AUTHOR

'You'll have to write an author biography of course.'

'Oh? Why?'

'Because people will want to know something about you before they lash out on buying one of your books.'

'You think so, do you?'

'Just do it, okay?'

'So what do I tell them?'

'For a start, you should mention that you've written four plays that were professionally produced and toured throughout the UK.'

'Should I say anything about all the temp jobs I had, like working in the towels and linens stockroom at Debenhams or as a fitter's mate in a perfume factory?'

'No, definitely not.'

'Motorcycle dispatch rider?'

'You were sacked, weren't you?'

'Boss said he could get a truck there quicker.'

'Leave it out then, but make sure they know that *Dishing the Dirt* is the sixth book you've written. And don't forget to put in something that shows you're vaguely human.'

'You mean this kind of thing: "I'm currently in Greece with my wife, Penny, two cats and three rescue dogs and working on a new novel and a couple of screenplays".'

'It'll have to do, I suppose, and then finish off with your website and social media stuff.'

'Oh, okay then.'

- visit my website at
  http://www.rob-johnson.org.uk

- follow **@RobJohnson999** on Twitter

- check out my Facebook author page at
  https://www.facebook.com/RobJohnsonAuthor

- follow me on Amazon at
  http://viewauthor.at/Rob_Johnson_Author

OTHER BOOKS BY ROB JOHNSON

LIFTING THE LID

(Book One in the 'Lifting the Lid' series)

There are some things people see in toilets that they wish they hadn't. What Trevor Hawkins sees might even cost him his life...

When Trevor hits the open road in his beat-up old camper van with his incorrigible dog, Milly, his quest for adventure soon spirals dangerously out of control. The simple act of flushing a hotel toilet transforms his life from redundant sales assistant to fugitive from a gang of psychopathic villains, the police and MI5.

Then there's private detective Sandra Gray, who could cheerfully throttle him for turning a well paid, piece-of-cake job into a total nightmare. Or could she?

"A superb adventure-comedy." - Jennifer Reinoehl for Readers' Favorite

"The story is just so much FUN!" - Joanne Armstrong for Ingrid Hall Reviews

"The twists and turns kept me on the edge of my seat, laughing all the time." – San Francisco Review of Books

http://viewbook.at/Lifting_the_Lid

Also available as an audiobook from Amazon and Audible

HEADS YOU LOSE

(Book Two in the 'Lifting the Lid' series)

The assignment in Greece might have been the answer to Trevor and Sandra's problems except for one thing. Someone was trying to frame them for murder... with a watermelon.

'Money for old rope,' Sandra had said when they accepted the job of looking after the ageing Marcus Ingleby at his villa in Greece, but when a neighbour brings a gift for the old man, the prospect of spending the rest of their lives in a Greek prison becomes a terrifying reality.

Meanwhile, Ingleby has problems of his own. During his seventy-odd years, his cupboard has accumulated plenty of skeletons, one of which is about to be rattled by a couple of ex-cons and a retired police inspector from his murky past.

"A highly entertaining, well-constructed screwball comedy." - Keith Nixon for Big Al's Books and Pals

"Masterfully planned and executed... It tickled my funny bone in all the right places." - Joanne Armstrong for Ingrid Hall Reviews

Shortlisted for a Readers' Choice Award 2015 (Big Al's Books and Pals)

http://viewbook.at/Heads_You_Lose

CREMAINS

(A comedy crime caper)

Seeing an elderly woman crushed to death under a baby grand piano is not the best start to anyone's day, and Max Dempsey's is about to get a whole lot worse.

When petty crook Max Dempsey finds himself deep in debt to dodgy undertaker Danny Bishop, he's prepared to do almost anything to pay it off and keep all of his fingers.

But he's likely to lose a lot more than his fingers when he agrees to do a "little job" for Danny and unintentionally crosses a psychopathic Greek gangster.

Cremains is a comedy crime caper that twists and turns its way towards a conclusion that even Max himself couldn't have predicted.

"It definitely kept me guessing, but also laughing. Both good results." - Big Al for Big Al's Books & Pals

"A hilarious comedy that keeps you on the edge of your seat... and there are loads of twists and turns as the story hurtles towards an explosive ending." - Anne-Marie Reynolds for Readers' Favorite

"A unique and witty storyline complete with a cast of quirky characters that keep the reader engaged from page one to The End." - Pamela Allegretto (Author of *Bridge of Sighs and Dreams*)

http://viewbook.at/Cremains

QUEST FOR THE HOLEY SNAIL

WANTED: Gainful employment of an adventurous nature but without risk of personal physical harm. (Can supply own time travel machine if required.)

When Horace Tweed places an advertisement in a national magazine, the last thing he expects is to be commissioned to travel back through time in search of the long extinct Holey Snail.

But this isn't just any old snail. The *helix pertusa* is possessed of an extraordinary and highly desirable property, and Horace's quest leads him and his co-adventurers to Ancient Greece and a variety of near-death encounters with beings both mythological and not so mythological.

Meanwhile, Detective Chief Inspector Harper Collins has her hands full trying to track down a secret order of fundamentalist monks whom she suspects of committing a series of murders – the same monks who are determined to thwart Horace in his quest.

"Fans of Douglas Adams' *Hitchhikers' Guide to the Galaxy* will enjoy *Quest for the Holey Snail*." - Awesome Indies

"The writing in *Quest for the Holy Snail* shows the author is a talented wordsmith with a penchant for Monty Python-esque humor... Overall, the writing is excellent." - Lynne Hinkey for Underground Book Reviews

http://viewBook.at/Quest

A KILO OF STRING

(A travel memoir)

"Fabulously funny - a real must for lovers of all things Greek."

After living in Greece for thirteen years, writer and reluctant olive farmer Rob Johnson has got used to most of the things that he and his partner Penny found so bizarre at the beginning. Most, but not all.

A Kilo of String is the story-so-far of Rob and Penny's often bewildering experiences among the descendants of Sophocles, Plato and Nana Mouskouri with occasional digressions into total irrelevances.

"Witty and very funny. I really enjoyed this book. The author clearly has a love for the country and the people." - *USA Today* Bestselling author Kathryn Gauci

"Had me howling with laughter... I am so excited to have found this wonderful author." - Effrosyni Moschoudi (author of The Lady of the Pier series)

"The author's entertaining stories, interesting anecdotes, and humor make this book an excellent read for everyone." - Mamta Madhavan for Readers' Favorite

A Kilo of String **is loosely based on Rob Johnson's podcast series of the same name at** https://rob-johnson.org.uk/podcasts/a-kilo-of-string/

http://viewbook.at/A_Kilo_of_String

Also available as an audiobook from Amazon, Audible and iTunes

"CREMAINS" OPENING CHAPTERS

I hope you've enjoyed reading *Dishing the Dirt* and that you might be interested in reading one of my other novels. To give you an idea what to expect, these are the opening chapters of *Cremains*, which is a comedy crime caper that's similar in style to my *Lifting the Lid* series but with completely different characters.

CREMAINS - CHAPTER ONE

It's not every day that you see some old granny crushed to death under a baby grand piano, and I'm truly grateful for that. I really am. But the even bigger shock was that this woman – a complete stranger – would be coming back to haunt me in the days to come. Not in a spooky, walking-through-walls kind of way but something a lot more real and far more dangerous.

The inevitable small crowd had gathered round on the pavement to have a good gawp, of course, and not one of them was lifting so much as a finger to get the poor cow out from under the wreckage. Probably too late anyway. All that was visible of her was her blue rinse and one arm of a slightly less blue housecoat.

Two blokes in orange overalls were standing a few feet away from the ghoul brigade and staring up at a second-floor window of the four-storey apartment block. There was some kind of winch arrangement just above the window with about ten feet of rope dangling from it. At the bottom of the rope, half a dozen strips of webbing swayed gently in the breeze. Best guess? The two blokes in Guantanamo jumpsuits had been delivering or removing the joanna, and the old biddy had been standing right underneath it when the harness snapped. Wham, bam, and raspberry jam.

I'm not a great one for too much of the blood and gore, as it happens, so I carried on up the opposite side of the street without breaking stride. Second turning on the left and glad to see the BMW in its usual spot and with all its wheels still attached. Not that this is the sort of area where even the Rottweilers go round in pairs. Far from it, in fact, and I've got the mortgage repayments to prove it. On the other hand, leafy suburbia is exactly the type of place that some of the thieving little ne'er-do-wells like to target in the hope of richer spoils. Well, they can count me out on that score for a start 'cos I'm totally bloody skint right at this moment, although I'm expecting my fortunes to improve quite dramatically in a few short hours from now. Unless, that is, Alan and Scratch have made a complete bollocks of things, which, based on past experience, is not at all beyond the realms of possibility.

I took the rolled-up copy of *The Times* from under my arm and dropped it into a bin on the corner of the street, noticing that I'd built up quite a collection since it had last been emptied. Lazy bastards. It's not as if they don't get a shitload out of me in Council Tax.

I fished the plastic clicker thing out of my suit jacket and scored a direct hit on the Beamer's rear window, causing the usual clunking sound as the doors unlocked, and the hazard lights flashed. What do they call them? Smart keys, isn't it? Not so bloody smart the time when the battery ran out on the stupid piece of crap and locked me out until I remembered the strip of metal inside it that worked like some kind of pretend key. Late forties hardly qualifies me as one of those grumpy old gits who's constantly moaning on about how much better everything used to be in *their* day, but you knew where you were with a proper key, didn't you? Smarmy gimp at the showroom told me this was a top-of-the-range BMW and I couldn't have a proper ordinary key even if I paid extra. Told me if I was dead set on having a car with a key, 'Perhaps sir might want to consider a second-hand Morris Minor instead.' Cheeky twat.

I climbed in behind the wheel, plonked the briefcase

on the passenger seat and tossed the rolled umbrella over into the back. Haven't needed it for days now, but it helps me look the part, that's for sure.

I fired up the engine. Nice purr. Almost worth the obscene amount of cash I had to fork out every month just for that sound. Carla would have had a blue fit if she knew I even *had* a Beamer, never mind that I was already way behind on the payments. As far as she was concerned, all we'd got was a four-year-old Honda Civic that spends most of its time sitting in the driveway. Still, there's a fair old bit that Carla doesn't know, and I'm definitely aiming to keep it that way.

CREMAINS - CHAPTER TWO

The High Street was already buzzing with Saturday morning shoppers, and it was a pig to find a spot to park. The last thing I needed was to draw attention to the fact that I'd even been in the area, and a parking ticket would certainly have done that. Even worse if the car had been clamped or towed away. A bit of a walk wouldn't do me any harm anyway. Not that I'm within a million miles of being a lardy bloater, of course, even though Carla's always on at me about shedding some weight. A pound or two off the waistline maybe, but not exactly a candidate for a three-times-a-week trip to the local gym. Sod that for a lark.

I deliberately walked straight past the shop without so much as a sideways glance and stopped in front of the next one. The plan was to pretend to be checking out the contents of the window display while I listened for any undue noise. But then I realised I was staring at a window that had been completely blanked out and remembered it was one of those sex shops – private shops, they call them nowadays – so I carried on to the hairdresser's next door. Not much to see here either except for a bunch of women getting their weekend hairdos done. Better not hang around here too long or one of them might clock me for a peeping tom with a shampoo and blow-dry fetish and call the cops.

I couldn't hear what I'd been listening out for from this distance, so I doubled back to the shop I'd ignored and took the key out of my pocket. A proper key. Still no noise out of the ordinary, so I shoved the key into the lock and turned it. Except it wouldn't. Turn, that is. I tried the handle, and the door swung open with the slightest of creaks. Christ almighty, the bloody idiots hadn't even bothered to lock it.

Once upon a time, the shop had been a gents' outfitters, but it had gone bust months ago. Presumably, the modern world hadn't any need for gents' outfitters any more, or maybe there just weren't enough gents left to be outfitted. Either way, I'd taken out a short lease on the place a few weeks ago in the name of a bogus company I'd set up specifically for the purpose. Not that I ever had any plans to run it as a shop, of course. God, no. I had something else in mind altogether, and this was going to make me a whole lot richer than flogging a bunch of ties and the occasional suit.

The light was dim inside the shop, partly because I'd had the door and window completely obscured with sheets of newspaper – from the copies of *The Times* I hadn't binned – and partly because the air was so thick with dust, you could have grown spuds in it.

Better get out of these togs sharpish or Carla will go into meltdown if she has to take another suit to the dry cleaner's.

I ducked down behind the counter that butted up at right-angles to the window and pulled out a bulging carrier bag. I was just about to take off the suit jacket and lay it on the counter top when I spotted the half-inch layer of dust that had settled on it. I scanned the rest of the shop for somewhere I could temporarily deposit the jacket, but apart from a few shelves bolted to the wall and also covered with dust, there was nothing. Not so much as a hanging rail with a bunch of coat hangers that must have been here when the gents' outfitters was still up and running. Bailiffs must have cleared pretty much everything that wasn't nailed down – and probably quite a lot of the stuff that was, apart from the counter.

I considered my options for a couple of seconds. Not even for that long because there was only one. If I didn't want the suit to end up making me look like a nuclear fallout survivor, I'd just have to put the overalls on over the top and hope to Christ I didn't roast down there. So, out they came from the carrier bag – grease monkey green rather than Guantanamo orange – and I had them on and buttoned up to the neck in a flash. Well, not quite a flash exactly, on account of twice nearly falling flat on my arse when each shoe got snagged up in a trouser leg.

Making for the far corner of the shop, I noticed several pairs of footprints in the carpet of dust, leading in both directions between the front door and where I was heading. Buggers must have been in and out a fair few times since I left them here last night. They'd better not have been sat swilling ale in some club or other instead of getting on with the job in hand. The sound I'd been listening for earlier was clearly audible now and getting louder with every step I took, so they obviously hadn't finished yet.

The swirling dust was getting even thicker too, most of it coming from the top of the metal spiral staircase that led down into the basement. These things are lethal at the best of times, never mind when you can hardly see a hand in front of your face, so I grabbed the handrail tight and took the steps one at a very steady time. At the bottom, I pushed through the heavy blankets we'd hung up the night before to muffle as much of the noise as possible, but they hadn't created enough of a seal to stop some of the dust escaping.

My eyes had already begun to sting like crazy, and the air was almost unbreathable down here, so I whipped out my handkerchief and clamped it over my nose and mouth. I squinted through the haze and my streaming tears to see Alan sitting on the floor with his back

337

against the wall nearest me and Scratch on his knees, drilling into the wall on the opposite side of the basement.

'Bloody hell, you two,' I shouted. 'What if I'd been the cops? You hadn't even locked the sodding door.'

But even Alan, who was only six feet away, didn't hear me over the din of Scratch's massive drill.

I yelled a second time and then went over to Alan and tapped him on the shoulder. Dozy sod nearly jumped out of his skin, and as his head spun round, his left hand flew up to his neck and he let out what sounded like a yelp of pain.

'What's up?' I said.

He pulled down the paper breathing mask to expose the only part of his face that wasn't encrusted with a thick film of cement dust. His lips moved, but I couldn't make out a single word.

'Knock it off a minute,' I yelled at Scratch's back.

Nothing doing, so I picked up a small piece of rubble and chucked it at him. Got him right between the shoulder blades, but whether it was the vibration from the drill or not, he didn't even flinch. Another piece of rubble – a lot bigger than before – and this time he lowered the drill and turned to face me.

He pulled down his own mask, and you didn't have to be much of a lipreader to make out the "fuck d'you do that for?" part of what he said.

I gestured to him to switch off the drill, and moments later, the sound of silence filled the basement with an almost eerie calm.

I looked back down at Alan. 'So what is it?'

'Done my bloody neck in, haven't I?' he said with an extra wince and giving his neck a bit of a rub, presumably to emphasise the point.

'Again?' I said. 'You're always doing your neck in.'

'Bloody martyr to it, I am.'

Scratch snorted. 'Martyr to being a lazy little bastard, more like.'

It was a remark that didn't make much sense, but the gist was clear enough. And it was true. Alan would swing the lead any chance he got whenever any manual labour was involved. He was about the same age as me and probably a fair bit fitter. A couple of inches on the short side and built like a weightlifter. No great coincidence, of course, because that's what he used to do in his younger days. Claimed that's where his neck problems first started and why he had to give it up. But bad neck or not, there was work to be done.

I gave Alan a sympathetic pat on the shoulder, which sent up a fresh cloud of dust from his overalls, and went over to check on the progress.

'What's the story then?' I said, stooping to get a good look at the hole for myself.

Scratch cleared his throat like he was trying to dislodge something the size of the piece of rubble I'd thrown at him. 'Another half hour or so should do it, I reckon.'

The hole in the wall was roughly circular, a couple of feet in diameter and about the same deep.

'It'll have to be bigger than that if you're gonna get through there,' I said.

'Off you go then, Max,' said Scratch, and he laid the drill down and pushed himself upright.

Now, I'm about average height for a bloke, but Scratch has got a good head and shoulders on me and a physique that's totally in proportion to his height. The man is bloody enormous, and what with the shaved head – a vain attempt to disguise the rapidly advancing baldness – and a busted nose, looks like a right thug that you really wouldn't want to run into in a dark alley. But that's where you'd be wrong because Scratch wouldn't hurt a fly. Not unless provoked. And if that happened, you – or the fly – would be in serious trouble. Come to think of it, though, the fly would probably be OK since it's unlikely that Scratch would risk being within swatting distance of it in case he was allergic. For a guy of his impressive stature, it had always struck me as weird that he should have so many allergies. Whatever it was, if you could touch it, smell it or swallow it, it was odds on that Scratch would come out in a rash. Hence the nickname. Apparently, however, he didn't have too much of a problem with cement dust.

'Any spare masks?' I said.

Scratch shook his head and took off his own. 'You'll have to use mine.'

It was already thick with caked-on dust and probably well past its usefulness, but I guessed it was better than a handkerchief, so I slipped it on and picked up the drill. Christ, it weighed a ton, and the vibration when I started in on the hole made my brain rattle. This was the first time I'd used the thing on account of having to get off home soon after we'd got everything set up the night before. Both being single, Alan and Scratch didn't have a Carla waiting to give them an earful about being late for their tea, but I'd promised them I'd do my share when I came back today.

Mind you, what did Scratch reckon? Another half hour or so? Jesus, I doubted I'd last more than five minutes.

CREMAINS - CHAPTER THREE

At bloody last. Finally there was light at the end of the tunnel – or at least an opening the size of my fist at the far end of the hole. Scratch's "half hour or so" had turned out to be well over double that, even though we'd worked non-stop in shifts. Alan had moaned like hell all the while he was having his go, of course, but thanks to the din of the drilling, Scratch and I could hardly hear him.

'Here, I'll take over,' said Scratch, presumably fired up with renewed enthusiasm now that the job was almost done.

Even so, I wasn't about to object, and I gladly handed him the drill.

The work was a lot easier from then on with Scratch chipping away at the far end of the hole and pausing every so often so I could pull out the loose rubble or push it through the other side. Ten minutes later and the hole was about the size of my head. Ten more and it was big enough for me to get my shoulders through with a bit of wriggling. The dust began to clear, and my eyes swept across the pile of rubble in front of me.

Holy shit. What the—? Feet. Human feet. In shiny black leather. The sharp points pointing straight at me. Thin stiletto heels nearly six inches long. My gaze crept stealthily upwards, eventually reaching the tops of the black leather boots and the pale skin of a pair of thighs. Then more black leather with little straps and buckles at regular intervals. Twin bulges of white flesh trying to force their way out, partially obscured by forearms clad in long black gloves. A coiled whip in one hand being slowly and rhythmically tapped against the palm of the other. Thick, black leather collar studded with viciously long spikes. Glossy scarlet lips, pouting slightly. Black leather eye mask and a bob of gleaming black hair.

Jesus Christ, what was she doing here?

Panicked, I darted my eyes to left and right. Wood and metal contraptions everywhere with ropes or chains dangling from most of them. A wooden X-shaped frame with a man strapped to it, spreadeagled and totally starkers apart from a black rubber hood that covered his face and head completely. Red welts criss-crossed his massive man-boobs and equally enormous belly.

I switched my focus back to peering upwards at the pouting red lips and the black eye mask. But the lips were no longer pouting. Instead, they'd spread into a kind of lopsided, leering grin.

'Who's been a naughty boy then?' said the lips, and there was a sharp "krakk!" as the business end of the whip struck the floor of what was pretty obviously not the vault of a bank.

END OF FIRST THREE CHAPTERS OF 'CREMAINS'

To read on, please go to:
http://viewbook.at/Cremains

Made in the USA
Middletown, DE
07 February 2022